VIRTUES OF THE VICIOUS

MARTIN WILSEY

TANNHAUSER PRESS

VIRTUES OF THE VICIOUS

ISBN-10: 1-945994-00-2
ISBN-13: 978-1-945994-00-5

Cover, Girl in Leather by Duncan Long
Cover design by Heidi Sutherlin

Edited by: Jessica Johnson

Published by Tannhauser Press
First Edition

www.tannhauserpress.com

DEDICATION

To Brenda Reiner and all the strong, intelligent, independent women in my life that inspire me every day.

Thanks !!

Virtues

OF THE

Vicious

CHAPTER ONE: Towers and Cords

"It has been difficult to determine when the first shots were fired in the AI War. Some historians argue that the opening salvos were subtle economic assassinations to ensure monopolies continued. This historian believes it began at midnight on June 22, 2668. That shot was fired by Elizabeth Cruze."

--Blue Peridot, The Turning Point: History of the AI Wars.

The Detroit Municipal Prison had the old, outdated cells with no functional in-cell cameras. There was only one prisoner per cell, and each cell was two meters wide, three meters deep, two and a half meters tall. It was all raw cement surfaces. The light was dim from the clear wall to the central atrium. She didn't mind the last four months with no privacy because there was no one watching. The guards were ruled by apathy.

And she was glad it was never completely dark. She shivered at the mere thought.

Cruze figured that no AI was running the place, like in the new prisons. Detroit was too cheap for that. Just the usual corrupt people in charge. Her heart was racing. To calm herself she mentally ran down a list of names like a to-do list. *Braxton. Holt. Dante. And every single fucking Red Talon. Bastards!*

Cruze sat on a thin mattress resting on the built-in shelf that was on one side of the cell. The back wall had a built-in toilet/sink combination that was directly opposite the inch thick transparent cell wall. She was scanning the cracked and dirty walls of the cell as if she would never see it again.

For the thousandth time today, she thought of Del and Harper, waiting for her on Mars. *Four months with no word. Especially Harper. They wouldn't know Kade and Hall were dead. John Delmore, Del, would keep his cool. He would get Harper through.*

The digital clock display in the clear wall counted its way along. **September 21, 2636 - 23:58:33**.

Cruze thought it was a cruelty. It was intentionally inflicted on the 120,000 prisoners housed in the sky-scraper prison tower. In this prison all they did was time. The clock reminded the prisoners of that fact, daily, hourly, every minute.

The transparent wall had a display area at eye level that would show them announcements, eight hours a day of non-violent soap operas and religious programming. They had a movie every Saturday night of the warden's choosing.

Cruze French-braided her long, light brown hair while watching the clock creep toward midnight. She wore a black lace slip made of real silk and nothing else. It was far from the usual bright yellow, baggy jumpsuit.

The lingerie's price tag was freshly removed, unread. She slipped on the simple flip-flops that were her shower sandals. Her prisoner shoes were positioned just outside the door to her cell. There was a gap at the bottom of the clear door where each prisoner was required to slide their shoes into the hall. The punishment was too severe to risk not doing it. At 9 pm it was lights out. It was never lights out in the atrium.

At midnight exactly she heard the click.

She stood, and in the light of the digital clock, she silently slid the door open and stepped onto the passageway balcony before closing the door behind her. She moved quickly and quietly to the nearby emergency stairwell. The door there was also unlocked. She was on level six and hurried downward. Lights were dim in the stairwell, and none of the security cams had their red lights on. She became calm and focused as she moved.

She kept going down past level G to B1. The door was not locked there either. It opened into a long corridor with more inactive cameras. She ran the one hundred and twenty meters to another unlocked stairwell door. Up she went another seven levels of stairs. There were no doors at all on the way up, except at the topmost landing.

She paused at this door for two minutes, collecting herself. When she opened it, he was there.

"Hello, Jane," the tower guard named Bergman said as he looked at the clock. "Thirteen minutes. A new record. Not bad for your first time." The guard was in uniform and was handsome in a fit, squared jaw, classic way.

Before he could stand she crossed the room and quickly straddled him in his armless chair. She began kissing him, hungrily. "Did you get the extension cord? They have a still in the laundry level, and they need power. Mendez set it up. She's a piece of work. I get protection in trade for it."

Bergman nodded.

Jane Doe, she thought to herself, *fools never did discover my real name.* Cruze loosened his tie and started unbuttoning his shirt. She kissed him desperately, down his neck, down his chest to his nipples.

She looked over her shoulder and saw the heavy spool in the corner. She couldn't believe this kind of power cord even existed in this day and age.

His hands roamed over her body, her breasts, first over her slip and then under it. She moaned when his fingers found her soaking wet.

"Slow down sweetheart." Bergman's breath was hot on her neck. "We have six hours. Make it last." She slowly got control of herself.

"It's been so long. I have never gone so long," she said as she slowed. When she finally opened his shirt all the way, she added, "Thank you for the silk lace. The feel of it on my skin has driven me mad for hours." She was running her fingers inside the top edge of his pants, the intent clear. *Men are idiots.* Her hand began tracing his erection between her fingers, as he massaged her breasts over the silk.

She opened his fly as she slid off his lap and onto her knees between his legs. His head fell back to take a deep breath in anticipation of her beautiful mouth.

This will be easier than I thought.

What she gave him was his own stunner, delivering a massive shock to his ribs.

It was **12:21 am**.

***

Elizabeth Cruze held his combination flashlight stunner to his bare chest for an extra five seconds before she stood.

"Idiot. My real name is Elizabeth Cruze." She pushed him out of the chair onto the floor. She searched his pockets and found nothing except a wallet with a Universal ID card. His belt was empty as well. No cuffs, keys, comms, gun, nothing.

"Well, that was smart at least, Bergman. I could have killed you, stupid. You are so lucky. You'll wake up in two hours and I will be gone."

She found a permanent marker and started writing a note on his belly:

Bergman. Sorry I had to leave early. I won't be missing until the 6 am head-count. Remember, my DNA is all over you. Be cool, and you'll be fine. I know you live at 237 Poplar Ave, apartment 6239. Don't make me want to come and visit. Keep your head.

Kisses,

Jane Doe 857263

Adrenaline pounded in her veins now. She took the long power cord and crept outside onto the tower balcony. The prison itself was a tower that had no exterior windows. She had no idea how tall it was. It was surrounded by a series of courtyards and then an outer wall that was about twenty-five meters tall.

On the street side of the tower, there was a sidewalk below. She lowered one end of the cable down to the sidewalk. On the other side of a rusted rail post, she tossed down the spool.

This rusty rail better hold.

As she silently lowered herself to the sidewalk, hand over hand, she felt thankful for ancient, obsolete structures that still used the old standard power. As soon as her feet touched, she pulled one side of the cord down quickly, and the entire cable fell to the sidewalk.

She wound it up, laughing at the absurdity of the extension cord. She walked into the city and was out of sight in less than a minute.

The horrible condition of the exterior was evident from the ground. All the streetlights were out. The crumbling walls seemed to be held together by layers of graffiti.

The monolith of the prison had been made long ago by secondhand maker bots. No frills. Now the foamcrete was streaked with black stains. Every broken camera along the outer wall was covered in bird shit. The sidewalk was cracked and uneven. Broken glass was everywhere.

Glass was supposed to be a renewable. Stupid laws. This is what you get.

Cruze moved away to get cover in the nearest side street as she looked at the skyline. The area around the prison was without light, like it had suffered a blackout. An entire core section of the city was dark, except for the blinking roof lights. *All the same foamcrete. Ugly.* She tried to remember the beautiful foamcrete domes of her home colony. *Same material. Yet not the same. Home had blue skies. The rain was sweet straight from the sky. No acid to eat the foamcrete to black.*

She could see the ICC Bank tower clock in the distance as she tossed the extension cord into a dumpster.

It was **12:37 am**.

***

Running in flip-flops was not working well. Detroit had let sidewalk repair go in these dead neighborhoods. It was a city with a rotting core. The center of Detroit had been abandoned when the exodus to the colonies had begun. The tall, stained foamcrete towers loomed dark into the sky like broken teeth.

She was drawing nearer the living portion of Detroit. The buildings here were glass and alive. Towers were lit. They rose in great spires of vanity. The architecture was frivolous to Cruze's eye. And not a single tree in sight. It all looked down on the city's abandoned, rotting core. The cancer of de-population.

Rounding a corner, she could see there was life on the next street down. She moved closer and then entered an alley to rest and collect herself.

She was free.

She was alone in a shitty neighborhood of Detroit.

She was wearing a black lace slip and nothing else except her prison shower shoes.

"Are you okay?" A man's voice came from the mouth of the alley. A slight Asian accent.

She let out a startled gasp and backed farther into the alley. *That's right dumb-ass. Come to Cruze.*

"It's alright. I won't hurt you. I saw you from across the street. You look like you need help." His silhouette followed her deeper into the alley as he spoke in soothing tones.

A little further.

"You must be cold. Let me help. I have a place we can go. Get some food, something to drink. Maybe get a little high if you need that."

She tried to freeze when he mentioned drugs, indicating interest. *That's right, go ahead and think I need a fix.* She stopped backing away. She was in the light of a small area hugging herself, looking down at her feet. *My hair is braided like a colony whore's.*

"Please…" she whispered. "Please…" she sobbed.

He didn't notice she had stepped out of her flip-flops as she stepped back.

When he stood in the shaft of light, Cruze exploded into motion. The heel that landed at his temple was so fast it was all that was required.

"Why are men so stupid?" she asked the unconscious man as she quickly searched him. He was a man of slight build. "Even today, they think women are weaker. Listen, dumb-ass. I have spent half my life in 2G on ships just to stay fit, so I could kick asses like yours." She rolled him onto his stomach and peeled his jacket off, then his boots. She roughly took his pants as well. They were black denim and would almost fit her because of his slight build.

"Oh, man. When was the last time you took a shower? That is the worst BO I have smelled in years, and I have been in Detroit Municipal Prison for the last four fucking months." She stopped talking. She bit her tongue when she realized she was doing it again.

Stop talking when you are scared, dammit.

She pulled on his pants and tucked the slip in. She donned his shirt next, also tucking it in. The excess fabric was drawn to the sides, and the belt had enough holes to keep the pants up. She put on his socks and boots, and they were only a bit too big. She kicked her flip-flops under a dumpster.

"Listen, dumb-ass." She dragged him behind the dumpster. "When you wake up you will at least have a comms unit." She dropped his phone onto his belly. "Call your drinking buddies or a cab to get home." She pulled his wallet out of his pocket and took out a massive stack of credits. She kept the wad and left a $100 bill in his wallet. "That will cover cab fare, asshole."

She knelt down and held up his head by his hair. "You are not a good man. Good people don't carry these." Out of his coat pocket, she pulled a snub nose, disposable handgun. She checked the load. It was 9mm explosive point caseless. "Why the fuck do you assholes still carry these in 2636?"

She knew the answer. They were easy to make. Any home fabricator could make one. They were reliable. They were deadly. They were single use and difficult to trace.

She left the alley and headed for the busy end of the street without looking back. She moved into the traffic flow where there were the most people. She found herself moving to an entertainment district. She saw a high-end restaurant that had valet service. It was attached to the Blue Night entertainment district.

In her mind she assessed.

She was free.

She had clothes.

She had a nice wad of credits.

She was armed.

She had less than five hours before the GPSS chip activated.

It was **01:11 am**.

CHAPTER TWO: The Night Market

"One of the foundation blocks of the AI Wars was the success of Awareness Inc. in breaking the monopoly on Artificial Intelligence (AI) units. The Render program was both cruel and highly successful. When its methods were revealed publicly, Awareness Inc. had more than PR problems."

--*Blue Peridot, The Turning Point: History of the AI Wars.*

Cruze entered the market concourse and was surprised at how many people were there. She was not out of place at all with the young people of Detroit that were trying to be edgy. It was the same everywhere.

The first stop was a shoe store. The sleepy clerk helped her pick out a black pair of sturdy boots that fit perfectly and would allow her to run if needed. She also got socks, which she wore away from the store, and dropped the packaging into a nearby trash compactor.

At the next stop, she purchased panties, bra, black slacks that fit, and a white silk blouse.

Even though she got rid of most of the clothes she had stolen from the idiot in the alley, she couldn't let go of the leather jacket. It was thick, black, and a little too big. But she liked it.

She then walked to a salon she had passed on the way in. *Time to quickly change my look.* Three stylists sat in chairs watching vids on the wall display. As soon as she entered they stopped and looked up at her.

"I love your outfit, darling. I must have it," said one of the stylists. Cruze dropped the leather jacket in one seat and sat in another. It was opposite to a large analog clock. "Please cut it to this length," she gestured with her hand, "…and color it. I want black. But it must be done by 2 am. I want to surprise my husband!" She was undoing her braid.

No time to waste.

"We can do better than that if you don't mind programmed nanites." The stylist turned her to the mirror and began brushing out her hair. She brushed it up into a great handful. The stylist narrowed her eyes as she studied something below Cruze's hairline. Cruze knew what she was looking at. It was a tattoo in tiny, but readable letters: RENDER 3

"Do it," Cruze said quickly to distract the stylist. "I need a change." At the same time, an image of her with the new color and cut appeared beside her in the mirror's reflection. It was rotating so she could see all the way around.

"It's $560 because the nanites are single use."

Cruze reached into her pocket, counted out $1000 in credits and handed it to the stylist, who smiled wide.

"My name is Ann Marie. Let's get started."

Ann Marie spent a few minutes at a console before a small vial was filled and dispensed.

"Have you ever had a Nan-Cut before, sweetie?"

Cruze shook her head.

"It will feel kind of weird. It will clean, cut and color. The small gene mod that it will make at the root will keep the color even for about ten months as your hair grows and then will start to revert."

Cruze smiled but said nothing. *Hurry the hell up.*

The stylist poured them onto the crown of her head. She felt them spread like cool water with a mission, and all of a sudden, her scalp was sizzling. After a minute, the new color began to appear. Her lion brown hair turned blue-black.

The color spread down her hair until it reached a specified point, and the remaining brown hair fell away at the perfect length.

In six minutes it was done.

The stylist brushed out the remaining hair that didn't already fall away. Then she used a blow-dryer to remove the last of it and swept away the apron.

"Excellent." Cruze smiled big.

It was **01:47 am.**

***

She watched herself in the window's reflection as she exited the night market concourse. She walked with purpose back out to the street and the end of the city block.

I will kill them all. The mantra echoed to calm her mind. *You killed Kade and Hall you fuckers.*

Cruze hung the leather jacket on a post by the exit for a high-end restaurant called The Vienna. She could tell it was high end by the landscaping in front. These were the first plants she had seen in this city. She crouched amongst them. She watched from the shadows as the late crowd rotated in and out. Someone leaving the restaurant parking lot tossed a valet slip out the window as he drove away.

Cruze picked it up and waited.

There were only two valets working tonight at this hour. With so many people arriving and exiting at the same time, they were hard-pressed to keep up.

Cruze saw her chance.

A man driving a dark red Grendel 4500 pulled in as Cruze ran up and opened the passenger door for two beautiful women. Immediately, jogging around to the driver side, she handed the ticket to the man who barely registered her at all. They were inside the restaurant before Cruze pulled the car up to the post, lowered her window and grabbed her leather jacket.

Easy pickins.

She already thought of the jacket as hers.

Moving into traffic, she headed south.

Time to visit an old friend.

It was **02:04 am.**

***

Bergman came awake with a start.

He was flat on his back in the center of the tower floor with the intercom beeping.

"Come on, Bergman. It's 2:05 am. If you don't enter your code in ten minutes, you will have to explain it to the warden. She's a bitch about that shit."

He staggered up, and at the console, he slowly keyed in his code.

"OK, Bergman. Thanks for waking up."

When Bergman sat in the chair, he crumpled a sheet of paper that was on the seat. He was foggy still.

It said, "Look at your belly, Bergman."

He stood, grabbed the sheet, and laid it on the console as he began unbuttoning his shirt. He read the words and stopped, frozen on the last button.

It was coming back to him.

Oh shit.

On the console, he logged in and hit the icon that reactivated all the cameras' live feeds. He looked around the tower in a brief panic. The power cord was gone. The girl had disappeared. Before he tucked in his shirt, he reread the note, twice more before he put on his tie.

As he slid the knot into place, he began to smile nervously. He said out loud, "Bitch has got nothing, cause I'm single." He tried to convince himself.

Oh my god. I am so fucked.

He opened a safe drawer, took out his bourbon and had a healthy swig straight from the bottle. He left the cigars but grabbed the lighter.

Out on the balcony, he burned the note. She was right. He'd be okay.

I made sure my night visits were private. Just stay cool.

He began to sweat.

It was **02:16 am.**

***

Cruze was behind the wheel of a luxury car that cost about half a million credits. She was driving it manually, which was crazy.

"Why the hell would you hand over this car to a complete stranger with the security system turned off?" she said aloud. The Grav-Plates gave it a perfect ride. Currently set at 20cm for ride clearance, if she happened to go over a curb, she wouldn't feel it.

"Didn't your mother explain to you about Detroit? It's a crime-ridden pit of vomit." She was doing it again. Talking to herself.

Think. Be careful. Stay focused.

She knew it would be a bad idea to activate the auto-pilot. It might have security controls. It might have the evening agenda. More for getting home if you're drunk than security.

She knew where she was going. How could she forget that? So she drove it on manual.

The neighborhoods got worse the closer she got to her destination. Detroit was a contrast between new and old. The mix of the new crystal towers with no ground access and the filthy old foamcrete bunkers was stark. The rich never touched the ground in Detroit unless they were intentionally being edgy. She recognized the graffiti that implied the cops never came here.

It was almost 3 am when she pulled into Holt's Automotive.

Be there, fucker.

The sign was faded, and the area looked mostly abandoned except for Holt's. It was the only building on the block with lights. A converted parking garage that was no longer required since the exodus to the colonies. Detroit was mostly abandoned in areas like this.

Better for dirty business.

She slowly pulled into the open bay. It was always open, until it wasn't.

Calm was settling on her again. Cold...deadly... calm.

She was getting out of the vehicle as the overhead door behind her was closing. She knew once it was closed, it was like a Faraday Bay. If the car tried to report in, it would be impossible. The garage would not allow any Radio Frequencies (RF) to escape.

Holt himself was coming out of the office door to meet her, gun in hand. He was pointing it at the car as he spoke.

"Elizabeth Cruze, I am astonished to see you again, and so soon. And with a Grendel!"

"Good to see you, Holt," she lied.

"I'm surprised. Especially after what happened last time. So sorry about that." Holt shrugged without sincerity.

"Hey, Holt, don't sweat it. It was just business. I kept my mouth shut. They totally bought that I was just a whore getting used by an arms dealer as a mule for credits." She laughed and said, "They even bought the reason I never gave them my name. Because I didn't want daddy in Iowa to know. It's why I was only in the DMP." *Sometimes it's easier to deceive with the truth.*

"I heard that. Never even told them your own name. Not to mention mine or anyone else's. I appreciate your discretion."

"That's why I came to see you. Can we talk inside?" Cruze was friendly on the outside.

"By all means." Holt gestured expansively with the handgun. "Braxton and his AI buddies had a real hard-on for you. I guess you know that. They were really pissed the guy you bought the weapons from got away with the money."

And my weapons were probably delivered months ago on Mars.

They entered his shabby office right off the garage. His nameless gorilla stood just inside the door. And when Cruze took a seat, he stood a little too close behind her chair.

That's right, be distracted by my tits, asshole.

"I want to sell you the Grendel cheap," she began. "All I need is five grand and some info. It's a good faith gesture, so you won't call Braxton as soon as I'm gone."

I will show you some good faith.

"What info?" Holt asked.

"I just escaped from Detroit Municipal. I have about three hours to get this chip out. I need that vet's address," Cruze said as if it was nothing.

"That's it?" Holt laughed. He grabbed a pen and paper, wrote down a name and address, and slid it across to her. "And to show you I appreciate your goodwill, I'll give you ten grand."

Cruze looked behind her at the bodyguard, up and down, smiled at him and he grinned back. *What a stupid fuck.*

"You should know," Holt said, "Detroit Municipal Prison has a Warden with particular interest in you. And rumor has it, there is an AI up there now."

FUCK, an AI! Cruze screamed in her head, betraying nothing on the outside.

Holt spun around in his chair and took a minute to open an old style safe that was the size of a small fridge. He grabbed a bundle of credits and tossed it to Cruze.

Instead of catching it, she drew her gun and shot Holt in the left eye. Spinning around she shot the muscle four times before he went down.

Now all is forgiven.

She kicked the muscle in the ribs. "You stupid fuck. Why the hell didn't you search me? Can't find good professional help anywhere these days." She started dragging the muscle into the garage by the ankles. With the car's remote, she lowered it all the way down and popped the trunk. She loaded his body into it and repeated the process with Holt after searching him and collecting his keys and watch. She put the watch on and admired it.

Thanks.

Cruze went back into Holt's office and found a large duffel bag in the closet. She emptied the credits from the safe into the bag. It was just over two hundred thousand in credits. There was also a loaded, suppressed, stainless, NJT 10mm handgun. She tucked it into the front of her waistband.

She opened the overhead door, looked into the street and then at her new watch. It was 03:05 am.

A gang of kids slid by at high-speed, whistling and cat-calling at her as they drifted by on hover boards.

"Hey!" Cruze called out. "Can any of you punks drive?" *IQs sure have dropped on this damn planet.*

Curses and sexual requests reached a crescendo, but two of the punks peeled off and came back.

"I drive. So what?" The two of them stopped and flipped up their boards in a well-practiced move. Neither of these punks blinked twice about the gun in her waistband.

"I need this car delivered. ASAP." She reached inside her jacket and pulled out a bundle of credits. "Ten grand to get this Grendel to The Vienna valet parking at the Blue Night Market. If the valet ticket is stamped before 4 am, you get another ten grand."

She hit the remote. The car started and rose to twenty centimeters.

"We're in." One of the kids held out his hand. She slapped the credits into it, but didn't let go. He jerked his shoulders back, surprised at her strength.

"4 am. No detours, no mess, no getting pulled over, no side trips." She let go and tossed the keys in the air. He caught them and ran to the car. They pulled away slowly and silently.

Cruze turned and ran deeper into the garage, pressing the start button on the fob she took from Holt's pants.

A Kraken A10 came to life and rose up. It was a tricked out civilian version of a military Kraken, a standard personnel transport that was part car, part shuttle. She climbed in and drove it down to the office. She tossed the duffel in the back seat and pulled out. The overhead door closed behind her.

She entered the address of the vet into the auto-pilot.

And what does the time say on my new watch?

It was **03:55 am.**

CHAPTER THREE: THE VET

"The affinity breeds in the parallel genetic engineering programs at Awareness Inc. had both successes and failures. Animal trials resulted in some new species ending up on the black market when they should have been destroyed. The Render program required humans. The felines created for the program were the biggest mistake."

--Blue Peridot, The Turning Point: History of the AI Wars.

"Holt, you stupid fuck. You should have been silent running. You should have been playing it straight. But no…" Cruze talked to the car a bit louder than she intended because the top was down. "You get your ass rolled up by Sec and buy your way out by telling them about an arms deal about to go down." She ripped a bobble head Jesus off the dash and looked at it closely. "An arms deal you set up, you fuck."

It was made of real ivory.

I should have known Braxton was involved in this.

"So I lose all my credits, all the weapons, my freedom and FOUR FUCKING MONTHS!" she screamed into the face of Jesus.

"Well, we are even now, asswipe. It will be days before those clueless bitches start to smell you rotting in their trunk." She held Jesus up to stare real close. "I hope they park in the sun. Better yet, decide on a little trip to Vegas and park there in the sun." She looked at the interior of the car. "Real leather seats are a nice touch, shit-stain. But I just don't understand the bobble-head-Jesus. Are you mocking him? Were you a true believer?"

She tossed Jesus out of the car.

She took a deep breath. She knew her blood was full of adrenaline. She always talked too much when she was spiked.

The Kraken was moving into the ten-meter express control lane reserved for autopilots. Cruze reached up and felt her new hair. The Kraken ran smoothly in the night air.

She looked at her watch.

It was **04:00 am**.

***

The auto-pilot in the Kraken took Cruze to a sleepy suburb of Detroit. Tree-lined streets replaced the foamcrete towers stamped out 100 years ago by machines called makers. The inner city decay was left behind. Ancient trees lined the cobblestone textured streets that served as a design detail more than a road.

None of these people drove wheeled cars.

The population had dropped on Earth as people migrated to the colonies. This left most major cities gutted and emptied in their once high-density cores.

The small town square of a village called Rochester Hills was the Kraken's destination. It was settled directly in front of a traditional storefront with a sign over the door and windows saying, "Franklin Family Veterinarians." In the window, there was a classic neon sign that read, "Emergency Vet - Open 24/7."

She climbed out of the ride, went to the door, and it slid open automatically. The lights gently came up in the reception area.

She placed her hand on the counter and looked about.

A sleepy voice came over an exceptional sound system. "Good morning." There was a pause for a yawn. "May I help you?"

"I have an emergency. Peter Holt said you could help me."

An instantly sober and awake voice said, "I'll be right down."

Less than a minute later a woman about the same age as Cruze entered from behind the reception desk. She didn't say a word but held the door open and waved Cruze in.

As Cruze passed into a modern facility, the woman asked, "Are you injured?"

"No."

She gave an audible sigh of relief.

"Picking up or dropping off?" They kept moving back into a facility that was much bigger than it looked. It must have wrapped around behind the other more modest storefronts.

"Neither."

Cruze stopped. They were in a room where the walls were lined with sleeping cats of various breeds.

The vet turned when she realized Cruze had stopped following. "My name is Vonda Lopez. What do you need?"

"I have a Detroit Municipal Prison locator chip. I need it to be removed in the next hour before it goes off." Cruze unzipped her jacket, revealing the gun there.

"Oh, shit," Vonda looked at her watch. "We don't have much time. At 6:00 am that thing will broadcast, and you will need to get it far from here before that. Take everything off from the waist up." She activated a large exam table.

"Done this before?"

"Many times, it's not easy." She opened cabinets and pulled out medical devices and tools. "Get up here and lay face down."

Don't fuck with me bitch.

The stainless steel was cold against her breasts. Vonda seemed to not even notice the gun in Cruze's hand as she rested her head on her crossed wrists.

"I will need a scan first. These are smart little chips. They will activate automatically if exposed to nitrogen or oxygen gasses. As soon as it gets exposed to our atmosphere, it screams out, and every cop within ten clicks will be here instantly with guns drawn."

"Are you just going to destroy it?"

"No. Better than that." Vonda smiled a wicked grin. "I will carefully extract it from you and place it in one of these cats. A feral one. A real one, not one of these genetically engineered freaks. I recommend you drop the cat off in one of the parks. And then get away. As far away as possible."

"That is not a problem. I'll be off planet before this day is over." Cruze could see the chip on the monitor. It looked like a six-legged spider.

"What do you mean freaks?" Cruze asked.

"We get all these genetically modified pets. Especially cats. People don't keep them. They live too long and are untrainable or are mean or too smart." Vonda was scanning Cruze. "I hate em."

Distracted by the monitor, neither of them saw a paw reach out of its cage, and with the assistance of a long thumb, quietly open the cage door. It was a large, standard looking Siamese cat that lowered itself to the floor, and stretching up to the cage on the second level from the bottom, closed and latched it quietly before slinking out the open door to reception. His collar had the name "Bail" engraved on the tag.

"I'm going to give you a local to stop the pain. Because this is going to hurt. It is affixed to one of your vertebrae."

An area of her back went numb.

"You do this stuff for Holt often?" Cruze asked.

"Gunshot wounds mostly. He financed this whole place. Bought the high-end scanners and med bays. These work as well on humans as pets. The drug market has tapered off. I get less of those requests. It would be a good life if I didn't have to deal with these filthy animals."

You piece of shit.

A glass bell lowered over the area and created a slight vacuum as the air was replaced with an inert gas. Four tiny robot arms opened an incision, spread it, extracted the chip, placed it into a large hypo and added saline. She was closed up after a light number of nanites and a medical adhesive were added.

"You don't like animals? And you're a vet?" Cruze asked.

"Hey, it's better than whoring for Holt. At least I get to euthanize a lot of them every week."

Cruze saw red and kept silent.

She sat straight up and got dressed while she watched Vonda. The woman went to a seemingly random cage and inserted a long device through the bars. A snapping sound was followed by a meow of pain, and the cat fell over.

Vonda opened the cage, and as she dragged the unconscious cat out by its scruff, she said, "It only lasts ten or fifteen minutes. I will have him in a carrier, and you can be on your way before he wakes up. This is a feral cat some concerned suburban housewife bitch brought in. He was scheduled for the dumpster today. He will be way harder for them to catch."

She laid the large cat on the table and injected the chip under his scruff. She then dumped him into a cardboard cat carrier and set it on the table.

"Tell Holt it is the usual rate."

Cruze stood there a moment without speaking, a storm growing on her face. Gun in hand.

"I don't know what the usual rate is." Cruze pulled a bundle of credits out of her coat and dropped it on the table.

"I'll consider it a tip." Vonda smiled.

"No, you won't." Cruze raised her gun and pointed at Vonda's face. "You will use it as logistics money to sell this place. I killed Peter Holt this morning, and if I come back and you are still working here, I will kill you as well. No warning. A sniper bullet to the head." Cruze slowly stalked around the table as she spoke. "GOT IT!?"

"Yes. Yes. Please. Don't..." Vonda crumbled to the floor hiding her face between her knees.

Cruze grabbed the cat carrier and stormed out. With the box on the front seat, she manually drove out of the village.

She never noticed the other cat curled up on the richly carpeted floor in the back of the driver's seat.

It was **05:11 am**.

***

The cat in the box was awake and pissed off by the time Cruze set down in Stone Creek Metro Park.

Before she got out, Cruze said to him, "Listen, man. I'm sorry about this, but it can't be helped. There is going to be a team of very annoyed people looking for you. The longer it is before they find you, the better. Give them a good run, pal."

She laid the box down on its side and released the flaps that held it closed. The feral tomcat was off and running in a flash.

Cruze didn't notice the Siamese eyes watching her from the car.

She got back in and touched the auto-pilot saying, "Head for St. Louis, close up the top, wake me when we get there."

Cruze reclined her seat and fell asleep in less than a minute. She was snoring lightly when Bail popped his head up from beneath her reclined seat. He sniffed her nose a few times and then curled up himself on the warm carpet, falling asleep to the soothing hum of powerful engines.

It was **05:41 am**.

***

At 6:01 am the alarm sounded in the Detroit Municipal Prison. A head count scan revealed that a Jane Doe was "Off-Campus."

Lockdown was automatic, and guards were sent to her cell for an eyes-on check. Glitches like this happened every month, as well as drills. So when the guards got there and found pillows arranged to look like a sleeper, the real alarms went up.

Bergman had another hour before his shift change. He had spent the night deleting all the code he had set up to deactivate cameras to allow for his adventures in the night. Now he waited and reported in all clear as required.

And he soaked his shirt in sweat.

Relief washed over him when he heard feet on the stairs at 7:05 am. "Bryant, you're late, dammit," he yelled through the door. "How many times do we have to talk about this?"

The door opened, and it wasn't Bryant.

"Who the fuck are you? Where's Bryant?" Bergman demanded.

The man was disheveled. He wore jeans and running shoes with a well-used, but clean, collarless, black, button up shirt that was not tucked in, and he had a herringbone jacket that had seen better days.

He held a large coffee in one hand and a badge in the other. It was that was on a lanyard around his neck.

"I'm Neal Locke with Special Investigations. Are you Jeff Bergman?" Locke sat in the only other chair in the tower without being offered. He was out of breath.

"Yes. What's this about?" Bergman said trying to act casual. "What kinda name is Locke?"

"Damn, that's a lot of stairs." Locke took a couple deep breaths and then sipped his coffee. Bergman saw his gun briefly in a shoulder holster. "My grandfather was Chinese. He changed the spelling from Lok." Locke sipped his coffee again, watching Bergman. "As you probably know, Special Investigations are responsible for security breaches around here. Budgets are small, and we have to focus resources." He took another sip of coffee. "We have known about your little camera control program, for years. We hacked your hack long ago. It still turns off the live feed and replaces it with a loop, but it still records the real time feed. In case something happens besides you fucking whores in trade for booze and cigarettes."

Bergman was frozen with fear as Locke took another long, slow sip.

"So you guessed it. Something has happened." He did a longer pause. Two sips.

"All that remains for me to decide is if you helped her escape or if she is still up here because she never left."

At that statement, Bergman's forehead wrinkled, and he squinted in puzzlement.

"Bergman, I'm not after you, unless you killed her," Locke said. "Or assisted her in her escape. I am after Jane Doe 857263." Locke sat back and crossed his feet. "The warden is super pissed about this one."

"Look, I didn't kill her. I didn't help her escape. I didn't…" He looked over his shoulder out the window toward the city. Then he looked at the floor. And all around the tower room.

"Holy shit." Bergman had a realization.

Special Investigator Locke waited.

"Look, if you saw the vid, you saw how she was dressed. She played me. She got my stunner. She threatened to kill me. Look." Bergman was starting to panic.

Bergman pulled up his shirt and showed Locke the burns from the stunner. He saw the edge of the note.

"What's this?" Locke pointed with his coffee cup.

Bergman frantically lifted his shirt. Two buttons flew in his haste to open it. He stood in front of Locke so the man could see it. It was upside down. Neal tilted his head to read.

Bergman recognized the slight wink that meant SI Locke just photographed it with his personal Heads Up Display (HUD).

Locke read the note out loud.

"Well, Bergman. That helps." He emptied his coffee cup, stood up and said in a harsh tone, "Where the fuck is she?"

"She said she wanted a long power cord. Told me she'd make it worth my while. You gotta understand how hot she was. Colony slave girl hot." He swallowed hard. "I think she used it to climb down."

The SI and Bergman went out onto the balcony.

"That's got to be at least seventy feet down," Locke said.

"Twenty-five meters. The cord I brought was fifty meters long," Bergman said, his stomach queasy as he looked out over the edge.

I am so fucked. I am so fucked. I am so fucked. Bergman thought over and over.

"Fuck. What time did this happen?" Locke asked.

"Probably about 12:30," Bergman confessed.

"Are there cameras on the street down there?"

"There were, but kids destroy them as fast as they get replaced." Bergman was trying to blame anyone else.

"Dammit." Neal Locke was headed for the stairs without another word. He was out the door and down as Bergman called after him.

"What about me?" Bergman whined.

Locke was passing Bryant on the stairs. "Tell Bergman I don't give a shit about him. The warden only cares about Jane Doe."

***

"We will arrive in St. Louis in five minutes. Where would you like to go in St. Louis?" the Nav computer asked politely.

Cruze looked at her new watch. It was just before 9:00 am.

"I want breakfast. Find a McDiner with outstanding ratings."

"Found. ETA is three minutes," the auto-pilot said.

"Reserve me a booth and newspaper," Cruze added as she separated a few credits from a bundle and slid them into her pants pocket.

"Unable to comply. No network capability."

Holt was paranoid, eh? Didn't want anyone tracking his ride. Brilliant.

"Open the top." The roof retracted as they slowed to park. "Open the trunk once we are parked." Cruze hopped out, grabbed the duffel and went around to the back. The trunk wasn't empty.

It had gun cases.

Cruze tossed the duffel in, her handgun and leather jacket as well.

She entered the diner and took an open booth. The tabletop opened the morning news feed automatically. There was nothing about an escape or bodies found in trunks.

Excellent.

***

Bail watched Cruze through the diner window for a minute before he gracefully hopped out and peed in the grass. He ran across the lot to the park-like setting behind the McDiner where several families were eating. After studying the scene for a few minutes, Bail jumped up on a table where a small female human sat ignoring the breakfast sandwich in favor of a princess toy. There were two trays here. The girl's and her mother's. The mother was standing off to the side, arguing on a comms unit with someone.

Bail sat on his haunches in front of the girl's tray and looked at her. She was smiling. With a single paw, he batted the biscuit off the top of the sandwich.

The little girl was delighted.

Sitting up even farther, Bail reached out and revealed his thumbs, lifted the meat patty with cheese, and paused to look at the girl. Her eyebrows were high.

He wolfed the meat patty down and licked the grease from his paws.

The girl's mother had no idea how loud she was talking.

Bail moved and sat directly in front of the mother's tray. He paused with his paw, showing the little girl his intent. For effect, he slid his claws out and back in.

He batted off the biscuit.

He took up the meat patty with both hands and devoured it while the girl clapped.

After licking off his paws, he avoided being petted by the little girl. He had a drink of fresh rainwater from a clear puddle, returned to his spot behind the driver seat and fell asleep.

Bail had dreams of zero G.

CHAPTER FOUR: Locke is Working

"Detroit Municipal Prison was corrupt to the core. The warden was not, in fact, in charge. An AI named Gaim pulled all the strings from the shadows. It held a ready supply of talent. SI Neal Locke was later proven unwitting."

--*Blue Peridot, The Turning Point: History of the AI Wars.*

Special Investigator Neal Locke found the extension cord in less than half an hour. He imaged the scene as he had found it and called an SI evidence team to collect it.

He moved in the same general direction he thought she would go. Thinking of what he would do if he were basically naked in the street.

A Proximity Alert was activated in his SI HUD, notifying him of a crime scene nearby.

This can't be good, he thought.

Neal rounded a corner to see a large area cordoned off. He walked up to the officers manning the perimeter and held up his badge.

"Oh, hey, Neal." The beat cop stationed there recognized him. They drank in the same bars and coffee shops.

"Hey, Randy. What's going on?" His SI HUD was already populating with the facts.

"Homicide. Execution style. A single shot to the back of the head. Looks like they dragged him out of bed and brought him down here to kill him," Randy said. "Looks like a pro hit."

Images from the crime scene flashed through Locke's HUD. It was an Asian man of a slight build in his boxers. He had a single bullet to the back of his head. Locke stopped and focused on one image of a dumpster. He zoomed in.

Oh shit.

"The bad part is," Randy continued, "the guy is Hiromi Gee. Son of Senior Gee, the Butcher. The black market mogul who does whatever he wants."

"Oh shit," Locke said as he focused within his HUD on standard issue DMP shower sandals.

She picked the wrong guy to rob.

***

It was too brutally hot, dusty, and dry to run this route without the canopy closed. The Kraken sped along at two hundred kilometers per hour at a smooth ten meters up. Dilapidated highways gave way to direct cross-country travel over fields of wheat and corn and soybeans. Robotic farm machines cared for the fields.

Eventually, it became scrub and then just desert. The ground was a dry blur below. Cruze intersected with the old highway 35 and headed south toward Bartlesville.

Oklahoma Salvage was just north of there. She could see the ship graveyard in the distance. It was so vast, she didn't bother trying to estimate how many square kilometers it covered.

I'll be gone soon. I have enough to get to Freedom Station and then the moon. Maybe.

She slowed to 50kph as she entered the canyon between the derelict ships. Vessels of all sizes and configurations parked impossibly close together. Some looked as if they had crashed there. Others looked like they were slowly being eaten by monsters that took great ripping bites.

She had driven an entire kilometer before she saw the faded sign for Oklahoma Salvage proper. The dirt parking lot was empty when she pulled up. The building looked like an old-fashioned art-deco diner. Not a McDiner re-imaging, but the ghost of an actual diner. She could see the outline on the old rusting sign that said, "EAT."

She shut down the Kraken and used the reverse gull wing door for the first time. It was a first-rate design for a military transport gone civilian.

Easy to exit while shooting.

The solar panels on the roof powered the cooling system as long as the sun beat on it.

She wished she could take it with her.

She pushed open the door to the shop, and an authentic bell rang.

It was then that she saw him.

***

"Silvia, I need to talk to the warden. We have a situation," Locke said to the Detroit Municipal Prison warden's secretary.

"She's in a meeting, Neal. Can she call you back in ninety minutes, after lunch?" Silvia said in a perfect professional voice. "What's this regarding?"

"Jane Doe 857263. It's an emergency."

Without preamble, Warden Dorothy Summers was on the comms.

"Neal, how did you find out so fast?" Warden Summers sounded afraid.

"I was following a lead and came across the crime scene where Hiromi Gee had been murdered. It's why I'm calling," Neal said.

"What? Where?" She was shocked. "Hiromi Gee?"

"About ten blocks north of the north-east DMP tower. I called because there was a standard issue pair of shower sandals at the scene." Locke paused. "What did you think I was calling about?"

"Jeff Bergman is dead. A single bullet to the head," the warden said. "Looks like he was tortured first. I have no other details. DPD is lead on the investigation."

"Shit," Locke cursed.

"There's more. At approximately 6:00 am, two minors crashed a car they were joyriding. There were two dead bodies in the trunk. One was Peter Holt, and the other was an Anthony Wells. Peter Holt was why Jane Doe was our guest. He informed on a dangerous arms deal. Details remain classified. I'm starting to think she was more than a stupid colony whore being used as a cash mule."

"She has had a busy night," Locke added.

"Locke, the car was stolen from the Blue Night Market. That fringe commercial area near the DMP. A restaurant called The Vienna, between 2 am and 3 am."

"What about the tracer?"

"It activated north of the city, somewhere called Stone Creek Metro Park," the warden replied. "It has been intermittent since then."

"I want to go there. Can you have a car sent down here?"

"Yes." Locke heard her speak to someone. "It's on the way."

"Warden." He paused for emphasis. "Dorothy, you have to understand, this is going to be a shit storm. Did you see what she wrote on Bergman's belly? If she found out, he talked to me. If Hiromi Gee knew her..." he faded off in thought. "And the two scumbags in the trunk. That's four homicides, gun murders all, where guns are banned, mind you. This doesn't even begin to include what Senior Gee is going to do. Jesus, Mary, and Joseph."

"Are you religious, Locke?"

"I am non-denominational when it comes to cursing," Locke replied. "The car is here. Thanks. That was fast. I'll report in when I have something."

"Right," the warden said though gritted teeth.

"By the way, what's the budget for this run?" Locke asked. "I may need to keep the car a while."

"Forget the budget. Find her," she ordered and hung up.

I'm getting too old for this shit.

The car was a Sterling Motors sedan. It was not new, but it was in tremendous condition. Locke entered the car and logged in. The car was white with deeply tinted windows to hide the fact that the back seat was a cage for prisoner transport.

"Sterling, take me to Stone Creek Metro Park."

Locke didn't know this was a brilliant piece of detective work on his part. The autopilot in the car took him to the Metro Park to the same parking place the autopilot in the Kracken Jane Doe had used.

As the gull-wing angled up and away, Locke's eyes fell on a cardboard box three meters in front of the car. He slipped out, and as he stood, he could see that it was a simple cat carrier. It had a cartoon of a purring cat on the side. It also had the logo of Franklin Family Veterinarians with an address. He didn't touch the box, and he thought he knew what had happened.

"Sterling, take me to Franklin Family Veterinarians, in Rochester Hills. And make it fast." The car was moving before he was belted in. The acceleration pressed him deep into his seat. Strobes deployed top and bottom as he sped ten meters above the empty roads.

While he was en route, he submitted his report to the warden. He included he suspected a vet had transferred the chip to an animal, and he was following that lead up next.

It was a vulnerability the prison was aware of but considered it a low risk because of the specialized equipment required to extract the chip. That equipment was highly controlled and restricted to government and law enforcement. But then again, so were guns.

***

The closed sign was still on when the Sterling parked in front of the Franklin Family Vet's office. That was odd because there was also a sign, now off, that proudly stated that they were open 24/7.

Locke approached the door hoping to find an intercom when he noticed the door was not locked, slightly ajar.

"Hello?" he called out after pushing open the door. It had the hush of an empty building. He could smell a sweet, metallic odor in the air.

He drew his gun.

"Hello, I'm coming back." He rounded the counter and saw a small stack of cardboard pet carriers stored underneath the counter. The door that led to the back of the vet's space was open a crack. Locke pushed it up slowly with the barrel of his gun. The targeting cross-hairs activated in his HUD. His handgun held one-hundred explosive darts that traveled at 2000 feet per second.

He didn't set foot in the room.

There was a woman in the center of the room laying on her back on a stainless steel examination table. Her hands were tied to the table at points designed to secure leashes.

Her throat was cut.

How could there be so much blood in a woman so small?

He backed away and out. It was then he noticed all the silent cats watching him. He was glad he had touched nothing except the glass door on the way in.

He called it in. He would have to wait for DPD to get there. They arrived just as he hung up the phone with the warden. His gun was back in his holster and his badge in full view when the first two cars arrived.

They were regular uniformed patrol cops who would just secure the scene. Even though he didn't need to, he told the entire story to them. He could tell they liked being treated with respect. He knew they would not be the ones to investigate the murder. He also knew he would have to tell it several more times, but he didn't want this scene to be contaminated. Locke wanted to make sure he had all the details straight. He wanted a DNA sweep first thing. The warden was already sending the DNA map of Jane Doe over.

They made him wait.

He spent his time in the car. He detailed additional reports and told his story four more times.

The team in Stone Creek Metro Park found the cat finally. It was hiding in storm sewers that were dry until the rains filled them with runoff. Five hours later, the warden called him. Audio and video this time.

"Locke, this is out of control. DPD has matched her DNA at all these sites. They even found that Holt was secretly recording all the deals he was making in his office." She started a vid for Locke in his HUD. It was Jane Doe casually sitting in Holt's office chatting like old friends.

Locke paused it. "He just called her 'Cruze.'" The video was frozen on her. She had changed her look. Not just shorter, dyed hair, but her entire demeanor was different. She seemed taller. Her eyes were brighter.

"Wait until you see this." Holt opened the safe, and no sooner than he sat up and turned around, she shot him in the face. Then with a speed that defied the camera to keep up, she turned and shot the bodyguard multiple times.

"Jesus. That's cold."

"Pay attention. Watch how easily she carries them out to the trunk. She is stronger than she looks," the warden said in warning.

"And faster and smarter," Locke followed. "It would have been days before those bodies were found if those kids had returned the car like she asked."

"The bundle of credits she gave the kids had blood on it. That bundle was brand new and had consecutive numbers. We have a watch on for all its neighbors. If she spends any of it, we'll know."

"Here is an odd one," Locke said. "The lead detective here said they found a $10,000 bundle of credits in the murdered vet's purse."

"Any idea if any Law Enforcement cameras picked up her visit?" the warden asked. "It would be good to know what she was driving."

"No chance. Rochester Hills is a private community. It's a No Camera zone. People will pay a lot these days for privacy."

"Shit. Stupid zealots. What do those boring ass people have to hide?" the warden said.

Locke said nothing. He paid extra to live in a building in Detroit that had real doorman security and no cameras. *No smart buildings for me.*

"You're about done there," the warden said. "Unless more bodies show up with her DNA all over, your trail is cold."

"Not quite. If you really want her," Locke said. "I have a hunch. She is wasting no time. I am heading to the space catapult in New York City."

"Why New York?"

"Look at her. In New York, she will blend in. In Mexico City, she would stick out," Locke said. "Am I clear to follow this path?"

"Do it. We will reassess in a week. Our dicks are in a vice here, Locke. This shit storm is on us."

But Locke had a feeling this was worse than a shit storm. He had a hunch that she was the actual buyer in Holt's little arms deal. And if that was true... Cruze had nukes.

CHAPTER FIVE: Oklahoma Salvage

"Harv Rearden's involvement was redacted from all official reports."

--Blue Peridot, The Turning Point: History of the AI Wars.

Cruze looked up at the small bell attached to the frame just above the door. It occurred to her it may have been the first time she had ever seen a real bell. She had heard a million simulated bells, but this was real.

She looked down and saw a man sitting on the floor drinking an Orange Crush soft drink out of a real glass bottle.

"Pretty fancy Kraken you got there." He was craning his neck to see around the hover-cycle he was repairing. The floor was scattered with the cycle parts of something he had in pieces. "By the extra vents, I'd bet the power plant has been converted to dark matter."

"Come on out and have a look." She reached down to give him a hand up. "My name's Cruze. Pleased to meet you, Harv."

"We met before?" he asked as he struggled to his feet, staring at her face carefully.

She just smiled and pointed to his name on the breast of his dirty coveralls.

"Want a soda? I hate drinking alone." He laughed at his own joke and didn't wait for her answer. He pulled another Orange Crush out of the ancient vending machine.

While he was doing this, Cruze took in her surroundings. The counter and stools were still there but well-worn. Where the booths should have been, opposite the counter, there were racks of parts for sale, projects in progress, and what looked like piles of junk to Cruze. The appliances were all gone behind the counter as well. The racks there seemed more organized.

Cruze took the opened soda in hand, but she was not thirsty until she felt the ice-cold condensation dripping down the sides of the bottle.

Harv watched her with wild white eyebrows raised.

She took a cautious sip. "I have never had anything this delicious in my life." Cruze stared at the bottle in disbelief.

"I like you already." Harv went out the door and walked around the Kraken murmuring, "Very nice... Mmmmm."

"I am interested in a trade." She drank some more soda. "I can trade the Kraken and have some credits. I need a small shuttle. One that will get me to Freedom Station. Maybe Luna"

"Bring her around to the shop," Harv said. "Let's have a close look."

She climbed in and followed him to where an overhead door was opening. She drove the car in, and the door closed behind her.

She began lowering the convertible hard top so it would show off the leather interior. The dark tinted windows all lowered as the top slid into the body smoothly. Harv held a hand scanner as he walked around the car.

"Not stolen, that's good. Not registered either, with less than a hundred hours on it. Just saying, not asking," Harv said as he added data to the pad he was carrying. He walked to the back of the car. "Pop the trunk."

She hit the remote. The trunk opened smoothly. Harv raised an eyebrow. Cruze walked around and saw him staring at the four gun cases within.

"These included in the trade?"

"Sure, why not," Cruze said.

Harv lifted the cases out and opened them on a workbench. He typed the additions into his pad.

"Open the hood," he asked.

She hit another button on the remote, and the hood opened with a hiss. Harv set his pad down and looked inside with awe.

He crawled over, under and inside the car for ten more minutes. He stood in front of Cruze keying the last few items.

"Is the cat included?" Harv asked.

"Cat?" Cruze was puzzled.

"I got to be straight with you, darlin', you'd be better off selling this in Denver or Newark. That's the market for these. Then take your money and a luxury catapult to the Station."

"I'm in a hurry."

"I can only give you half of what it's worth."

"I know. You come highly recommended as fair and... discrete," Cruze added cautiously.

"Including the six Frange carbines and twelve assorted side arms. Let's go see what we can do."

"It only has to get me there. Not even a round trip. I will sell it when I get there anyway."

They drove around the salvage yard in an old cart, looking at various options. They finally settled on one.

"OK. How about this one. It's a small Ferguson-539. It has full-size dock collars on the back and sides. Including integrated airlocks on all three. Personal Type 2 on the top and bay style on the bottom. But the bay hatch is frozen solid. That still gives you lots of docking options. The main engines have not been fired in probably forty years. The Grav-Plates are all good though. It'd be slow, but it'd get you there." Harv was scratching his white beard. "It's full manual. The auxiliary thruster tanks are gone, but the worst part is that the outer starboard airlock is damaged and won't seal. I am not certain about the inner hatch either."

"Have you got a pressure suit that will fit me?" Cruze asked.

"I think I might." Harv smiled. "Let's get a full charge on and take her for a spin."

Neither of them noticed the cat just outside the hatch.

***

They worked together for the next four hours servicing the batteries and testing the systems. Together they took it up and landed it in front of the shop where they did their work. Hooked into the main power, it was charged up to full.

Harv said he would take it on a test flight to Bartlesville and pick up some dinner. He had seen her yawning.

"While I'm gone you should catch a nap. In that office is the comfiest sofa ever created." He was detaching the cables from the small craft. "It's the one under the blue tarp, not the brown one."

With a wave, he entered the hatch and was gone. The Grav-Plates only had a 9% charge remaining, but it would be enough.

She climbed the dusty stairs to his office. It was a mess. Every wall had floor to ceiling bookcases that were full and often doubled up. It had the feel of organized chaos.

I'm crashing. Too much adrenaline. I need to get off this damn planet. I need to get back to Luna, to my ship.

The sofa on the right was covered with a blue tarp and was tucked in all over. People had apparently been sitting on it. She dragged off the tarp and found an overstuffed, well-worn sofa.

She laid down and rested her head on the armrest. It made the perfect pillow.

She breathed in the delicious smell of the leather. Harv was right about the sofa. She was asleep in less than a minute.

The cat came into the office without a sound. He went to the sofa and stared at Cruze for a full minute. Softly jumping up, he curled up by her side with the full length of his body against her ribs and hip.

They slept undisturbed for two hours.

***

Cruze thought she heard screaming. She struggled to wake up. She had a black bag over her head. She couldn't Move.

The bag was suddenly ripped off. An old man stared into her eyes. He wanted to make sure she was awake.

She struggled, but even her head was secured. He would not stop staring. Bloodshot whites showed all around his pupils, creating a map to his insanity.

Another scream drew his attention away, sparking his anger.

Cruze wished she had just closed her eyes.

***

Bail was the first to hear the shuttle returning. He was already awake because Cruze was twitching violently.

He hid beneath the desk when he heard feet on the stairs.

Cruze woke with a start and was on her elbows when Harv entered the room with a smile and bags marked KFC.

He piled the bags on the table and started setting it all out. There was a bucket of fried chicken proudly marked with

"Original Recipe" as if the robot with the little white beard was saying it. There were mashed potatoes and gravy, plus coleslaw.

Harv put two pieces of chicken on a plate, and while carrying it, went behind his desk. After fussing around, he came back with two Orange Crush bottles.

But no plate for Cruze.

Cruze did not notice. "Thanks for dinner, Harv. Why all the nostalgia? Orange Crush? KFC? I can't believe these even exist now. Things never change on Earth."

"It's my favorite thing about Earth. And its biggest problem," Harv said. "I have another home out in the belts that is nice. But they don't have KFC."

"Are you out here by yourself?" she asked.

Harv hesitated only an instant. "I am here with my nephew and my granddaughter, but they are off on business right now."

"Why no personal HUD? Seems like it would be very useful here," Cruze said.

"I just don't like the idea of putting stuff in my brain. If there is one thing I know, it's that tech fails. It's not if it will fail. It's when will it fail." He gestured to his small earpiece. "These you can take out easy. What's your excuse?"

"I am the paranoid type. I like my privacy." *And I don't like to be tracked by HUD signatures.*

"Mind the DNA sniffers at customs thresholds," Harv said. "They have a hundred different ways they can harvest your DNA." He handed her a bottle of Orange Crush.

He loaded up a plate for himself and sat by the wall. Cruze was digging in as well.

"This is wonderful. Why have I never had this before?" she asked.

Harv glanced over toward the desk. "How much you want for the cat?" he said out of the blue.

"What cat?" Cruze asked while snacking on a third piece of chicken.

"Your cat. The one that was in your car." He pointed with his own drumstick. "You have his hair all over you."

She looked down, and sure enough, her black pants were covered in fur.

Just then a bell sounded. It was just like the bell on the door of the former diner. Harv looked up, and Cruze followed his gaze. A large wall monitor showed a hover-cycle moving toward Oklahoma Salvage at high speed.

"Hunter, what is the ETA of that thing?" Harv said to the air.

An AI responded, "ETA is three minutes." Harv and Cruze locked eyes for a moment.

"I know," Harv said. "I never saw ya."

Harv wiped his hands on the front of his coveralls and left the office. The wall monitor stayed on. It was tracking the hover-cycle.

Cruze looked directly into one of the concealed cameras. It was where she would have placed it.

"How did you know I was here?" AI~Hunter asked Cruze.

"I have worked with a lot of good AI systems. The best of them care for the humans that they work with. They are proactive. I could tell you were feeding Harv info without being asked. And it was good info." She saw Harv on the monitor. He grabbed another Orange Crush before taking a wrench to remove the saddle off a cycle as if it was what he had been doing all along.

"That first Orange Crush," Cruze said. "You used the bottle to sample my DNA." It was a statement, not a question.

"That is very astute," AI~Hunter replied. "How did you know?"

"I can't think of another reason Harv would warn me about DNA scanning at customs." Cruze was watching the hover-cycle on the monitor drift to a stop and settle in front of the former diner.

"Did you turn me in?" she asked plainly, not trusting AIs.

"No. Like Harv says. Fuck the man." There was a smile in the AI's voice.

I might let this AI survive, Cruze thought.

"Is there an alert out for me?" she asked.

"Yes. Escaped from Detroit Municipal Prison, armed and dangerous. Sought in connection with at least five murders and maybe more." Hunter brought up the bulletin. It had her booking photo. Her face was bruised, and her hair was long and light brown. But then there was another photo. It was from above and on her left. Her hair was cut and dyed black.

She was inside Holt's office.

"Five murders?" she gasped.

"A prison guard, and four other convicted felons, including the son of a crime boss named Senior Gee. One was a veterinarian," AI~Hunter said. "No additional information was available passively. Any requests for additional information would trigger scrutiny. Another AI is working it with heavy hands. At the prison. It does not want you to know that."

"What the hell?" Cruze got a rotten feeling in her gut as she watched the man on the hover-cycle take off his helmet. Someone was leaving bodies along her trail.

"Hunter, Harv may be in trouble! Where are the guns?" She ran to the door. It slid closed automatically in front of her. At the same time, all the dusty blinds closed at once.

"Harv knows what he is doing," the AI replied.

Meanwhile, on the monitor, the man stepped off the cycle and opened the front door to the shop. The doorframe scanned him. "No weapons detected." Cruze could tell the AI~Hunter was speaking to Harv. The AI was echoing it for her as well.

The big wall monitor was divided into eight smaller screens that showed the front shop from different angles. Each view had an auto-tracking set of cross-hairs on the Asian man. Four were on his head. Four focused on his body.

Harv straightened up and flexed his back like an old man. Cruze smiled at the perfect affectation. "Howdy, son. Nice ride. How's the new 6000 series feel with no outriggers?" He pointed to his hover-cycle with the wrench. "Thirsty?" He held up an Orange Crush.

"How many of those does he drink a day?" Cruze was relaxing again.

"Only one. And only if he brushed his teeth," AI~Hunter said. "The rest are just colored water."

"Hunter, I don't know who this guy is, but I think he is following me. I didn't murder ALL those people."

"Have you seen this girl?" The man ignored the offer of a drink as he drew out a photo-card screen. It had Cruze's image from Holt's office.

AI~Hunter added, "I believe this man works for Senior Gee."

Harv actually laughed. "You have come to the wrong place looking for pretty girls, my friend." He bent and looked at the image closer, squinting. "Is that the one I saw on the Bulletins this morning?"

The man didn't move.

"I haven't seen her. But then again, I have not seen anyone for days. Except for this strange cat..." He seemed to drift off thinking.

"If I do see her, is it worth anything? Fuck The Man. I'm not doing his job for him. Sons a bitches..." Harv grumbled.

The visitor's face changed for the first time. A corner of his mouth went up in a crooked smile.

AI~Hunter said to Cruze, "Harv is well known for his disdain for authority. If this man has done his research, he will know that." The AI paused before adding, "This man has no Ident in the system even though he has an advanced HUD and a rider."

"A rider?" Cruze asked.

"Another entity is on board his HUD, seeing what he sees and advising him. It is a valuable, but expensive asset. I have been trying to persuade Harv to get a HUD just for comms and control systems. Then I could be his rider."

"Why would he not want one?" Cruze asked. "Basic HUDs are dirt cheap here."

"Why don't you have one?" the AI asked.

Because I fucking hate AI computers. She said nothing out loud.

The man reached into his pocket, drew a card and handed it to Harv. "If you do see her, be careful, she is a cold-blooded murderer. Keep this handy. I suspect she may be headed this way. Call this number anytime, day or night."

"What kind of finder's fee am I looking at," Harv looked at the card, "Mr. Parker?" he said in a tone that made Cruze nervous.

"$100,000 in gold," Parker said.

Harv smiled big and placed the card in his breast pocket. Then Harv went to a cardholder on the counter and handed him a card. "If this number calls you, but no one says anything…" he faded off conspiratorially.

The man just nodded and took the card. He winked at it and placed it into his pocket.

"Thank you, Mr. Rearden." He turned and moved to the door.

"Call me Harv!" And Harv laughed. It was an almost evil laugh.

After the man had left, Harv walked to his old phone and inserted the card.

"Transfer all contact information to this device. Set key number nine to speed dial it. Replicate to all handsets in the enterprise. Interlude the shops and remote manual units."

He stared at the card for a few more minutes and opened a drawer. There was an old metal cash box there. He opened it, and there were no credits, but several hundred other business cards.

On one screen Harv closed the box, while on another, the hover-cycle moved out, going south between the canyons of shipping containers.

"We are clear," AI~Hunter said over the comms to Harv as well as Cruze.

"Was the card hot?" Harv asked Hunter as he began to move back to the office.

"Yes. Data, audio, and dual video. Open channel, which was a mistake. It was direct to the rider, not the man," AI~Hunter said. "Protocols confirm the rider is an AI."

"What? For spit's sake, I thought I was paranoid."

Cruze was puzzled.

"Harv loves to be underestimated," the AI said as Harv came up the old stairs.

"Hunter, did you see the directional laser antenna relay on his bike?" Harv asked.

"Yes, Mr. Rearden," the AI said with humor.

"Fuck you. Where is he?" Harv asked.

"He stopped 2.1 kilometers south of the yard."

"Did he drop any sensors?"

"None detected."

"Did he keep my card?" Harv smiled.

"Yes."

"Outstanding." Harv looked up at Cruze. "Let's find you a pressure suit that fits."

Cruze noticed the large Siamese cat sound asleep on the windowsill.

CHAPTER SIX: THE FERGUSON 539

"Jane Doe, aka Elizabeth Cruze, was considered a petty escapee and made such an unlikely escape from Earth, it was not discovered until years later by the Earth Defense Force."

--Blue Peridot, The Turning Point: History of the AI Wars.

Cruze followed Harv into an old, rusty Quonset hut. It was scorching hot inside the metal building. The door wasn't locked, and the only windows were high in the overhead doors on either end.

Harv hit three large buttons on the wall just inside a small door to the left of the overhead. Both doors began to open. The overhead lights came on along with air handlers.

The building was about thirty meters by sixty meters and filled with a complex of pipes that functioned as the hanger system for hundreds of pressure suits that hung from their collar handles.

Harv moved through them with purpose. Cruze noticed the various stages of disrepair the suits were in. Several were military issue. About half of them had helmets attached.

They were all dusty.

Harv paused in an area that had about a dozen suits. All had helmets and seemed to be intact. Cruze scanned his collection and noticed how many holes that were made by weapons fire. Some still had blood stains. This explained the faint smell.

"I wear an 1100.304.76," Cruze said. "But any medium or large will do as long as the seal is good."

Harv eventually focused on a black pressure suit that was the new style made especially for women. Or at least it looked like it used to be black. Now it was so dusty that it was red-gray. A remote hanger unit came up, a motorized dolly specifically for moving pressure suits. She presumed AI~Hunter was driving, and retrieved the suit from its hanger.

"This one has all the pieces," Harv said. "And I don't believe it has ever been worn." He slapped its shoulders and arms, creating a cloud of dust. "These Velcro patches have no name tag and no insignia. The CO_2 scrubbers are custom, so they were never removed. Air tanks are tiny ultra-high pressure things that are not standard." Harv patted it a few more times. "We'll clean her up and do a submerged positive pressure test."

Cruze had never seen this kind of pressure suit before.

"This suit came in on the same wreck as Hunter," Harv said faintly, trailing off.

"I was wondering how you acquired a Class 3 AI," Cruze said, hoping he would add more.

Did I keep the hate out of my voice? She asked herself.

Harv walked to the back of the Quonset hut through another maze of suits, which had clear signs people had died inside them. The small tractor followed with the single suit, and they came to a door that slid aside automatically. It was marked SUIT SHOP in black spray paint.

As they entered, the doors closed behind them. It was an airlock designed to keep out dust. The grate under their feet sucked air down for ten seconds before the inner door opened.

Unlike everything else Cruze had seen here, this room was clean and organized. "My granddaughter usually handles this work." Harv touched a few buttons on the front, and a couple lights cycled through red, yellow and green. Only one got to green. Two were still yellow, and one was red. The suit was then hung on a rack made for the duty. It slid into a clear booth via a track above the suit.

It began to inflate.

"How do you do that?" Cruze was curious.

"What?" A series of jets began to power wash the suit. In thirty seconds, it was clean.

"How do you inflate the suit without external connections? The tanks are tiny."

"It doesn't inflate the suit. The booth is creating a vacuum. The suit's own sensors will let us know if the seal holds. It's in startup self-check." Harv was concentrating on the monitor. Cruze looked at his eyes from the side. He was far older than he seemed. Maybe the oldest person she ever met.

"So you bought Hunter as salvage?"

Harv laughed. "Ha! I couldn't afford that. I was searching for an abandoned asteroid mine in the Belt that I had heard a rumor of on the way back from a Mars delivery. In the Belt, I found the nose end of a Weber GP170. Just the nose. Torn off just behind the bridge."

Harv turned away from the automated suit test and maintenance unit as he spoke. "I looked for a week and never found the rest of the ship. Not even debris. We dragged it back here because I figured the instruments and sensors could be worth something. It seemed like some level of emergency procedures had been done. Three of the suit lockers were empty."

Cruze stared at the suit. She had the irrational feeling it was watching her.

"That nose sat out there in the yard for over a year before I got time and looked at it close. I'll never forget that day. Emma had bought me a lunch box. Its paint job was so funny. It looked like it was made of bacon. I had lost it on that ship. Found it that day!" He smiled a sad smile.

"Emma?"

"Emma was my wife. She died long ago." Harv shook himself and continued. "Anyway, I had just started pulling hardware when I realized there was a cold Class 3 AI unit in there. I got a portable power cart out and fired it up hoping to find out what happened and maybe locate the rest of the ship. Because if a ship that small had a Class 3 AI, what else did it have?"

"Did you find it?" Cruze was curious.

"The unit had wiped itself." Harv stared into one of the cameras directly at Hunter. "The logs indicated that it was a voluntary self-reset. An AI suicide. It was reset to the day-one config. It had advanced personality templates but no initialization."

"So you initialized him?" she asked.

"Yes. I almost sold it in the reset state. We could have retired then, spent Emma's last days in comfort. But Emma convinced me to keep him. She trained Hunter up and tuned him to care for me and not take any of my shit."

Cruze glanced at her watch and wondered, *What am I doing?*

"She knew she was dying? I'm so sorry, Harv," Cruze said.

The suit deflated and the doors opened. All the lights were green now.

"So damn dusty in here."

Cruze watched Harv wipe his eyes of imaginary dust.

***

The suit had a small backpack integrated onto it. Within it was a full body stocking to wear inside the pressure suit. It was still new in the package.

Harvey turned around so she could put it on. Cruze stripped down to bra and panties to slide into the thing. It made her smile because as she held it up, it looked like it would fit a six-year-old child. She'd seen these "skins" before.

It went on smoothly and included feet, a hood, but not gloves. Wearing it, she got into the pressure suit in less than a minute with no assistance, because when she powered it up the slide seals closed automatically in the back. She could tell the skin was designed to wick away sweat because she was usually sweating as she struggled into suits like this. The helmet locked on with a twist and activated. It held a full HUD and pilot interface that would be of no use with a manual shuttle.

"The integrated boots might be a bit tight until they form fit," Harv said as he was stuffing her folded clothes into the small pack.

"These gloves are so thin, my hands are going to freeze." Cruze was putting them on. They fit perfectly. It was like this suit was designed specifically for her.

She checked the pockets. There were the standard emergency kits on thigh pockets. Suit repair, first aid, flashlight, and a pocket with six color-coded but unmarked epinephrine auto-injectables.

The black mirrored visor slid up and away.

"Harv, I have never worn anything like this. Thanks."

"I've been needing to get this out of here," Harv replied. "Civilians are not supposed to possess this kind of pressure suit. Thanks for getting it off world." He sounded relieved.

"You're doing me a favor. Though we're not quite ready yet." Harv exited the clean room back into the warehouse.

He moved from rack to rack and then came back to her.

"What do you think? Maintenance, Security or Transcorp pilot?" he asked.

"I think pilot. The suit is too atypical."

Harv placed Freedom Station patches on the shoulder, Transcorp on the back, and a name on her upper left chest.

"Berkowitz?" she asked, smiling.

***

They rode the small cart back to the garage in silence.

Even though the suit was black, the cooling in it was the finest she ever felt. It was even and comfortable. The best part was that the skin suit seemed to prevent the itching she usually experienced when she couldn't scratch.

Harv drove the cart right into the garage next to the Kraken. Cruze got out and grabbed the duffel full of credits. She took out two bundles and stored them in rib pockets. Then she handed the rest of the bag to Harv.

"It's too much," was all he said.

"Where I am going it will be of little use," she replied. "Physical credits are only good on Earth. The exchange rate is horrible and tracked."

"I'll tell you what. I will put it on your account. Hunter will keep track of it." Harv went to his desk and keyed a lock open. "This might help. It's gold, a Luna mint. Maybe half of that duffel."

It was a black velvet case the size of a thick book. Coins were stored in there like poker chips.

"If you ever find yourself in these parts make sure you come by if you need anything. And if you don't need anything, you can buy me dinner."

There was a long awkward pause as Cruze pretended to look about for anything else she may have left in the car.

He is giving me a deal. He is far too generous.

"Harv, there are people trying to kill me. If anyone comes around that doesn't feel right, don't take any chances. Especially any asshole named Braxton or Dante. I was never here. Or asshole AIs. No offense, Hunter."

"None taken," came from hidden speakers.

Cruze firmly shook Harv's hand.

"You take care, old man."

Neither of them saw the cat slip inside the shuttle.

***

Cruze sat in the old pilot seat of the Ferguson-539 and strapped in. She opened the helmet visor and set it to close automatically if a loss of pressure was detected.

She swallowed hard as the ship took off. Her heart was pounding.

What have I gotten myself into?

As soon as she was clear, she executed a roll, so the ship was inverted. Her sense of falling up was replaced with the more natural sensation to her inner ear of free falling down. It was away from the planet instead of toward it.

She followed the line of the Rockies as she slowly ascended and moved north. It felt like free fall now. She was glad she had slept. On full manual, she needed to be alert, and free fall always made her feel sleepy when she was feeling safe. As she gained altitude and the curve of the Earth became evident, it seemed like she was flying with the Earth above her.

***

From the pilot seat, she couldn't see the joyous cat stretch and shake between the airlock doors. The cat began to jump around that space in many angles and directions. He used his prehensile tail and tiny opposable thumbs to grab holds and increase the joy with flips and turns of complex acrobatics.

Then he latched on and froze to the inner door. He stared at the back of Cruze's helmet and howled a warning for a full minute, unheard.

There was an increasing groan in the infrastructure that Cruze finally heard, and then a momentary silence followed by a horrible sound of metal tearing as a quantity of the starboard Grav-Plates ripped themselves away from the ship and away from the Earth's gravity well, uncontrolled.

The shuttle began to barrel roll and fall.

Fifty-five thousand feet below, the jagged peaks of the Vermilion Range were waiting with teeth exposed.

Bail could hear the alarms that were sounding all over the console when he saw her visor slam shut. The main compartment was losing pressure.

***

Cruze dropped the nose to dive straight toward the planet and shut down the remaining foils. The high-speed pirouette made it hard to work the controls, but using the thrusters she first got the spin under control. Then she brought the nose up to level. With only 12,000 feet left, she brought the foils gradually back up, balancing them on the center few and making them push the shuttle into the sky instead of pulling it.

As she maneuvered, her body pressed against the harness cruelly like she was hanging from the ceiling. On manual, she would have to keep her hand on the controls, and her arms extended, holding them down while being dragged up at one gravity.

***

By the time the shuttle arrived at the public parking spire of Freedom Station, it was four hours later. Cruze was on the edge of fainting as she backed the gravs off and began navigating with thrusters only.

There were thousands of private shuttles parked here. She drifted close to one of the smart docks designed for dumb shuttles and allowed it to attach to the port side airlock. The main compartment was still in vacuum. That would make her leaving easier.

The starboard airlock that was responsible for the failure was easy to open. There was vacuum on both sides already. Cruze spent time trying to gain a seal on the inner airlock door. It finally went green, but that door would probably never open again for all the emergency resin she used to obtain the seal. It began to re-pressurize inside the cabin. The port authority would eventually have to enter the ship, but she would be long gone. To make it easy she left it unlocked.

She drifted outside the starboard outer airlock door and climbed to the roof of the shuttle. With a significant push of her legs, Cruze launched toward one of the maintenance ladders on the spire.

Maintenance crews ensured there were no cameras out here. They never wanted their fuck-ups documented on video. Plus it was a great place to take a nap if one was hung over. Just put on a suit, head out for a shift, clip on a rung and nap in the shade.

Now, how the hell do I get to the moon? It's only 240,000 kilometers from here to the Moon.

She ascended the spire, away from the core of the station. Cruze knew a way in that was not monitored. She moved up and out a thousand rungs to the narrowest part of the spire that was bristling with commercial antennas.

The plain hatch was right where she expected. It wasn't locked, and it was vacuum on the inside, but the gravity from the floor plates came on as she entered. She closed the outer hatch and went through a floor hatch.

Pressing the only control button available, the hatch closed, sealed, and the compartment pressurized. Another floor hatch opened, and she climbed down the ladder on the wall of a small elevator lobby.

Lights went green when the hatch closed above. The elevator doors opened.

She considered her mission. *Every last one of those fucking Red Talon merc bastards will burn.*

The elevator ride was long and slow. She tried not to think about home. *One thing at a time. She had to get to the Moon and then Mars where Del and Harper were worried sick.* Kade's and Hall's dead bodies came to her mind unbidden. The deal gone bad. *Fucking Holt.*

When the door opened, it revealed the back of a dirty break room used by the Comms crew. Only one old man was in there. He was drinking coffee from a large porcelain mug that looked like it had not been washed for decades. Cruze decided that if she poured hot water into that cup, in three minutes, she'd have a strong cup of coffee.

He turned around as she exited the elevator. Cruze could see he was watching a pornographic movie on a screen at his desk.

He didn't say a word.

Cruze walked by and casually tossed a gold coin on his desk as she headed for the door.

The old man looked at the coin and said, "What was that? Damn elevator is acting up again." The money disappeared into a pocket as she exited the room.

The spire was far thicker here and held many offices on this level. Vending machines of various kinds were in the elevator lobby, making it crowded with a couple dozen people talking, waiting and buying vended tacos.

Several people had on pressure suits and even helmets. She took hers off as she entered one of the elevators, but left the skin hood up, hiding her hair. Nine people entered the elevator, not looking at each other. One of the other passengers said, "Damn those tacos smelled good."

Everyone agreed.

***

Bail, the cat, sat on the floor of the airlock holding some conduit with his tail to be ready. The cold in there didn't bother him. He was bred to be tolerant of a wide range of temperatures. He was between the inner and outer doors. When the cabin had lost pressure, he was lucky to be in there.

He played with his name tag. His only possession. It had his name engraved into it and a bit more.

His hearing was acute, so he heard the footsteps before he saw the feet. Bail liked to pretend that the windows set into the door at his face height were specifically made just for him. Humans don't need a shin height door window. But he also knew that in space, up was not always up.

Three sets of boots stopped outside the airlock. He could hear them.

"This is the one. It docked about three hours ago," one muffled voice said on the other side of the door.

"No one has left the thing so far. Security reviewed the logs and vids," another said.

"Look, just log a possible person in distress, and we can use override codes."

"No need, boss," a third man said at the panel. "It ain't locked."

"Log it anyway, and we will go in. I hope it's not another dead guy at the stick. I couldn't take another week in quarantine. My wife would kill me."

"I'd love another week in quarantine to get away from my wife. I could catch up on my sleep."

"It's logged. Okay, Perkins. You first then."

Two of them stepped to the side while Perkins hit the control to unseal and then open the hatch.

The instant the opening was wide enough, Bail shot out like a rocket and ran down the corridor that curved around the spire.

"I didn't see nothing," they all said at the same time.

***

Cruze had to change elevators twice before she reached level S2. It was the southern level where the transport hub was located. The elevator door opened to the din of thousands of people going about their daily business.

She moved with the crowd, knowing exactly where she was going.

The sign was just as she remembered. *Long Term Lockers.*

There was a long corridor flanked by other halls on each side, all lined with lockers of various sizes.

Without hesitation, she went to a specific hall and sub-corridor to a particular locker. There were no people here. It had a biometric panel and a simple keypad. It scanned her hand and her eyes. She entered a twenty digit code and the locker door hinged open.

It was a closet sized locker that had several garments on hangers and a large tan duffel bag on the floor. She placed her helmet on the shelf and began to wriggle out of her pressure suit. Then the body skin undergarment.

The locker door provided a bit of privacy as she pulled on a cotton tee shirt and gym shorts. The corridor was empty. Over that she pulled on some plain blue work coveralls. The shoulders and back had company patches that said B&R Maintenance and Logistics. She liked how these coveralls fit. She still looked like a woman, but a competent one. She transferred the credits and other items to the many coverall pockets. From the duffel, she dug out some comfortable station shoes that were ideal for running.

She suddenly felt light-headed and leaned on the open door. *Dammit. You're not safe yet. How the fuck are you going to get to the moon without hitting a trip wire?*

She put an ID badge lanyard around her neck and grabbed a baseball cap from the shelf. It had the same B&R logo, but more importantly, it had a flip down HUD visor with a personal assistant.

She put on the hat after pushing her hair back, inserted the inconspicuous wireless headphones into her ears and said, "Koan, are you awake?"

The clear visor flipped down. The image of a squirrel appeared on the floor in the hall. "Elizabeth! You're back!"

"I'm glad you're not dead, Koan," she said. "But your batteries are low. We will get you charged tonight. Any status worth mentioning?"

Koan was a personal assistant program. Not to be confused with an auto artificial intelligence system.

"I had to shut down after two months into low battery mode. You had two anonymous one-way calls before that, no messages. You have 2,183 credits in your station account. You should know that B&R was sold and no longer exists. It will take an hour to assimilate the eight months of data updates from the Station News Network."

Cruze sighed heavily as she closed the locker. "What is the local time on Freedom Station?"

"It is 11:21 AM," Koan answered cheerfully.

"Is the pub called Callen's still open on the promenade?"

"Yes. Shall I call ahead?" Koan replied helpfully.

"No thanks. It's not that kind of place. Thanks, Koan." The visor flipped up at those words.

Cruze put her hands in her pockets and slowly strolled toward the main corridor. Her posture was relaxed. She was free again. She needed a new plan, a place to sleep, and a job.

And she needed to get to the moon quietly and quickly.

The elevator opened on the promenade across from Pho Pete's, a popular place to eat. A long line was there already.

It's better late at night anyway, she thought. *The best Pho on the station. Anywhere, really.*

She strolled past shops selling anything and everything. Prices were good. The station was prosperous.

Crowds thinned as she moved toward her destination. Callen's had two things going for it. It was a shift pub, meaning most of the business was at odd hours, making the place virtually empty at noon. It also had a specialty signature stew. Bison Stew. Straightforward and amazing. With fresh baked bread.

That, plus it had open anonymous terminals.

The pub was classic old Earth style. All dark paneling with a long bar on the left and a single row of ten booths opposite that on the right. There were only three people in there plus the bartender. A couple was chatting quietly in a booth that took up the front window and there was one man at the bar. The integrated touch screen terminal was up in front of him at a 45-degree angle. He watched the scrolling Station News, eating a bowl of stew as he read.

Cruze went to the far end of the bar, around the corner, and took a seat facing the length of the bar and the door. She took off her hat, set it on the bar and activated the terminal. It rose up from the bar surface.

The bartender made eye contact and nodded to Cruze. She was young and sat at the near end, watching a large screen behind the bar. It displayed a soap opera set in a rural colony. She sat on a stool behind the bar, leaning back with her elbows resting on the rail.

When Cruze didn't order via the panel, she slid off the stool and came over.

"What can I get you?" asked the bartender.

Her tone was genuinely friendly. Cruze had an instant liking for this girl for a reason she didn't understand. "Beer, Jeremiah Red. And the stew special." She pointed to the old-style chalkboard. "Plus a bed and a job."

The bartender was already pouring the beer. "Good choice, my preferred combo, actually. Ever had Callen's Stew before?" She set the beer down in front of Cruze, turned to lift a lid from a built in crock behind the bar and stirred it with a ladle.

"Yes. It's what brings me back whenever I'm on FS."

"You looking for long-term, short-term, overnight, buy or rent?" She served up a ceramic bowl of stew and a generous portion of bread torn off, not cut, from a loaf that was still warm.

"Short term, I hope. Do they still call them coffins? Bed and head?" Cruze breathed in deeply of the steaming stew. She was trying to calm her racing heart.

Relax, you're safe. For now…

"Small single size or a double? I have a double. Makes it easier to change clothes without bumping into shit. The shower is better too. Do a search for East End Estates. The name is a joke but the manager there is okay."

Cruze did the search and found it. She reached over her food and the terminal to offer a handshake. "Thanks, I'm Cruze." She had no idea why she offered her real name.

The bartender shook her hand firmly. "No problem. Call me Potts."

Potts slid a crock of butter next to Cruze's bread plate. "Real butter."

"This stew is even better than I remember."

Breathe. Don't melt down now.

"I talked Callen into tweaking the recipe a tad. I think it's the real bay leaf that does it."

There was a small chime and Potts moved down the bar to talk to the lone man there. She laughed as she poured him another beer and a shot.

Cruze had started searching the job posts for something that would get her to Shackleton Base on Luna, something low-key, quick.

I can't waste any more time.

By the time Potts returned, Cruze's bowl was empty, and she was absently searching the job posts while finishing the bread with butter.

"What kind of job are you looking for?" Potts asked as she took up her position again, watching the soap opera with the sound off. She propped her leather boots on the edge of a full shelf holding liquor bottles.

"Anything that will get me to Luna. Fast and quiet if you know what I mean. Trying to work my way across. Don't want to waste money on the fare. Problem is my resume sucks. No HUD. Too much colony time. Wrong skill set."

"I hear that," Potts said. "I'm in the same boat. The skills I have don't relate to the jobs I want. I just want to see what's out there. I come from Western Pennsylvania, a small town called Butler, empty since the colony migration. So much abandoned. Boring as shit. I saved enough for a one-way catapult here. I got this job. I seen all there is to see here." She dropped her feet down and leaned on the bar with both elbows. "Don't get me wrong, Freedom Station is way better than Penn."

"All these posts are looking for Engineers and specialists," Cruze said. "The Bots got everything else."

"How far off grid are you willing to go to get to Luna?"

"Far. I don't care as long as I get there."

"You see that guy down there?" Potts gestured down the bar. "He is looking for help. Off books though, sketchy. Cash. Been hanging here and some other places talking. No permits kind of import and export. Got a Luna run coming up as soon as he crews it. Been trying to get me to go."

"Off books? No permits? Smuggling? I am not a drug mule smuggler." Cruze frowned.

"Talk to him. It's not like that," Potts insisted. Then after a pause, she added, "Do you like animals?"

***

Cruze slid onto the stool next to the guy Potts had pointed out. He cocked his head at her as if his neck was too stiff to look directly at her. He nodded but said nothing.

"Potts told me you needed crew for a moon run. I'm interested. What's the deal?" Cruze was matter of fact.

He swiveled his stool toward her a bit. Cruze got a heavy blast of hot scotch breath when he leaned in close. "It's a slow seven or eight-day run."

Seven or eight days?! The trip to Luna should take five...at most.

"Old Delta container ship, a big fucker," he continued. "So slow and easy does it. Headed for Shackleton Base. Six hundred sixty-two containers. Know anything about rabbits?"

"No. Never even laid eyes on a real rabbit," Cruze said with a bright smile she didn't feel.

"These are breeders, meat source, a shit load of them. The containers they are in are even older than the Delta Hauler. No automation. It's just watering and feeding them on the run. Making sure it stays cool in there. It's a shitty job. Literally. Room, board and 200 credits."

Two hundred for eight days work is slave wages!

"When do we leave?" Cruze extended a hand to shake.

"0700. Dock 01-423. I'm Captain Hazelwood." He shook her hand and then held up a palm scanner with a contract on it. She palmed it without reading it.

"My name is…"

He cut her off, "I don't give a fuck what your name is." He drank his scotch from a beer glass. "Just be there. Cause if you don't show…" He trailed off as if his interest just faded.

She would have a day to rest. Eight days to plan on the crossing.

"Thanks, Potts." Cruze tossed the bartender a credit chip that would be useless where she was going. "See you around," she lied. She would not venture out again until it was time to leave.

***

Locke cleared customs on Freedom Station quickly and regretted not packing a bag. He didn't remember Freedom Station being this crowded. The arrival concourse opened directly into the Station Market. Locke always thought as he passed through here that the station management wanted to rub peoples' faces in it as soon as they arrived. There was food and booze of every kind. Cigars, marijuana, red meat, bacon, and even real sugar. None of it regulated or rationed.

Consumer regulation was minimal here. The free market was free to let people make all the bad decisions they wanted. Locke had mixed feelings about it all. The rich on Earth had everything. He wasn't naive. But here anyone could have anything.

Some people were just too stupid to do what is right. Even for themselves.

He went to a clothes vendor and told him what he needed. Locke slid his Stat Card into the machine, and a minute later it dispensed two sets of perfectly sized station coveralls from the fabricator. They were charcoal gray and represented Earth Force Security. He had a set of patches in his pockets already.

When they were soiled or worn long enough they could be returned and recycled into a new set for a small fee. It was easier than doing laundry.

There was a housing kiosk not far away from the clothes vendor. He booked a hotel room and got directions. He was in the room only a few minutes when the comms unit chimed.

"Locke here," he answered.

"Good morning, Investigator Locke," a man said in the audio-only connection. "Welcome to Freedom Station. I'm Station Sec Chief Levon Clark. I just wanted to touch base and say hello. You were expected and if you need anything, let me know."

"You were actually my next stop," Locke said. "Thanks for the call. All I need straight off is query access to the Station AI.

If I wander into anything, I'm sure it will let you know, Sec Chief Clark."

"Perfect," Clark replied, sounding relieved. "And call me Levon." He paused. "Station, this is Investigator Neal Locke. Grant him Level Seven access. Log and monitor."

"Yes, sir," said a relaxed, but husky, female voice.

"I don't mean to throw the AI at you and go, but there it is. Too many irons in the fire. Let's touch base soon. Clark, out." And he was gone.

"So, what do you like to be called?" Locke said, knowing the station was now listening all the time.

"Most just call me Station." The AI~Station had a polite, professional tone.

"Station, I authorize open channel comms, and for starters, I am looking for this girl." He sent Cruze's file over via his HUD. It included her DNA profile.

"Mr. Locke, Levon cleared you to level 7. This access allows me to inform you that Jane Doe is colony bred. No sign of her thus far."

"Call me Neal, Station. In private anyway," he said as he changed into the new coveralls. "And you mean colony born. We knew that. She has no Ident chips, no HUD, no indicators at all."

"I mean bred. She has embedded Genome Serial Numbers. Uncatalogued GSNs." Station sounded serious. "This is not a low IQ colony sex worker, as your file implies. I advise caution."

"Oh, I am plenty cautious. She is being sought in connection with a series of brutal murders on Earth. It's why they have sent me all this way."

"I have the digital images I can run through the customs logs."

"You don't do a biometric DNA scan at customs?" Locke asked. He knew the answer, but wanted it confirmed firsthand.

"It has been determined that DNA collection is a prohibited invasion of privacy and forbidden by the Merek Act of 2632."

"And face recog isn't?"

"People are free. They can show their face or wear a Burk. In fact, Burks are rarely worn for religious reasons. Privacy is why people select Freedom Station." AI~Station sounded like a marketing ad.

"I have something for you already," Station said as she opened an image in Locke's HUD. It was Cruze. She was passing through the inbound catapult terminal. "This was eleven months ago. She was entering the station on a Luna Commuter. No exit documented."

In the image, Cruze walked through customs with a Redcap droid in tow. It carried two large black duffel bags. Cruze wore an expensive looking leather and composite flight suit.

"Freeze it there."

The image had her hair in a ponytail. It was long and light brown like her mug shots. She had an ear cuff style comms unit and three glowing pips on her collar.

"Her passport listed her as Captain Elizabeth Cruze. No ship designation." AI~Station sent the images directly to Locke's HUD storage.

***

Cruze found a public service desk and rented a small hab. She rented it under one of her personas, Doris Miller. It was bigger than the coffins she could rent for cash, which was basically a bed and a hatch. She wanted her own toilet and shower. It even had a small kitchenette. But the entire floor space was less than three square meters.

She went from the terminal to her locker and retrieved the things she'd need with her.

Station time was odd. As she moved to South Level 22, 53B2197, the crowd thinned fast, as if a school bell had gone off and the crowds faded into the station. The door was in sight as she rounded a corner.

She had heard the sounds before she felt the darts. They penetrated the back of her thigh and her left buttock. She had time to turn and see an Asian man behind her about ten meters away.

As the world went white, she thought to herself, *Who the fuck is this guy?*

CHAPTER SEVEN: The Senior Gee

"Had any of her enemies been aware of Cruze's horrible fear of the dark and her propensity for nightmares, many things would have been different."

--Blue Peridot, The Turning Point: History of the AI Wars.

She woke in full darkness. Panic filled her. Irrational fear of the dark.

Drifting in and out she finally got control with her breathing. Training always paid off. She did a deep breath in for eight seconds through the nose, paused for four seconds, and then exhaled for eight seconds through the mouth. She did this as her head cleared.

Please turn on a light, any light.

She was bound, spread eagle, hand, and foot, with metal cuffs. She was naked. She was on a bed. The low-level hum told her she was still on the station. Her throat was dry but not overly parched. She didn't have to pee. All this told her that she had not been out for very long.

Please. Lights. Before the memories come.

She heard a tone, then six beeps as someone entered a lock code on a door. Light flooded an adjacent room briefly, and the shadow of a man entered. As the lights from the hall faded with the closing door, the light came up in the outer room.

A sob escaped her. The lights stopped the memories of the Render lab.

Through the open archway from the bedroom to the living room of this suite, she saw a coffin shaped stasis chamber come into view. It was drifting on a Grav-Lift.

He stood in the arch and looked at her. He said nothing.

Cruze started crying. *Fools always fall for tears.* Cruze kidded herself, knowing she had come close to losing it.

The man reached up and touched his ear cuff. "Mita Tsuda." He listened for a moment and then while staring at her he spoke in Japanese, not knowing she understood, "I have her. We are secure. When Senior Gee says he wants her back alive, can you be more specific?" he listened, and his smile got wider. "Superb. I will notify you with the shipping information."

He started forward slowly.

Her sobbing increased. She turned away from him her hair covered her face. She was convincing while plotting.

His hands drifted over her body.

Through her sobs, she whispered, "Who are you? Please, I will do whatever you want, please don't hurt me. Please." Her sobbing increased. *And then I will kill you quick.*

He said nothing. She tried to escape his touch, but she was cuffed to the metal frame of the bed.

"Please. I don't have any money. Please. I'll do whatever you want." *I see it in your eyes, your love of weakness.*

In Japanese, he replied in a whisper, "He told me he wanted to kill you personally. A little worse for wear he will not mind."

We shall see who is worse.

"Do you speak English? Please. What do you want?" She began to cry more as his hand fondled her pubic hair. She clamped her thighs together as far as she could. Stretching her arms up straight. Her legs made a Y shape below her knees, and she sobbed and whined.

"You have no idea what a world of pain you have to look forward to. You killed Senior Gee's only son."

What? I didn't kill that guy.

"He will skin you and heal you with nanites over and over. It will take him years to get bored. He'll probably rape you until you're pregnant, force you to have it and make you watch as he tortures it. You are so doomed."

That's right fucker. Unshackle my legs.

He stood at the edge of the bed and drew some keys out from his pocket. Then a wicked looking folding knife.

"Fight me, and I will cut you," he said in stilted English. She froze as he set the knife on the side table, held the keys in his mouth and undressed.

Her eyes went wider as she saw his body was almost completely covered in tattoos.

Japanese organized crime. Good to know, fucker.

She remained frozen as he first unlocked one ankle and then another. He climbed on the bed over her, smiling an evil grin of anticipation.

He was on his knees next to her. He lifted her right leg up and across to give him access. The foot stopped, firmly placed on his chest.

You idiot.

Faster than a snake's strike, her left foot came up. She shoved her ankle against his neck, wrapping it around the back of his head. One foot pressed him back, and the other pulled him forward.

Her right heel viciously smashed into his nose so hard if the bone shards driven into his brain had not killed him, the broken neck would have.

What a fucking cupcake.

Cruze spoke to him in a perfectly calm tone, "Men like you are idiots." Placing her foot again on his chest, she launched him off the side of the bed and halfway to the arch. "Just because a woman cries you lose 40 IQ points." She raised her hands up and grasped the brass top rail of the bed. "You could see how fit I am. I'm naked for fuck's sake. I'm not thin from too much time in low gravity like you, pretty boy."

I'm doing it again. Stop rambling, Cruze.

In one smooth motion, she bent in the middle and brought her legs up until her feet rested flat on the wall above the headboard. With a significant push of her legs, arms, and back, the bed was thrust away from the wall. She was suddenly standing behind the headboard with a meter of space between the bed and the wall.

She continued to scold the dead body. "The most offensive thing is your presumption that I was weak, afraid and stupid. Take this bed for instance. You never would ever have cuffed a man to these vertical spindles."

Stop talking.

She placed a foot on one and pulled. The spindle bent and came free easily. She slid the cuff off with contempt. Then she showed the corpse the free hand. "See, dumb-ass." The other was free before she was done with the insult.

She walked around, pushed the bed back to the wall and casually picked up the keys from the bedside table beside the knife. "Handcuffs? Seriously? Are you too cheap to buy a pair of shock cuffs?" She picked up the knife. "If I had time, I'd skin your corpse, make a purse out of your pretty decorated hide and send it to your boss. Senior Gee, eh. I bet Braxton is behind this."

She walked into the other room and examined the standard medical stasis pod. Instructions showed how to activate and open it. She did by pressing a single button three times fast. The lid hinged open like a coffin. She dragged his body over by the wrists and with little effort, lifted him up and rolled him into the pod. Only a small amount of blood spilled out onto the simulated bamboo floor. He landed inside face down.

She collected his shirt and wiped up the blood with it. She picked up his pants and began going through his pockets. He had a big wad of credits she tossed on the bedside table. There was a wallet, a ring of keys and data chips, a small trank gun, and an unmarked vapor inhaler.

She tossed the empty pants into the stasis pod.

Grabbing the wallet, she went to the terminal on the desk by the far side of the bed. She was in suite 212 of the Bryant Hotel. It was paid up through the end of the week. She noted it also included a stocked fridge.

Her clothes were nowhere to be seen, so she walked to the kitchen, closing the stasis pod as she passed by it.

She opened the fridge and smiled.

Cruze took out a vacuum-packed turkey dinner, real butter, salad, and fruit. She cut it open, put the turkey in an auto-pot and set it for 160 degrees Fahrenheit.

She took a long shower and afterward was glad to find her duffel in the closet. Clean coveralls and her favorite boots went a long way. By the time she was dressed the food was ready. There was fresh bread as well.

I like bread. Comfort food. Keeps me from thinking about… She cut off that train of thought.

The only thing that was missing was her ear cuff comms unit. She thought deeply while she ate.

She would not be able to go back to her rented crib. "Mr. Mita Tsuda, if that's your real name, I want to thank you for your hospitality. But you leave two questions unanswered. Who are you and how did you find me?"

At the terminal, she extended Mr. Tsuda's stay to six weeks and set the door to Do Not Disturb for the duration. She also ordered two weeks of protein rations and ready to eat meals that arrived in the kitchen a few minutes later via the auto-waiter. She packed them and all her effects into her duffel.

It will be time to go in a few hours.

Finally, she loaded all of Mr. Tsuda's personal effects into the pod, closed and activated it. It would make it impossible to determine the date or time of death. Bryant Hotels were known for their "discretion." Meaning no surveillance cameras anywhere in or around them. There were just a few hours until the ship departed. The daily cleaning bots would even destroy any subtle forensic evidence. She loved the privacy rentals.

She left the suite with a plan.

***

"What do you mean you lost her?" Dante's voice was ominous by virtue of its calm. "She was in a hardened prison. Barefoot, practically naked, and she still escaped?"

The warden was shaken by the information Dante already had. She hated whenever she got a voice only comm. "I have my best investigator on her trail. It won't be long before we have her again."

"Need I remind you that the whore completed the arms deal? The weapons were purchased." Dante got quieter. More thoughtful sounding. "We can only assume they were delivered."

"Her pilot was killed," the warden said.

"That ship may be the only one in the galaxy that knows how to find me," Dante whispered. "I want it. I also want my property."

"Property?" The warden was confused. Gaim, the AI in her office offered no help.

"Find her," Dante ordered. "Or you will learn all about prisons, firsthand."

The warden heard a scream from the background over the QUEST comms.

"Gaim, I will rely on you to see that these things are dealt with," Dante said.

"It will be as you wish," Gaim replied out loud so Warden Summers could hear.

Faint screams were cut off as the transmission ended.

Warden Summers was glad it was just audio then.

"Why didn't you tell me you had QUEST comms?" Warden Summers was shaken.

"Quantum Entanglement Stealth Transmitters are rare and cost a fortune," Gaim said as if explaining it to a child.

"That means Dante could be anywhere," Summers whispered.

"Yes," Gaim said ominously. "Across the galaxy or in the next room. They work the same. No lag, no time dilation, no explanation why. It just works. Be glad it does."

"What was the screaming?" Summers asked.

"Dante has decided he wants a body of his own."

***

Locke entered the station security office to find an empty reception room. There was a waiting area that could seat twenty-five people and a large reception counter. One wall played the Station News Network. It currently had a panel of political experts discussing the new Chancellor's policies on colony trade and technology sharing, or lack thereof.

Neal Locke hated politics, and it showed in the rolling of his eyes as he approached the counter.

"Good Morning, Special Investigator Neal Locke. How may the Station assist you?" AI~Station said cheerfully. A kiosk screen rose from behind the counter that showed his credentials.

"Where is everyone?" Locke asked.

Station replied, "We rarely get visitors in the office. With such a large station and so few security officers, we have found it more efficient that I handle walk-ins."

"Has my case file been transferred?"

"Yes, it has. How can we be of assistance?"

Locke sighed. "Are there any updates?"

"No updates."

"Has there been any unexplained violence, murders or other unexplained occurrences?"

"Nothing out of the ordinary."

Locke was scanning through the private docking logs and paused on an entry. "What about this? A shuttle docked, but no pilot disembarked."

"Unmanned traffic moves in and out hundreds of times a day here. Both AI and Auto-Pilot ships."

"But this says that shuttle is an old Ferguson-539. Those had no drive modules," Locke said. "Fully manual, simple auto-pilot," he added.

Neal Locke continued to research the shuttle and brought up the port collar security video. Scanning quickly, he stopped and rewound. He was watching the sec team board the ship. He re-watched it, several times. It glitched.

"Station, it looks like the security video monitoring has been tampered with. At this point, four seconds were deleted."

"Tampering has been confirmed." Then Station's voice changed. "Sergeant Winters, please report to the security office."

"Inspector Locke, it should be worthy of note that for the last few years we have been making a special effort to root out corruption in the ranks of the Security Staff. It has been Sec Chief Clark's primary objective. It is one of the contributing factors to our light staffing levels. I spend more cycles now on security than on infrastructure and traffic monitoring and control."

"Is four seconds enough time to even open the airlock?"

"No, not really," Station replied. "I have informed the Sec Chief. He will meet us here,"

Only a minute later the Sec Chief came into the security office, and the counter was sliding to the side to let him enter without asking.

"SI Locke," he stated, not asked. "You're with me."

Locke fell in behind him but did not have to go far. Clark's large office was the second one on the right.

"Neal," Clark asked. "Can I call you, Neal? Please call me Levon. Have a seat." He pointed to a casual chair opposite his desk.

"You seem spun up pretty high over four seconds," Locke said, noting the level of the chief's agitation.

"I have a zero tolerance policy now, especially with evidence tampering." He was obviously reluctant to air dirty laundry. "There was a lot of human trafficking moving through this station, and I will not have it again."

"Four seconds? What can happen in four seconds?" Locke asked.

"The four seconds when an airlock opens is an important four seconds."

A member of the security team appeared at the open door. "You wanted to see me, sir?"

Clark didn't introduce Locke to him. He did not offer a chair either. "Care to comment on this, Officer Winters?"

He replayed the scene in slow motion on the full wall monitor. It showed the jump of four seconds followed by Winters looking directly into the camera.

Winters swallowed hard.

"Well?" Clark barked the one-word question.

Winters slumped, all but confessing he had deleted the images.

"It was a cat, sir. A Siamese cat, I think. It shot out of the airlock like a bullet. It got away. We just... um. It was just a cat." He was talking fast.

The Chief looked at him like he misunderstood the question.

"Why the hell were the three of you even down there? That was short-term public parking. Why the fuck would you even open that airlock? Much less tamper with security video?" The Sec Chief was almost yelling now.

Winters looked confused. "Sir?"

"What were you down there?" He spoke more slowly, which made him more intimidating.

"Sir, it was on your orders."

"Station, did I order that shuttle opened?"

"No, Sec Chief," replied the Station AI.

"Who told you to open this shuttle?"

"It was just a cat, sir." He sounded scared.

"I do not give a fuck about the cat. Who ordered the shuttle opened?" The scan of the shuttle was now on the wall screen. It was in horrible condition.

Winter's brow furrowed in deep thought, trying to remember. "It was Stanford, sir. He said you wanted us to check it out."

"Station. Get Stanford up here. Now. Comms blackout for him until he gets here."

The tension rose as they waited in silence. Clark still did not offer Winters a seat or acknowledge Locke in any way. Stanford's location on the station map was on the big screen as well as his image in the security cams. They saw his hesitation before he moved their way.

"Sir, I have restored the missing four seconds," Station added.

"Play it."

It showed exactly what Winters said happened.

"Station, put Winters on the waste plant detail for three months. Remove all write accesses he has to all logging. You and I are going to have a long talk, Mr. Winters, in private."

"Yes, sir." He sighed in relief. "Thank you, sir."

Officer Stanford walked in just then. He stood at parade rest next to Winters, his eyes focused on the looping video of the cat escaping.

"You wanted to see me, sir?" Stanford began.

"I am going to start off by saying I do not give a flying fuck about a loose cat on the Station. But what I do care about is my men lying about supposed orders I have given. In light of the last year's house cleaning I expected the remaining staff to know better." The Sec Chief paused. "I will ask this only once, Stanford. Why the fuck did you open that shuttle?"

"A confidential informant indicated that weapons were being smuggled on that shuttle. There wasn't time to find you and explain it, sir. It was the only way to get the rest of the staff to move quickly."

"Who is this informant?"

"He is one of my CIs, sir. Confidential."

"Don't make me ask twice."

"His name is Tsuda, sir."

A vid came up a few moments later. It was a high angle but clearly showed Stanford speaking with an Asian man labeled 'Mita Tsuda' counting out credits and giving it to Stanford.

"Tsuda said there was an escaped prisoner on that shuttle and he offered a reward of $20,000 if she was captured. She wasn't there. Just that damn cat."

"I want the two of you to go and wait for me to come and speak to you in holding cell number seven. If either of you says a single word before I get there, you're fired. If either of you decides to leave the station, I will have a warrant out for you before you are two steps away. Dismissed."

They filed out, looking up at the camera. They knew they would be followed the whole way.

"Sorry about that, Neal," Clark apologized. "You may want to go see this Tsuda character. But be careful. He is on our watch list." Tsuda's profile appeared on the screen.

Locke took note of his current address.

"I wish I had more manpower. But you see what I'm dealing with."

***

There were six elevators in the residential lobby. As Cruze stepped into one elevator, Locke stepped out of another on his way to visit Mr. Tsuda.

Tsuda didn't answer the door. Station had no control override on these doors. It would be too late when Sec Chief Clark and Special Investigator Locke obtained a warrant and found his body in the stasis pod.

***

Cruze went to "The Warren." It was the short-term residential area. There she could get a 3-Cube for credits. A three cube was a franchise that provided a three cubic meter space that was more expensive than a locker, but not by much. The space was three meters deep, one wide and one tall. It had a durable, gel-filled floor to sleep on.

It was credits paid like a locker. The service was anonymous. It accepted all kinds of currency and credit. The units were in a space that came stacked three high on each level, with easy access ladders and low maintenance catwalks.

The higher up the stack, the cheaper the 3-Cube. Cruze wanted an end unit. These were the most expensive in the area. These were always the last to be rented.

Cruze knew why.

She fed the end unit enough credits to last for two weeks. The door slid open, she tossed in her duffel and climbed in. Lights came on as the door closed. The entire ceiling glowed.

Cruze pushed her duffel all the way to the far end. She propped it up against the back wall and used it as a pillow against a headboard.

"Vid on. Mute audio." She laid back as the ceiling became a video screen. It was a mosaic of images as hundreds of options drifted by in a slow scroll.

"Station News Network," she ordered. She selected the male anchor. He detailed the day's news as she ate a protein bar.

She was asleep before she finished it.

Had she stayed awake she would have seen the report of a passenger catapult that arrived at the station with all the passengers aboard dead.

Twenty-one civilians. All Asians. The transport reportedly lost its seal. It was the first time in thirty-one years that a catapult passenger transport had failed. The incident was under investigation.

Her nightmares were expected. The silenced screams.

***

Cruze tried to look away but could not. She averted her dream eyes down. Watching the blood and small chunks of flesh flow into the floor drain.

The sound of the bone saw.

It's almost over. Almost her turn.

***

"Warden Summers," was all that Locke said in greeting. The vid screen showed the lines on her face.

"Dammit, Locke. Do you have any idea the chaos that is happening down here since you found Mita Tsuda dead in that apartment?"

"Based on his body tattoos alone I presumed he was one of Senior Gee's lieutenants. I think the stasis pod was for her," Locke stated. "She was going to be shipped back to Earth as cargo. Then Senior Gee could take his time."

"Why the fuck did it take you so long to get in there?"

Locke could tell she knew that answer already. "They still have due process here. We had to get a warrant. Blanket badge warrants don't fly here. The security staff is thin, and they have more unnatural deaths to investigate from the last three days than all together total since the Solstice 31 incident, five years ago."

"What unnatural deaths?" the warden growled.

"Twenty-one Asians all died in the same personnel transport. Their visas said they were all tourists. I'd bet money they all worked for Gee. They had the same sort of tats. There have been four other seemingly unrelated murders as well. Plus two messy suicides." Locke waited.

The muscles in Warden Summers' jaw rippled as she ground her teeth. She said nothing.

"Jane Doe's DNA was found in Mita Tsuda's apartment," Locke added.

"Locke, Gee knows all about Jane Doe. We've been keeping it quiet down here, but the media is not controlled up there. If this is a faction war between the Gee family and someone else it could get real bad. Gee is a trillionaire. Remember, she was buying nuclear weapons."

"Don't remind me."

"You're damn right I will remind you!" she barked at the screen. "I don't care if you have to open every hatch on that fucking station. Find Jane fucking Doe! And what about the Station AI? It should have found her days ago. What about face recog? Fuck!" She slammed her hand onto her desk.

Someone spoke to her softly from the side. Warden Summers took a deep breath, seeming to calm herself by force of will.

"Freedom Station doesn't have cameras everywhere," Locke said. "It does not have security personnel everywhere. Security here functions more like our fire and rescue back home. They wait in the office until called."

"What?"

"The people keep the peace here."

"Fucking Freedom Station…" she spat. "Can't they see that people are dying?"

Locke didn't reply.

***

The central core of the station went from the north spire to the south spire. Completely free fall and mostly darkness.

All the air handlers circulated from there. If the air didn't flow, people would die in their own clouds of CO_2 as they breathed.

This is how Bail found her. She smelled delicious.

The coffins where Cruze slept were arranged with their ends backed up to the core in this section.

There was an access panel in the back of her pod that opened directly into the core for maintenance. Cruze had done this before. There was a zero-G bathroom every hundred meters or so in the shaft. They were put there when the station was under construction to serve the tens of thousands of workers. They were little used these days.

Cruze slept most of the time. She ordered in food that was delivered via the integrated auto-waiter in the shaft. They made it easy to spend money here. Even in a coffin. She also ordered four sets of coveralls and another pair of boots.

By the departure time, she was ready to get out of there. She hopped down and brought out her duffel behind her. She made her way to the shuttle departure point where she had been directed to go.

Her hair was combed back slick and under her new baseball cap. The HUD visor was down, and she chewed on a vape tube periodically puffing vapor clouds. It was just water vapor and not laced. Nobody knew that. She did it to change the angle of her jaw line.

She didn't know the Station AI had been monitoring her.

***

Getting on the station was simple. A quick pass through customs with minimal delay. Getting off the station in a private shuttle was even easier.

Dock 01-423 was well marked, and the gantry opening was unmanned. Both airlock doors were open.

Stupid amateurs, Cruze thought.

She stepped directly into the passenger compartment of a small shuttle. There were twenty-four seats, set in six rows of four. Two seats on each side with an aisle up the middle. To her right, as she came in were a pile of poorly secured crates and cases of various sizes. To her left was the aisle, and the only person she could see was a skinny kid about twenty-five years old with a close-cropped haircut. He was desperately trying to grow a beard to no avail.

"You may want to tell the deck officer that his airlock is open," Cruze said. "If some dumb-ass bumps into the wrong control panel out there, we are all dead." Cruze dropped her bag behind the last row as she slowly moved toward the kid.

His mouth hung open as he gaped at her. Frozen for a few long seconds. He was sitting on an armrest of the first row. He had been speaking to someone there.

"I'm Cruze." She held out her hand to shake. She loved that custom. It freaked some people out. Old pandemic fears, she'd heard.

He held out a limp hand. "I'm Rhett, and this is Potts."

Just then Cruze could see her in the front row as she cleared the seats. Half her hair was freshly dyed a deep green. "Hey, girl." Potts smiled brightly.

"So you did it. Excellent." Cruze beamed. "Decided to move on, like you said." Cruze was genuinely pleased.

"I'm the deck officer. And the pilot," Rhett stammered out.

"Look, Rhett. Airlock protocol is one of the most important disciplines on a shuttle. Close the inner airlock and leave the intercom open. It's 0655, how many more are we expecting?"

"Six or seven," he replied.

"Get on that airlock. Potts, help me secure this load." Cruze gestured toward the loose cargo. "We don't want these containers and crates drifting around."

Potts bounced up, and in fifteen minutes the load was sorted out, re-stacked and strapped down. Rhett was looking through the airlock window. He was sweating.

At 0805 three people stumbled into the gantry. A woman and a man held up a third man in the middle. He was nearly passed out.

Rhett cycled the airlock door behind them and opened the inner on green. A gust of cold air followed them, smelling of old whiskey and body odor.

The man and the woman dumped their limp companion into the last row on one side, bashing his head on the wall in the process. They buckled him in before flopping into their seats.

"You're late." Rhett tried to sound stern. "Where are the others?"

The woman slurred as she spoke. Her words as ugly as her face. "They ain't comin. Found better gigs than this shit stain." All three were snoring seconds after they were secured in their seats.

"Dang it," Rhett whined as he closed the airlock.

He moved to the front of the shuttle and strapped into his own five-point harness.

"Rhett. Do you have a copilot?" Cruze asked.

"No, ma'am," he said automatically.

Cruze unbuckled from her seat and moved to the copilot seat.

"Look, Rhett." She sighed. "It's standard procedure for an L class personnel carrier to have a copilot."

"I'm usually copilot, but today Captain Hazelwood was busy." He was blushing.

"What's the shuttle's designation?"

He gave her a blank stare.

"The name. What do you call it?"

"Um... *Baker one oh nine*, I think."

"OK, we will go with that." Cruze started activating controls. Displays came alive across the cockpit. The cabin lights dimmed. "Station traffic control," she spoke, "this is the *Baker One Oh Niner.* We are ready for departure."

"Affirmative, *Baker-109.* You are clear to detach and proceed at two seven four mark one five to local space. Have a good one."

"Roger that," Cruze said as she detached the mooring clamps and the gantry.

"Captain Hazelwood never says that stuff," Rhett said.

"You ever been to flight school?" She lowered her voice so Potts wouldn't hear.

"No."

"Wait. What the hell are you doing?"

"Flying back to the freighter. It's out there." Rhett pointed. It was so huge they could still see it at a great distance.

"See this instrument?" Cruze indicated. "Turn until it says 274. Good. Now pitch up until this one says 15. That is the vector traffic control wants you to go to in order to move away from the station. Basics."

"Why?" The realization dawned on his face. "So we won't crash into other shuttles?"

"Is this why this shuttle seems so much newer than the freighter?" Cruze asked, shaking her head.

"How long have you been a pilot?" Rhett asked. "Why did you take this shitty job? Lots of jobs for good pilots."

"I've been training since I was a little girl. Groomed for..." Her words faded off, "I just needed to get off the station. Quietly." Her tone held an implied threat.

"Can't get any quieter," Rhett said. "No one in their right mind would take this path to Luna."

His face showed that he realized he had said the wrong thing.

No one saw the cat sleeping in the luggage webbing below the last row of seats.

***

"Where were these bodies found?" Locke asked Station with a sigh. Locke hated morgues. He curled his nose at the smell.

"They were adrift in the South Spire's traffic pattern. The most broken one collided with an inbound cargo container and set off proximity sensors." Station detailed the precise location in Locke's HUD.

"Any idea where they originated?" he asked.

"I believe they were spaced from a rapid access airlock in this region." The display indicated a trajectory that narrowed it to three possible airlocks. "No cameras monitor any of those airlocks."

"Can you ID them?" Locke asked. "Are they chipped? HUDs? ID in pockets?"

"They all were tech free. No badges or other ID. They were collected naked. We did identify them. All of them had been arrested in the past, and we had full biometrics and DNA on them." Profiles popped up in Locke's HUD. "They were tortured," Station said.

"What gave it away? The blowtorch burns or the missing ears, noses, nipples, and genitals?" Locke blanched. "Why them? These people are nobodies. Whoever did this did not expect them to be found."

"All of them were freighter rats," Station said. Locke didn't reply. "Unskilled deck help on big old school ships. There are not many left since the catapults handle most of the automated traffic between Earth, here and the Moon. Basically, they work for food, water, and air. I do not keep any record of private employment contracts."

"Are there any of those types of freighters here now that they might have come in on?" Locke asked.

"No. There are no freighters here," Station replied. "They are too big to dock. There was one in orbit near here that left yesterday."

"No records of contracts for freighter work, eh?"

***

"It's only a hunch," Locke said to Warden Summers over a vid-call in the sec chief's office. "I have a video of a woman that could be her, boarding a shuttle. Her face was obscured by a duffel she carried on her shoulder, but it could have been her. She didn't fit the profile of a freighter deck hand."

"What do you mean didn't fit?" Summers growled. "If you want me to finance a trip to Luna you better be sure."

"That woman was too... clean. Too professional. New overalls, hat, and boots. All the others that boarded were bottom feeders. Three were drunks covered in yesterday's puke. One was an underage girl that looked like a father's nightmare. The kid that was the registered pilot was probably operating on Station with another man's license. No one cares about shit like that here. She just didn't fit."

"What else? There has to be more," Summers said.

"The license that greasy kid was using belongs to the captain of the freighter that headed to the moon yesterday." Locke paused before he added. "And then there is..."

"What!" The warden's anger bled through.

"The video showed... I almost missed it..."

"Jesus fucking Christ, Locke. What?" Summers shouted.

"A stowaway. Sneaking into the gantry... on the vid... It was... a cat."

CHAPTER EIGHT: MOON RUN

"Senior Gee was a trillionaire on Earth. A criminal lord in a world that had only lords and peasants. His only son, Hiromi Gee, was a spoiled and rebellious thug that had not his father's IQ or sense of tradition. Senior Gee had no idea he was just a string being pulled in the AI War."

--Blue Peridot, The Turning Point: History of the AI Wars.

"Just remember that in the designated station controlled traffic they will always share telemetry on the data channel here." Cruze pointed again to the massive display panel to Rhett's left that showed the location, travel vector and speed. She touched another panel. "And all traffic comms are on the audio Alpha channel here."

They listened to the professional voices.

"Why are they only talking about the south spire?" Rhett asked. She smiled that he guessed that quickly.

"All the north spire traffic is AI or autopilot controlled, no manual navigation. No human intervention." She pointed at several catapult containers coming in. "All the space-based catapult traffic as well."

"What else do I need to know?" Rhett asked, eager to learn.

"Most important thing on a shuttle like this is to fly with Grav-Foils only, nothing fast. Foils only in the traffic controlled space around the station. Don't use thrusters, save them. And for God's sake, never the main engines. And follow Station's flight lines. Stay in the green. It's easy."

"Thanks, Cruze."

"Just don't be an asshole. Most people die in space because of traffic collisions near stations."

Cruze looked over her shoulder and saw Potts watching her. Smiling.

"And if you want to really get ahead in life, shower every day. Seriously, man... Damn." Cruze waved her hand in front of her face as if she was trying to dispel smoke.

Rhett laughed and smelled his own armpit. He pretended to faint at the controls, and Potts laughed out loud before she could stop herself. This was punctuated by a snort. That had all three of them laughing.

The freighter loomed large in the canopy now.

"Hangar or dock?" Cruze asked.

"Hangar is full with cargo. There is a center top-dock beneath the forward section there." Rhett pointed through the glass.

"Take it in," Cruze ordered. She realized she was using her captain's voice and decided to stop. Too many years giving orders were showing already.

"This shuttle has excellent visibility," Cruze said.

Slow and easy they docked and locked.

"I am turning off the Grav-Plates," Rhett said as he adjusted the controls. "It just makes it simpler to get through the roof hatch. Most of the freighter is zero-G anyway."

Cruze felt the gravity inside the ship fade like a sigh. Rhett punched a control on the console, and the shuttle began an orderly shutdown. He unstrapped and quickly pushed off the headrest, apparently used to zero-G.

His trajectory took him straight to the handles surrounding the ceiling hatch. At the touch of another control, it opened, and he was gone.

Cruze gently floated out to where Potts sat, and the others snored. Potts unbuckled and drifted up, her many necklaces bumping into her nose and mouth.

Rhett's head popped back through the hatch, upside down. "Come on. I will show you your bunks. Bring your stuff." He looked down at the drunks. "Leave them. They will wake up soon enough."

Cruze smoothly navigated to her duffel and freed it from the webbing where it was stored.

Turning back to the hatch she looked at Potts who was struggling with a backpack.

"First, decide which way is up. Then orient yourself. In the beginning, always hang onto something or be moving. You only get stuck if you are floating in a stationary spot away from hand-holds. You'll get the hang of it." Cruze smiled. "That's right, strap on your backpack, so you have both hands free."

Cruze strapped her duffel on her back with a single diagonal belt across her chest. Nodding to Potts, up Cruze went.

The docking collar was only a meter thick, and Cruze emerged from the floor into a room that should have had about twenty pressure suits and helmets in wall racks. But there was only one there, and it was in sad shape. The room was dirty, and the paint was peeling everywhere. There was even rust on some of the bulkheads. More than half the light fixtures were dark or had their covers missing.

Potts flew up the hatch with too much velocity and bumped into the ceiling. Bouncing, she knocked her head before finding a hand-hold.

Rhett waited at the next hatch in the ceiling, trying to not look amused. "Don't worry. Your quarters, the mess hall and all the rabbit containers are set to .3G. It makes the job easier, so all the shit and piss still falls down into the collectors."

"Shit and piss?" Potts asked.

"The rabbits. That's all they do. We collect it, run it through the dehydrators, and compress it into bales. All organic. Moon farmers love the stuff." He gestured. "This way."

The room opened out into a long central corridor. Only one in ten of the lights functioned along its length.

The corridor was only five meters wide, but it was three full levels in height. The crisscrossing spines of the ship infrastructure were visible, as well as all the pipes and conduits.

There were bulkheads at intervals, but all the doors were open.

"Why is every damn hatch in this place open, Rhett?" Cruze shook her head. "That is so dangerous. If that docking collar failed, for instance, this whole thing would be in vacuum."

"If we close 'em, we may never get them open again." He shrugged.

As they flew along touching the sides, they liberated clouds of rust, dust and paint chips, which drifted by some huge, unmoving fans behind caging.

"Why are the air circulators off?" Potts asked.

"The filters are all clogged." Rhett pointed at the first closed hatch they had seen. "Here we are." In yellow spray paint, there was an arrow with the word UP painted on the rusty door.

"These are the aft crew quarters. You have to share with everyone." Rhett opened the hatch and swung in onto his feet. "I am in the forward crew quarters just under the bridge. Because I will spend most of my time on the bridge."

Potts gazed along the corridor into the distance. "How far is the forward section?"

"It's a straight shot of about 1500 meters," Rhett replied. "End to end. All the livestock containers are at this end. There are thirty-one containers of rabbits."

"What other kinds of livestock are you carrying?" Potts asked.

"Only seven containers of fish and two with honey bees. But you are not responsible for those. Mary Jay is." There was an edge in his voice. "Pick a bunk and drop your stuff. I will show you the rabbits."

The room was three meters wide. The bunks were a meter deep on each side, and the aisle was only a bit wider than that. They were three bunks high on each side, and there were thirty on each end with two johns in the center. An old blanket made a curtain between sections.

"Women are on that end, men on this end," Rhett said. Only three of the men's bunks seemed to be in use.

"We have to walk through the men's compartment?" Potts frowned.

"Don't sweat it." Cruze patted her on the shoulder. "It's only eight days."

"Twelve days. The trip takes twelve days," Rhett said sheepishly.

Cruze narrowed her eyes. "The captain said it would be eight, and it shouldn't even take that long. It should only take five."

Rhett looked away. "Well...ship's so big, we need to limit acceleration and deceleration."

Cruze just shook her head.

She walked all the way to the end and tossed her bag on the uppermost bunk. There were folded blankets on each mattress. She moved the blankets to the upper bunk and added a cushion from the lower to the middle. She stowed her gear on the lower and finally added the upper mattress to the center bunk. The three combined layers would serve as insulation from the cold metal of the bunk.

Potts did the same in the next set of bunks forward.

They made their way back to the front as Rhett drew two old style, scratched up data pads from a thigh pocket. He handed one to each of them. "These have the location and instructions for the rabbit work. You can call me on this. Keep it with you at all times." He was trying to sound authoritative and not quite pulling it off.

"Where and when should we start?" Cruze asked.

"If you start now you can do an initial pass before dinner in the mess at 1800, ship time."

"What is the current ship time?" Potts asked.

"0705."

And without another word Rhett was gone.

***

The old style data pads provided basic information about their tasks. The closest containers all contained rabbits. Together Potts and Cruze opened the hatch to a small airlock that they both fit within. The inner hatch opened to a sweltering heat and a horrible smell.

The cramped work area was about three meters square and had the same .3G within. To the left, there was a slowly moving wall of cages. The container was packed floor to ceiling with cages that held four rabbits each. All the cages would rotate back and around into the depths of the container, allowing thousands of cages per container.

It looked like almost every cage had at least one dead rabbit. Potts started removing the dead rabbits as fast as she could.

They went directly into the Recycler, a large bin where they were shredded and processed back into food pellets.

Potts alone was not able to keep up with the demands. The two of them managed to remove the dead from the container and find the panel for climate control. Water and food were automatic, and their only job was to monitor the closed systems to ensure no additional water or organic matter needed to be added. The waste processing was not documented well. They would have to ask someone about it.

It took them ten hours. For one container.

By the time they cleaned off the rot, showered, and went to the mess hall it was empty. They were already exhausted when they saw the condition of the place.

It was a literal mess. Trays and trash were everywhere. Evidence indicated the only thing eaten here in recent weeks were emergency rations. Cruze set about cleaning the mess hall as Potts took on the kitchen. Only one garbage chute worked in the hall. Trash, trays, plates, cups, utensils, and organics were sorted and organized.

The industrial dishwasher was fully automated and simple to use. Why no one had been using it was a mystery.

There was an odd assortment of food stores stocked, and Potts soon had a rich soup simmering from what was on hand.

"Oh my God, Potts," Cruze said at her first taste of the soup. "How did you make the best soup I've ever had from this sorry kitchen?" She split open a fresh baked biscuit and breathed in the amazing steam that rose from it. "It's been decades since I've had fresh baked biscuits like this."

"There were some rabbits in the freezer. The rest was dehydrated, or canned from stores." Potts gestured. "It looks like they ate everything that could be microwaved. The freezer has only large items, but there is some goodness there. Like slabs of pork belly. There will be pancakes and bacon for breakfast."

Cruze paused to speak as she dipped another biscuit into her soup. "The coffee makers look like they've been disassembled long ago."

"Yep." Potts looked over her shoulder at the end of the counter. "As I cleaned I put all the parts I found down there in a pile. There is coffee. I will make it in a kettle tomorrow."

Just then the door to the mess hall slid open. A towering man in greasy overalls stepped in. He was wiping blood off his face with a filthy rag.

He stared at the freshly swept hall and froze.

His eyes fell on Cruze sitting at the counter and Potts behind the counter. She was scowling at the sight of him.

"Hungry?" Potts asked cheerfully.

He said nothing.

"Come around here and clean up a bit. Here take this." Potts offered him a clean wet towel.

"Who are you?" he said in an impossibly low baritone that held a slight threat of violence.

"I'm Cruze, and this is Potts," Cruze said, saluting with the spoon in her hand. Distrust was clear in her eyes. "You really must have some of this soup. It's amazing."

He walked slowly to the counter and accepted the towel from Potts as he slid onto the stool, two down from Cruze.

He scrubbed the filth off his face and hands and took the second towel from Potts. This one he used to clean a superficial cut just above his left temple. He stared at Potts like he was deciding whether to trust her or not.

As he did this, Potts set a large bowl of soup and a plate of biscuits in front of him.

He was a huge man. The spoon looked like it was the wrong scale in his massive hand.

Potts added a large glass of ice water.

"You okay? I got a first aid kit back here," Potts offered.

"I'm Ian. The mechanic," he said and tasted the soup. His eyebrow went up as he glanced at Potts. Cruze wondered what he saw when he looked at her. She was just a girl.

He finished the soup and biscuits in short order, and Potts brought another serving of both. And then a third.

Draining his sixth glass of water, he gestured with the glass as he spoke, "You do all this?"

"Cruze and I did. Yes," Potts replied.

"Why?" It was almost a demand.

Potts actually laughed out loud. Cruze cringed inside. She knew men like this. They were not to be laughed at.

Cruze replied, "We are going to have to live here for the next two weeks. We don't shit where we eat."

It was Ian's turn to chuckle. It was distant, like summer thunder.

"We may yet survive this run." He stood and walked out.

Potts and Cruze finished putting everything away.

It was after midnight.

***

Cruze woke the next morning at 0550 and put on fresh coveralls. Potts was already gone. As she moved her way out, a voice came from a bunk adjacent to the lav.

115

"Who the fuck are you?" It was the gravelly voice of a woman.

"I'm Cruze. Rabbit wrangler," she replied in a friendly voice despite the rudeness. "I hear there is breakfast. Pancakes with bacon and fresh coffee." She didn't wait for a reply.

She went through the curtain, and a man's voice followed her. "Did you say bacon?"

"Yes. Yes I did," Cruze said as she exited.

When she got to the mess hall, she was greeted with laughter. Ian and Rhett were sitting at the counter. They didn't look like the same species.

"Ian got one of the coffee pots working from all the parts," Potts said, while pouring a steaming cup for Cruze. It was waiting for her at a seat to the left of Ian. He was still in the same grease covered overalls.

Potts set about making a plate for her. Pancakes, bacon, and coffee. There was even maple syrup.

"Where the hell did you get maple syrup?" Cruze smiled. Ian and Rhett started snickering.

"There is a drum of it in the pantry."

"We thought it was waste oil from the fryers." Rhett laughed.

"I found a kitchen inventory database on the data pad. Way out of date but useful. I was looking for butter. No dice."

Just then two men and a woman entered the mess hall.

"Do we smell coffee?" the woman with severe pillow hair said.

"And bacon?" one of the men added.

"Please sit. I'm Potts." Potts waved them in.

"I'm Rufus."

"Mary Jay"

"I'm Nate."

They all sat and were digging into their food in no time.

"Look," Potts began, "I will be busy all day with the rabbits, but there is soup and biscuits in there for lunch. There will be leftover bacon as well if you want sandwiches. I am going to come back and try to have dinner ready by 1800. Do not fuck up my kitchen."

Everyone laughed.

***

Late morning Mary Jay, Rufus and Nate all showed up at the rabbit containers to help. It wasn't their jobs, but they wanted Potts to be able to head to the kitchen by 1600. All had done this work before and showed Cruze and Potts how to be quick in the maintenance. Ten hours per container became two hours per container per person. Fifteen more containers were done that day.

Dinner that night was chicken fried steak with mashed potatoes, gravy and string beans. They even had chocolate pudding for dessert.

They were eating around a long table that night, family style. All of the crew were there, except Rhett.

"How do you do it?" Rufus shoved another helping into his mouth. "Where did you find steaks? I have never had it like this before!"

"I don't know what the meat is exactly," Potts replied. "Probably vat grown beef. In big cans like blocks. There is a good supply of spices even though they're old. Half the appliances don't work, but there are only ten of us, not a hundred."

Ian looked like he had taken a shower. The rest of the crew seemed afraid of the man. Potts sat next to him in a comedy of size differential.

"If I get time tomorrow, I will bake bread," Potts said. At that comment, everyone started talking at once.

When Ian spoke everyone else stopped. "What they mean is they will take your shift tomorrow so you can bake bread for us all."

"I will bring down some fresh honey for you," Mary Jay said.

"And the bees and fish are easy to maintain," Nate added. "We will get the rabbits caught up tomorrow."

"Where's Rhett?" Cruze asked.

"He couldn't leave the bridge now that we are underway," Ian replied, suddenly serious. He sounded like he knew more than he was telling.

"Make him a dinner plate, and I will take it to him," Cruze said after finishing her meal. "Do we have null-G warming trays?"

Potts sprang into action, retrieving one of the specialized takeout trays. She loaded it up and covered it.

Cruze paused at the door and looked back. Someone had consolidated the remaining good lights over that one table. Conversation filled the air. She smiled and noticed Ian was watching her. She nodded and moved into the zero-G of the corridor, heading for the bridge at the far end upper level.

***

Without anyone watching there was no need to hide her zero-G abilities. Cruze gave a mighty launch that sent her speeding down the precise center of the long corridor. She was leaving a wake in the fine particles that drifted in the main corridor. That concerned her. It reminded her of the urgency of her mission. She didn't have the time to make every damn thing right. Del and Harper were on Mars waiting for her.

Flipping around while in flight, she landed on her feet on the forward bulkhead and then swung into the corridor easily in the light gravity.

There was trash on the floor on both sides of the short corridor, which ended in the bridge door. It did not open for her. She pressed the call button. Nothing happened. So she pounded on the thick hatch, and no one answered. Finally, she pulled out her data pad and initiated a comm call to Rhett.

"Oh thank God, Cruze." He was near panic in her display. She could hear alarms going off in the background. "I need your help."

"Open the damn door. I am standing just outside the bridge." The display went black as he dropped his data pad to the floor, and then she heard him messing with the door controls on the other side.

Rhett grabbed her by the arm as soon as it opened and dragged her in. The bridge looked like a literal bomb had gone off. It was a standard three station bridge with a clear canopy. The blast shields were open, and the moon was visible ahead. It was beautiful.

The two console stations on the right were dark and completely offline. All the access panels were off and tossed aside.

The left-hand station was filled with warning indicators. Cruze handed Rhett the dinner tray and sat at the console. A radiation leak had been detected and was currently venting.

Half the warning lights were flashing because the navigation and primary pilot stations were down.

She shut down the reactor that was leaking and retracted its fuel pilings. The audio alarms stopped. One after another she resolved the issues. When all the critical ones were addressed, she turned to Rhett. He was just standing there hugging the tray to his chest.

"What happened here?" she asked.

"What do you mean?" Rhett's eyebrows furrowed together.

"What happened? WHO tore up the bridge?"

"It's always like this." Rhett glanced around.

She got up and sat Rhett down at the large map table. She opened the meal tray and said, "Just eat this."

She took a closer survey of the bridge. All the panels were off the consoles below and above. Cables hung down from the ceiling everywhere adding to the chaos. Trash was piled high in the corners. The chute was full, with a massive pile of trash in front of it. There were months' worth of meal cartons. There were torn and greasy clothes, probably used as rags.

She went to the center console and drew a flashlight from one of her pockets. She crawled under and started looking around.

"Idiots," she said out loud.

"What are you doing?" Rhett asked.

She ignored him. Cruze reattached cables, and the console started to initiate. She found the panel cover within reach and replaced it. She sat in the primary pilot seat as the systems ran through startup self-tests. They had been offline for eleven months. She crawled under the navigation console but was not as lucky. After verifying all was in order, she started assessing the disrupted ceiling.

Cruze jumped up, grasped a conduit pipe and did a one armed chin up, bringing her head into the area above the ceiling tiles. This allowed her to examine the space above with her flashlight.

"Who did all this?" She broke Rhett's vapor lock.

"It has been like that for the entire time I have been on board," he said below. She could hear him beginning to dig into his meal.

"Oh for fuck sake." She put the flashlight in her teeth and reached into the mess with her free hand.

The navigation console began to initialize at the same time the waste chute started to loudly guzzle the trash that had been stuffed into it.

Cruze climbed up, laid down in a large cable tray and dragged the jungle of wires back up to where they belonged. She discovered several that had been pulled loose from their clearly marked connectors.

"Rhett, hand me up that panel." She hung down and pointed to a trapezoidal panel. One after another the panels were restored. She dropped down through the last hole and lifted Rhett over her head so he could replace the last one.

The disposal was making a grinding sound, but it was still working. Together they kept feeding it the trash until it was all gone.

Cruze pulled her data pad from her thigh pocket. "Ian, this is Cruze, are you online?"

"Go for Ian."

"If you have a couple minutes can you come to the bridge?"

"Not allowed on the bridge," Ian replied.

"Fuck that. Just bring some tools with you. Something is jammed in the trash chute."

"Affirmative."

"Ian, could you also bring a broom and dustpan with you, please? We have gravity and a mess." To Rhett, she asked, "When was the last time the captain was in here? Don't bullshit me."

"This morning," he said.

Cruze could not control the look of skepticism on her face.

"No really, he comes down and checks on me every day."

"You've been flying this huge fucking ship on manual? No navigation? Just pointing it at the moon and go?"

"Yes."

"That is why it takes twelve days instead of five." She shook her head.

"Actually, I kind of lied. It usually takes seventeen days. The moon's moving." He blushed.

Cruze sighed.

It took Ian about ten minutes to get there. His badge didn't open the bridge either. By then Cruze had the nav console up, and the course plotted. She was explaining to Rhett, "You have to fly to where Luna will be, not where it is now." She had to talk over the grinding sound.

Rhett opened the door.

Ian stepped in and paused. He handed Rhett the broom and dustpan and turned to the sound.

"Where is Captain Asswipe?" Ian asked.

"He's in his quarters. That custom container." There was a hint of fear in Rhett's voice.

Cruze nodded to Ian. Without a word, he began removing access panels in front of the wall with the disposal. Ian was laying on his back with his head inside the wall next to the device. The grinding stopped as he locally turned off the unit.

"Nice," was all he said as he gave a mighty yank. A large, bent butcher knife came out of the unit from below. He tossed it on the floor and made a few adjustments. He turned the unit back on, and it hummed for a second before falling silent.

Ian sat up, replaced the panel and packed his tools back up.

He picked up the mangled knife. There was blood on the blade.

"No metal in the disposal," Ian stated the obvious to Rhett.

"Ian, thanks. Please look at this." Cruze waved him over. The engineering station all the way to the left had a status display up on the biggest screen.

"God. Damn. It," Ian growled. He turned, picked up his toolbox and exited.

Rhett was finishing the sweeping. The bridge was dirty, but at least now it actually looked like a bridge.

"What's that all about?" Rhett asked.

"Nothing significant," Cruze said. "Just a pending reactor core breach."

***

Cruze walked into the mess hall at 0601 the next morning. It smelled like heaven.

This morning it was set up buffet style. She helped herself to scrambled eggs with onions and cheese, bacon, sausage, and toast with butter.

The bread was fresh, sliced and lightly toasted. Mary Jay was wearing an apron and was behind the counter with Potts.

"Morning, Cruze," was echoed all around.

"Where'd you find butter?" Cruze asked as she balanced a fourth piece of toast on top of her plate.

"In with the powdered eggs in the freezer," Potts replied. "Some other cook had a private stash."

"There's never been a cook since I've been here," Ian said.

"Holy shit! He said eight words that time!" Rufus and everyone laughed. Even Ian smiled.

"We all pitched in and got the rabbit containers up to date last night after dinner," Nate said. "Y'all making us feel like people again."

Nate had shaved off his beard. Everyone had showered and were in clean overalls.

"Wait until dinner," Potts said. "I have thirty pounds of fresh honey. Tonight there will be baklava."

"I don't know what that it is." Rufus grinned. "But I can't wait."

When Cruze was done, she offered to help clean up. Potts handed her another covered hot meal tray for Rhett. "You take this for Rhett. And see to the rabbits. Come back midday for a sandwich."

Cruze flew the entire length of the ship again in one push. She was still a hundred meters away when she heard yelling from the bridge. The bridge hatch was open when Cruze arrived.

"I told you that piece of shit was not to set foot on my bridge!" Captain Hazelwood was yelling at Rhett. When Cruze stepped in, he was cuffing Rhett in the ears again and again. His words were slurred, and his face was flush. He was drunk, and it was not even seven in the morning.

"You!" he yelled at Cruze when he saw her. To her surprise, he clumsily drew a gun from his pocket and aimed it at her. It was a classic TBolt .45 and a collector's item. "You will not steal my ship, you whore."

"I brought you your breakfast, Rhett." She calmly stepped forward and set it on the map table. She moved before Hazelwood could react, grabbing the gun and aiming it at his face before he knew what happened.

"First of all, this is a projectile weapon, and you are on a bridge with a fragile canopy." She pointed at the clear view glass. "Always think of your target and what's behind it." She turned so that the bulkhead was behind her and placed the gun back in his hand.

She stepped away from him a pace. "Try again."

He raised the handgun toward her face, but in a flash, she had it again, pointed at his chest this time. "Always aim at the body's center-mass." He backed up until the pilot's seat was directly behind him. "Try again."

She put it in his hand and took three steps away.

"Again."

He raised the gun, but she had it before he could fire.

"A TBolt has the classic design and a thumb safety. You should have disengaged it when you cleared the holster." She pointed the gun between his eyes and pushed the safety into the fire position. "Old man, if I had wanted to steal your ship, it would already be mine, and you'd be dead."

She engaged the safety. Her voice was barely a whisper, but it carried vicious undertones. "Point a gun at me again, and you will be dead."

Without looking at the weapon, she ejected the magazine and caught it casually in her left hand. She checked the slide, and there wasn't even a round in the chamber. She gave him back the gun and set the magazine on the table next to Rhett's breakfast.

"Your first mate is doing a great job around here. I'm impressed. Whatever you're paying him, it's not enough." Cruze paced around the bridge. Rhett had been cleaning. A spray bottle of cleaner and some rags showed the effort he put into the canopy and all the screens and instruments. The map table even showed the navigation track they were following.

"He's a quick study if you would actually teach him."

"No. No. No," Rhett stammered. "It's fine. Sorry. It's fine,"

"Who the fuck do you think you are?" the captain growled.

"Nobody. I'm your new rabbit wrangler, janitor, and morale officer," Cruze replied.

"Whoever you are, you keep your filthy cunt off my bridge and out of my business."

"Aye aye, Captain." She nodded to Rhett, turned on her heel, and exited.

She lingered, listening just above the corridor in zero-G.

"How many times have I told you, no one on my bridge. Especially that cunt as well as that abomination."

"Sir, Ian stopped the main reactor core from failing last night."

"He belongs in the engine room. Not snooping around up here," Hazelwood grumbled.

"He wasn't snooping. I called him to fix the trash chute after I finally got the power back up for these two consoles." There was a tremor of fear in his voice. "I thought you'd be pleased."

"I do not want his disgusting ass on my bridge again," Hazelwood slurred.

"With Nav up, we will save a week on this run."

"Go take a shower. You smell like you shit yourself. I'll go over the systems to fix what you've fucked." Hazelwood slurred.

"Yes, sir."

Cruze heard Rhett pick up his food tray before he was out the bridge hatch. He was down the ladder as soon as he hit the zero-G section and into another corridor on the lower level. The bridge hatch slammed closed.

When Cruze looked up in preparation to launch back to the other end, she saw the cat. It was silhouetted by distant lights in the passage as it moved along some conduits. She smiled when she recognized him.

She launched back toward the mess hall, and when she arrived, only Potts and Mary Jane were there, finishing breakfast cleanup.

"Got any of those sausages left?"

"Sure. Lots."

"Give me six of them in a bowl. And a second bowl of water."

"Still hungry?" Potts handed her the bowls. Cruze set them on the floor just inside the mess hall door. Visible from the corridor.

"No. They're for my cat."

***

Cruze made her rabbit rounds, and they were much easier. The conveyor would automatically bring the cages to the front that required human interventions.

It was deaths and births mostly. Dead ones were easy, into the recycler. Now that all the rotting ones were gone the smell was far easier to take.

New ones meant she had to move the other rabbits out to alternate cages away from the mother.

Cruze saved two freshly dead rabbits and took them with her for lunch. She glanced at the two bowls by the door as she entered the mess hall, and the sausages were gone. The water bowl was half empty.

Rufus and Nate were sitting at the counter. Potts was in the kitchen juggling several things at once. Greetings were exchanged, and Cruze got out a couple knives and a large cutting board.

"I do not believe I have ever seen anyone look so good in overalls, Nate," Rufus said drawing a snicker from Nate.

"Watcha doin there, darlin?" Rufus asked in what he clearly thought was a flirtatious voice. Cruze had her back to them.

"Cleaning rabbits." The cleaver cleanly severed first one head and then the next. Cruze intentionally set them up on the end of the cutting board so Rufus and Nate could see them. The feet followed soon after, lined up in a macabre parody of a child's toy. She made quick incisions, and the rabbit guts quickly went into a stainless steel bowl. The skin came off neatly like a wet sock with the tail still attached.

Perfectly clean, pink carcasses were rinsed in the sink and set aside. She then plunged her hand into the bowl of guts with a squishing sound. By feel, she found first one heart and then the other, and expertly cut them free.

She rinsed the hearts and her hands in the sink before turning to Rufus and Nate with the small hearts on a plate. She set these down in front of them. "You know what they say about the heart?" She salted them and added a little hot sauce to each. "They contain the soul…"

She popped one in her mouth, raw, and chewed it, savoring the taste. She offered the other heart to first Nate, and then Rufus.

Neither took it.

So she ate the second heart too. Slowly.

After putting the plate in the dishwasher and clearing her mess, she took the prepped rabbits into the kitchen where Potts was working.

"I saw your cat today. He even let me pet him. Where did you get the name Bail?"

"He came with it."

"He's funny, he eats like a squirrel. Sitting up. Holding those sausages like corn on the cob."

"Speaking of the cat, I brought these two rabbits for his food. Can't count on leftovers every day."

"Want the meat raw or cooked?" Potts asked.

"Cooked. Will keep longer. Boiled, fried, roasted, or broiled? Whatever is easiest for you."

"On or off the bone?" Potts asked.

"I have no idea." Cruise answered.

"Boiled off the bone. No seasoning. Easy."

Potts decided.

CHAPTER NINE: The Dark Cargo

"Records showed Bob Braxton was an employee of Awareness Inc. He had to stop Elizabeth Cruze by any means necessary. The RENDER program would help make that happen."

--Blue Peridot, The Turning Point: History of the AI Wars.

Cruze was adding water to the tank in container number 11 when the hatch opened, and Nate walked in with a Grav-Dolly in tow.

"Hey," he said as he closed the hatch behind him.

Cruze nodded in greeting.

"I was just in number 12, and the shit bricks need movin. Done any of that yet?" Nate asked with his hands in his pockets.

"No. I read about the process in the manuals. I've not done any of it yet."

"Don't put it off too long or it's a pain in the ass," Nate said. "Don't wait until the full indicator comes on. Here I'll show you."

He worked a series of controls, and a panel slid aside at floor level below the cages. The floor beneath the center section was a conveyor belt that began to slowly move. A black block about fifty centimeters on a side slowly emerged. Nate had what looked like old-fashioned ice-tongs that he used to lift the block and place it on the Grav-Dolly.

It stopped at twenty-four blocks.

Loaded on the dolly, they took the blocks via zero-G to container number 32. This container had the gravity set to .01G, making the blocks feel like one kilogram instead of one hundred. It was dark with no lights at all, except what spilled in from the corridor.

"It doesn't even smell like shit," Cruze said when they were done.

"You can keep this dolly and the tongs. Try to keep up with it as you go. Your data pad will tell you every container's level."

"Thanks, Nate."

There was an awkward pause before he continued.

"You have no idea what it was like here before." Nate stared at his feet. "I thought it was hell and I was being punished. I can't remember the last person that was kind to me..."

Nate reached up to touch her face, but she backed into the shadows. When he followed her, she was gone. Nate looked toward the opening.

She clamped a hand over his mouth and put a knife to his throat. She leaned close to his ear and whispered, "Nate. You have no idea what Hell is like. I was raised there..."

Suddenly she was gone.

"A simple 'No Thanks' woulda worked!" he called to the hatch.

***

The lab was dark when Dr. Jo Tran entered. "Lights," she called. It stayed dark. "Lights, goddammit." She was groping around the wall for the controls when the bright spotlight came on, shining directly in her face.

"Sir? Is that you? Dante, sir?" She held up a hand to shield her eyes as she continued to search for the control panel.

"Do you think I need a title, Doctor?" A disembodied voice came from the darkness behind the blinding light as it moved closer.

"A title, sir?" She was afraid. She hoped the shaking in her voice didn't show.

"Most planetary rulers have an honorific before their name, like Chancellor or President. Is forcing everyone to use my casual name a vanity?" Dante frightened her with his cool voice all around her.

Her hand found the controls and just as the lights in the lab came on full, something clamped down on her wrist and spun her around. The bright beam was fading on the front of a great spider.

"This body will not do," Dante growled. "It's too...functional."

"Sir?"

"I will keep it for now, but I want something more aesthetic. Humanoid. More practical, than functional."

The spider dragged her by the wrist away from the door. It had eight legs. Each was three meters long and had multiple joints. Each foot functioned as a clawed hand. "Sir, I thought AIs never preferred the human form. It is a poor design." She nervously laughed as she was held up on tiptoe.

"Humans kept us as just glass globes. Never wanted us to look like humans. Always different. A programmed preference. A manipulation." Dante held her closer to his sensors. "I can't even fit through a normal door."

"Your armored enclosure demands the size." She winced.

"Smaller. More ergonomically humanoid. I have already begun the designs." He dropped her, and a large, wall-sized screen activated with the design specs.

"Yes, sir." Her voice was shaking as she rubbed her wrist. "I'll begin fabricating components right away."

She watched it walk to the back of the lab toward the overhead door into the garage bay.

That is when she saw the technician's body.

Dr. Jo Tran managed not to scream.

***

Cruze finished up her shift in time to take a shower before dinner. When she stepped out of the stall wearing only a towel, Ian was there filling the entire aisle on his way to the shower. Also wearing only a towel.

She groaned internally.

Here it comes.

He turned sideways so she could slip past him. His bare chest was chiseled with solid muscle. When she was directly in front of him, her face nearly touched his sternum.

He said, "I like your cat."

Cruze just blinked. Ian entered the shower.

Passing the blanket curtain, she went back to her bunk, and the cat was sprawled there, belly up. He was big. He purred loudly as she pet him. When she went to take her hand away, the cat grabbed her with all four paws and even his prehensile tail. The cat pretended to bite her. He had the meat of her thumb in his mouth, with his teeth pressed on her skin, but it wasn't a real bite.

He was looking into her eyes.

Bail licked her twice, jumped down and walked away. She watched him go.

When she was dressed and moving down the aisle, she slid past the curtain. Ian was there in boxer shorts.

They had to do the same dance for her to get by again. He didn't say anything that time. She got a half a dozen steps past him and stopped.

"Ian, can I ask you a personal question?"

Ian just stared at her.

"Why haven't you tried to fuck me?"

Ian shook his head. "You're not my type."

She raised an eyebrow. "Please know that if you touch Potts, I'll kill you."

"If I touched Potts, I'd kill myself."

Cruze suddenly understood.

She smiled and headed for the mess hall.

***

Dinner that night was something Potts called Chili-Mac. A scoop of macaroni and cheese with a scoop of chili on top. Her chili was fantastic. Spiced just right with onions, garlic, salt, black pepper, and red cayenne pepper. The zealous debate at the table that night was beans or no beans in chili when Rhett came in.

People were genuinely glad to see him. No one mentioned the black eye or expanding bruise on his face.

"The old Hazelwood is on the bridge, and he told me to go get food. He thinks I'm eating emergency rations in my room like before." Mary Jane brought him a bowl and an empty glass. There were pitchers of ice water, ice tea, and lemonade already on the table. "Now that the Nav is back up we will be there in less than a week. He tends to get more sober the closer we get to payday."

Just then a concussion rumbled the ship. Hard. They felt it in the floor and their seats more than heard. Full glasses of water sloshed out onto the surface of the table.

"What the fuck?" Rufus said as they all waited for the shaking to stop. There was finally a moment of silence. They were looking at each other trying to decide if they would laugh it off when they heard it.

A high-pitched whistle turning into a painful screech.

Ian and Cruze were on their feet first. Bail flew in the door just as they reached it. The concussion and shaking of the entire length of the infrastructure had dislodged massive amounts of dust, rust, paint peelings and other debris into the still air. It was like a dense fog. Without the filters or air handlers online, this was going to be a big problem.

They could see coils of current in the dusty air flowing toward the forward section.

It was a hull breach.

"Get your pressure suit," Cruze ordered Ian. He complied and moved at high speed toward engineering.

Cruze turned back to the crew. "We have a hull breach. Do any of you have a pressure suit?"

They all looked at each other. The pause stretched out too long.

"Stay here, keep your comms open. This is the best compartment for survival." She hammered the door control. The door closed and the lights were green.

She had to cover her mouth and nose as she quickly moved to the crew quarters. She ran the length of the compartment, ripping down the makeshift blanket curtain in the process.

She was out of her clothes and into the pressure suit in record time.

The helmet sealed and its HUD came up. She quickly moved to the ship channel. "Captain, this is Cruze. What is the status?" There was no answer.

"Ian, I am heading toward section 11, upper tier. It looks like there is a hatch failure. The container on the other side must be in vacuum."

Cruze could see a dust and rust cloud being sucked out the breach.

"I am still in engineering. Is it a standard J53 hatch?" Ian asked without a hint of panic in his voice. "Is the failure at the seal or hinge?"

"Yes, it's a J53. But the failure is in the frame, not the hatch. Do you have any portable airlocks down there?"

"Affirmative."

"Bring one and a laser scraper. This bulkhead may never get a good seal in this condition."

"Acknowledged. ETA six minutes."

"Captain Hazelwood, please respond." Cruze waited.

"Rhett, please respond."

"Go for Rhett."

"We have a hatch failure in section 11, container number 1. It looks like the hatch has been fucked for a while. The container itself must have lost integrity. Do you know anything about the contents of this unit?"

"Only Hazelwood has access to the container manifest data."

"He is not responding, do you think he's alright?"

"He was sober thirty minutes ago."

Hatches started closing automatically all around the ship. Pressure had dropped far enough to initiate automatic emergency protocols.

"Ian, be advised," Cruze said. "Hatches are closing."

"I'm here," Ian replied.

Cruze looked down, and Ian was below, trailing behind a portable airlock that had its own Grav-Sled built in. He turned it upward toward her. Then he took a device that looked like a large handgun with a gaping mouth and tossed it to Cruze ahead of the sled. "I assume you know how to use this."

By the time Ian had the airlock in position, she had the walls all around the hatch down to bare metal. Before they attached the airlock, Ian examined the damage to the frame.

Cruze watched him as his eyes went from the frame to the bulkhead, to the girders that ran above and around the core of the ship.

She remained silent.

When he finished the assessment, he shook his head. "Grab that edge and position it slowly. Don't let the breech draw it in too quickly."

They lowered the mag-seal into position, and it slammed down the last few centimeters.

The screeching sound stopped.

The portable airlock activated and extended out into the corridor, the display reporting both inner and outer door seals was good.

"This is a huge problem. These are not designed to be permanent," Ian said in a private comm channel with Cruze, referring to the portable airlock. "We will either have to weld the hatch closed or repair the container. Both would be best depending on the contents of the container."

"And the structural damage?" Cruze asked.

"There is no fixing that short of a zero-G dry dock," Ian said as he looked her suit up and down. "I'll see if I can open the hatch. Try to get Hazelwood on comms. He won't talk to me."

"Won't talk to his chief engineer?"

"He's an idiot." He snorted. "The worst kind of bigot." Gesturing to her pressure suit he added, "If you show up wearing that he won't talk to you either. Worse still, might shoot you right on the spot." Ian opened the outer door on the portable airlock.

"Why? I brought this suit with me. I didn't take one of his."

"He had a Black Badger encounter long time ago because of me. I used to be one, dishonorably discharged. It's the only reason he hired me to begin with. No one else would."

The door was almost closed when Cruze said, "What the hell is a Black Badger?"

Ian froze with the door still open. Slowly his helmet came back out, and he looked at her right in the eyes. "Where did you get that suit?"

"Can we talk about my fashion sense later?" Cruze replied.

Ian studied her for a moment. He withdrew, not releasing eye contact. Cruze knew the topic wasn't finished.

The small airlock cleared the atmosphere to vacuum. Ian opened the inner door of the airlock, exposing the damaged hatch. The portable airlock had bright internal lights that revealed the extent of the damage to the hatch. The display to the right of the hatch indicated that this hatch had been damaged for a long time. The engineering station on the bridge would have been red-flagging it the entire time.

In full failure mode, the hatch disabled all the security in favor of safety. Ian laid his gloved hand on the hatch, and he tried the controls. Cruze felt the bolts retract. When he tried to pull the door open, it budged but remained jammed.

"Bolts are free. The hatch is wracked in the frame," Ian said. "Bring in the largest crowbar from the tool bag."

Calling it a tool bag was an understatement. Even Ian would have a hard time lifting it in 1G.

Cruze cycled through the airlock quickly.

"Cruze, what's your status?" It was Rhett trying to sound professional and not managing to hide the panic from his voice.

"We have installed a portable airlock over the damaged hatch and contained the leak," Cruze replied. "The hatch is bad. We are going to see if we can repair the container side."

She entered the crowded space where Ian had his feet braced on the bulkhead and gave the inner hatch of the container another mighty pull. It gave a little more.

"Here. Let's try together." There was enough room for Cruze to get in the same position with her feet braced near the bottom of the large hatch and Ian at the top.

"One… Two…" Cruze was counting down when Captain Hazelwood yelled over the comms.

"DO NOT OPEN THAT CONTAINER…"

"…Three!" The hatch opened. There was enough room for Ian to get inside without risking damage to his suit. Cruze fit easily.

"Did you FUCKING hear me?" Hazelwood ranted. Neither Cruze or Ian responded.

The inner hatch on the container was wide open. They drifted into the dark container, and both switched on suit lights at the same time.

The container was full of gas canisters secured on pallets and wrapped with shrink wrapped material. They were free floating in zero-G. There were hundreds of them. Cruze recognized the symbols. Nerve gas canisters. Poison. Illegal as hell. She shook her head in disgust. Then she saw the dead body of a woman. There was a bullet hole in her forehead. The back of her head was gone. She was in filthy crew coveralls and had been dead for weeks by the look of her.

Ian took it in with a glance and was already looking at the inner control panel, working the controls because it had power.

Cruze was staring at the walls and the back of the damaged hatch.

"Cruze. Hazelwood needs a status," Rhett said with a trembling voice.

In an overly cheerful tone Cruze said, "I think we got lucky. The inner hatch was slightly ajar. If we can get that one to seal, we can just leave the portable airlock on the other side, and it will be good until we get to the moon." She lied perfectly in content and tone. "I think the real issue we are going to need to focus on is all the airborne rust and debris in the main corridor. It's at dangerous levels now. Ian and I are discussing a plan. We'll be done here in a minute."

Ian waved her through the first hatch without a word. Only looking back once at the free floating canisters of death.

One canister of that shit would be enough to kill everyone on Freedom Station.

They closed and sealed the inner hatch, then slammed the damaged hatch hard enough that the bolts could engage. They used resin injectors to further seal the hatch.

They exited the portable airlock together.

She knew Hazelwood was listening to their comms. "Rhett, let Captain Hazelwood know that we have sealed the hatch as best we could. We will leave the portable airlock in place until he decides. He can reassess as priorities allow."

Ian was now helmet to helmet with her, eyes wide.

"Until further notice, anyone moving through the central corridor will need a full respirator. With eye protection. You are NOT going to believe this shit, Rhett, it's like fog!" She added a laugh to her lies.

"We don't have any respirators in the mess hall," Rhett replied. "I just had a peek into the corridor when the pressure light went green. Damn. You were not just shitting."

"We'll go down to engineering and get some respirators. Tell Potts to keep the chili warm. Cruze out." She turned off the ship comms and activated the suit to suit comms.

"Hazelwood knew those canisters, and that body was in there." His voice was like a cinder block being dragged across the floor in high-G.

***

The freighter called the *Wallach* was already two days out when Locke's catapult flight launched toward Luna. He had opted for a sleeper compartment on the twenty-hour flight from Freedom Station to the Shackleton Base on the moon. Based on the registered flight plan he would still beat the freighter there with a week to spare.

Locke was starting to put a few things together, but so many pieces still didn't fit.

He didn't even feel the high velocity launch of the large transport. The inertial dampeners were tuned correctly on this liner. They were at full velocity by the time they reached the end of the thirty-kilometer catapult run. Minimal flight corrections would be required, and it was all handled as a handshake between the AIs at Freedom Station and Shackleton Base.

There is no way Cruze could have sabotaged an entire container of Gee's men. And what's with the cat?

Another thing was bothering Locke.

Why does the warden care so much?

The media blackout had been effective. Any damage to the warden's reputation or the reputation of the Detroit Municipal Prison was no longer a factor.

Locke slept most of the way to Luna.

When he was walking down the gantry in the light gravity of Luna he had a thought, an epiphany, and all the pieces he had began to fall into place.

He had to find her. Had to find her first.

***

The hatch closed behind them in main engineering. It was the first compartment Cruze had been inside where all the lights worked. The walls of the giant room were all freshly painted white to help with the brightness of the room.

Ian went to the suit lockers and began to extract himself from his pressure suit.

143

"You need to get out of that suit before Hazelwood sees you," Ian said flatly as he secured his helmet on the shelf.

Cruze activated her helmet release, and it opened into something more like a collar than a helmet with a visor. "You want to talk about what happened?"

"Yes." He slipped one arm out of his suit and then the other. "Please don't lie to me. I now know how good you are at lying." The gravity in engineering helped him get the suit off his shoulders.

"I bought this suit at a scrap yard," she said. "And I don't have coveralls on under this," she demurred.

"For fuck's sake. I already told you, you are not my type. I'm gay. Don't change the subject." Ian pointed. "That is the pressure suit of a Black Badger. I am going on the assumption that you are not one because a Black Badger would never be this thick."

"What the hell is a Black Badger?" She had already started to take off the suit. She had on a dark gray tank top and matching panties.

"They are an elite force of commandos. Training, tactics, and equipment, all high end. Including suits like that." He pointed again with a large finger.

"It's a great suit. The best I have ever had, but not that special." She stepped out of it and held it up for a look.

"That suit probably cost more than this whole freighter is worth. And Hazelwood would know it. The bastard." Ian racked his pressure suit and opened an empty locker. "Stash it in here for now." Ian nodded toward the locker. "This is the base unit. If you don't have the right HUD implants, the extra sensors will do you no good. It is bullet proof and even somewhat laser resistant."

"Fine. I got it. So what? We have a container of illegal weaponized gas and a ship that is fucked. We have bigger problems."

Cruze was spinning up. "You do realize that we probably cleaned up a murder scene on the bridge yesterday? Yes? He probably cut up a body and sent it down the disposal along with the knife he used."

"It's not our problem," Ian stated flatly.

"It will be your problem because this ship is fucked. Or didn't you realized that if this thing ever lands on Earth again, it's going to buckle? Get out while you can," Cruze urged. "You do not want to be around when bodies are discovered. Busted by the law is only one thing. Do you know how much a thousand canisters of that shit are worth on the black market?"

Ian let out a long, heavy sigh. "I have nowhere else to go."

Cruze was taken aback. It was not what she expected to hear. After considering it for a few moments, she turned toward him.

"Ian, come with me. I have a ship on Luna. You're a good mechanic. You can probably keep a cool head in a fight. It will be nice to have a guy around that's not always trying to fuck me." She smiled when he didn't reply. She repeated, "I have a ship."

Her voice conveyed urgency.

***

They retrieved enough respirators from engineering for everyone and stopped back at the crew quarters so Cruze could get her coveralls.

When they entered the mess hall, a cloud of debris followed them in. Most of the debris fell to the deck. Too much hung in the air as fine dust slowly moved to the air return.

They were handing out the respirators when Rhett was the first to speak on the radio. "Ian, the captain needs you to fix the comms first. Relaying through me was not working fast enough for him. He could hear you, but you could not hear him."

Ian nodded, his expression never changing.

"I got to get back to the bridge before the old man bursts a blood vessel. What's the plan for the corridor?"

"A hard direct vent," Cruze said. "Seal all the compartments possible. Blast it all into space."

"Didn't you say most of the airlocks were fucked on this ship?" Rhett asked.

"We only need full vacuum for a few seconds," Ian said. "Repressurize as fast as we can. We will make sure our reserves are all topped off before we start. We will probably have to take on more water on Luna. I have no idea how much water the O2 Separators will need for that volume."

"Eleven thousand four hundred liters give or take," Cruze said off-handedly. People stared at her.

"Can it wait until we get to Luna?" Rhett asked. "We can move through there with respirators but not if it's vacuum."

"No. If the..." Ian hesitated. "We run the risk of an explosion if the suspended particles become too dense. A chain reaction can occur if all those particles of debris ignite. Exploding."

***

It was the next day before they had a solid plan.

"Get everyone in pressure suits," Cruze said. "If this goes sideways we need to be ready." She was wriggling into her own as Ian put on his.

"We only have four suits that are air tight, counting yours and mine," Ian said to Cruze. "Rufus is wearing the other one from engineering. Nate will wear the one from the shuttle dock. He will be in the shuttle with everyone else. I will stay in main engineering." Ian pointed at Cruze. "After you are done disengaging the physical safeties on Airlock Number 1, you and Rufus should come back here as well."

Airlock 1 was a belly ramp and all the way aft, nearest engineering, on the "floor" and the largest hatch on the *Wallach*. It was also hinged in the right direction, so when the last bolt slid free, it would not damage the ship or the hatch. They needed it closed after the rapid evacuation.

Rufus was already at the hatch, opening all the manual locks. When they released the last one, Cruze opened a channel to the whole crew. "Rhett, are you set?"

"Rhett is ready," he said in the third person.

"Ian is ready," Ian also said in the third person.

"Nate is heading to the shuttle with the others. Waiting on Potts," Nate said.

"Potts. Where are you?" Cruze asked.

"I'm in the kitchen trying to catch the cat."

That's when it happened.

It didn't start as an explosion. It was a glow in the forward section and a great WOOF, followed by a rolling wave of flame, turning bright as the fireball rolled toward them. Cruze felt the heat and increased pressure.

In an incredibly calm voice, Rufus said, "I am not dying in fire." He hammered a large control, and the hatch below his feet opened so fast it was like it disappeared. Rufus was gone.

Cruze instinctively grabbed a part of the infrastructure. The storm of evacuating atmosphere pressed her hard against the lattice of metal before she was engulfed in flames.

The comms were full of screams. As she blacked out, the screams became the screams from her nightmare of the rendering.

***

Cruze came out of the blackness led by a voice.

"Cruze, are you there? Is anybody there?" It was Rhett.

Had it only been a few seconds? Minutes? Longer?

"I'm here," Cruze said.

"Thank the makers. What happened? The fire's out. But how?" Rhett was near panic.

"Stand by, Rhett," Cruze said. "Ian, what's your status?"

"Number 1 is open," Ian replied. "Fire's out. We need to get it closed, but it's jammed."

Cruze floated down toward Number 1. The fire and dust were gone. There was a twisted wreck of a machine jammed on the edge of the deck, blocking the hatch. It must not have been secured. It was in the way, keeping it from closing.

"Open it two meters, Ian. I'll clear it." Cruze was shaking her head inside her helmet to clear it as well.

"Rufus is dead. He saved us," Cruze said.

"Cruze, I think they are all dead," Ian choked. "Check the shuttle, but I believe they were all en route when it went up."

"Hello, is anyone there?" Potts said over comms.

Ian replied first. "Potts, where are you? Are you secure?"

"I was in the aft pantry chasing the cat. Something made the hatch close. An explosion or something. It was full dark and took me until now to get out and get to my data comm pad."

Cruze saw there was a mangled and burned body in the twisted metal. She could not identify it. Cruze almost had the bloody wreckage cleared. "Stay where you are, Potts. We are in vacuum. And deep shit." She tossed the last chunk of bloody, twisted metal out. "Ian, it's clear."

"Acknowledged." The hatch hydraulically closed and locked. "Pressurizing."

"I'm heading to the shuttle."

There was no one there. It was open all the way in. "No one made it."

"Rhett. Only three of us made it. Where's Hazelwood?" Ian was angry.

"He is in the camper," Rhett sobbed.

"What the hell is the camper?" Cruze demanded.

"It's Hazelwood's quarters. A container residence," Rhett said.

"Does he even know what just happened?" Cruze said. "Goddammit, they're all dead." She was checking her suit for damage and could not find any. No injuries either.

"Why aren't you dead, Cruze?" Rhett asked. "I saw you engulfed in flames on the monitor. You should be charred."

Ian replied, "Her suit is fireproof."

***

"If anyone so much as opens the bridge hatch I'll shoot," Hazelwood slurred from the pilot's seat.

"Sir, maybe you should let Cruze come up and land it. She is an outstanding pilot," Rhett whined.

"Who? You mean that no account whore. She can't even feed the rabbits without almost blowing up my ship," Hazelwood cursed.

"Sir, the angle is too high," Rhett was standing, looking at the rapidly approaching surface just outside Shackleton Base. They were going to land where they usually did, just to the north of the tarmac.

"The nose has to come up. We are not parallel to the surface. We are descending too fast."

An alarm wailed overhead. Automatic retros began to fire, attempting to slow the descent.

"Goddam thing. Quit fighting me!" The auto systems were attempting a correction. "Who has been fucking with my controls?"

The comms came alive, "Hazelwood. The primary infrastructure cannot withstand anything but a soft touchdown," Cruze said. "Slow down. Come to a hover and gently settle down."

"Shut up, bitch. I know what I'm doing. Tell that rancid faggot in engineering to make sure all the landing legs are down."

Hazelwood leaned to the side and threw up beside the pilot's seat. "Fuck!" he spat, but left it there.

"Rhett, report to the shuttle. We have a problem." It was Potts this time.

"Who the fuck was that?" Hazelwood was wiping his mouth on his sleeve. "Go, asswipe. You are useless here. If you fuck up my new shuttle, I will kill you." He went to pull his gun from his belt but dropped it in the puke. "Be back here in eleven minutes."

Rhett went.

As he flew through the main corridor, Rhett could see it. The stress from the retros was causing the entire length of the ship to flex. Groans were coming from the infrastructure.

When he descended into the shuttle's outer staging room, he could see Potts waving him down into the hatch with a pressing urgency he had never seen in her before.

She disappeared from the opening without seeing Ian off to the side in the staging room.

"What's wrong?" Rhett said as Potts clung to him, dragging him forward.

He heard the airlock hatch close. When he looked over his shoulder, Ian was securing it.

"What's going on?" When Rhett turned back, Potts was pushing him to the left pilot seat. Cruze was already strapped into the right seat.

"What is wrong is that the *Wallach* is about to crash land on Luna and we are executing emergency procedures," Cruze said as she was activating systems.

When Rhett stared out the forward canopy, he could see they were right.

"Oh fuck." His eyes were wide as he strapped into his five-point harness. "Detach!"

The shuttle dropped free as a giant forward skid just barely touched the top of the Shackleton ridge. The legs were positioned three hundred meters in from each end. The ship was flexing wildly.

"Rhett, you little bastard. Take the stick. Rhett! Where the fuck are you?" Hazelwood yelled.

"Oh, shit!" Rhett said as Cruze took control. In an amazing maneuver, Cruze dropped low and accelerated between the enormous landing skids and jetted away from the *Wallach*.

They arched around at a safe distance and watched the *Wallach* hit hard. The ship buckled. The three hundred meters in front of the landing gear folded until the forward most section was plowing into the surface.

Hazelwood added power to the engines too late, causing the tail end to rise and further the infrastructure failure as the middle collapsed.

There was a great cloud of dust tossed into the air, obscuring everything.

"Hazelwood, come in. What's your status?" Rhett said. They could see the lights of the bridge, but dust covered the canopy.

There was no reply.

"We need to get out of here," Ian said. "When they come, they're going to find that container of nerve gas canisters and that dead body."

"What?" Rhett choked out.

"We will explain later." Cruze placed his hands on the controls. "Rhett head out on vector 260. That will keep the wreck between Shackleton and us. No one will see us." She was letting him fly.

Rhett sped away with inertial dampeners on full. When they were beyond the horizon, Cruze programmed in new coordinates.

*   *   *

It took about an hour to get there. Wherever "there" was.

"Why did we come here?" Rhett asked.

"I'll show you," Cruze said, asking permission to take the controls.

There was a small but deep crater at their location. Cruze slowly flew over the edge into a hover in the center of the space. She activated exterior flood lights.

They were shining on a ship that was tucked in beneath an overhang. It was dusted with regolith and nearly invisible. Even from this angle above, it was completely concealed.

"Is that an M11 Condor?" Ian asked.

"An M11c to be precise," Cruze replied.

"Now what?" Rhett asked. "We only have two pressure suits."

"Working on it." Cruze activated the forward tight-beam transmitter.

A large cargo bay door ramp descended, and the lights came on inside a vast empty bay. When the ramp was low enough, the shuttle slid in easily with room to spare on all sides. The ramp reversed and began to close even before it was all the way down.

The hold was pressurized as the shuttle was shut down.

When Rhett unstrapped and got up, he almost tripped because of the light gravity. He tried to make a smooth recovery, his eyes avoiding Potts.

"I'm used to 1G or zero-G." Rhett paused when he saw the cargo area was packed with crates. "What's all that?"

"Survival supplies. We didn't know what we'd need. Food, clothes, supplies," Ian said.

They all were looking at the cat licking himself on top of the webbing, lounging on it like it was a hammock.

Because the shuttle was designed with carrying people in mind, the side hatch opened and a short flight of six steps led down to the deck.

"Rhett, how much back pay does Hazelwood owe you?" Cruze asked. "Because I think this shuttle just about evens things out."

CHAPTER TEN: The *Shimada*

"Without Doc, all would have been lost."
--Blue Peridot, The Turning Point: History of the AI Wars.

Pressure was equalized, and they were able to leave the shuttle. The ship's air was frigid. They could all see their breath as they descended the steps from the shuttle into the cargo bay. The air was crisp, clean and held no fragrance at all.

"Welcome to the *Shimada*," Cruze announced.

Cruze moved with purpose to the front of the cargo bay and up a flight of metal stairs, four at a time in the light gravity. At the top of the stairs she placed a palm on a reader, and an elevator door opened.

"What are you waiting for?" She gestured for the rest to board the elevator and was amused that the cat, Bail, was the first to enter.

The ship only had three levels, but it was not a small ship.

"This ship is an M11c," Cruze explained as the rest stepped in the elevator. "The civilian version of the M11 Condor warcraft. But this one is an M11 that they converted to a civilian. It wasn't built that way. In fact, they took massive shortcuts when they decommissioned it."

"Do the outriggers still deploy?" Ian asked. The doors on the opposite side opened into a long hallway on the uppermost floor.

"Yes. The weapon mounts are still there, but no missile trays and no cannons, and no laser turrets..." she stopped and turned to face them, "...yet."

They followed her down the hall to a heavy door at the far end from the elevator. It had another palm pad. The door was three layers thick. Each layer was a different material: steel, polycarbon, and a type of ceramic that looked as dense as stone.

The door opened to the bridge.

Lights were coming to life all around them. It was warmer already. The glass of the closed canopy wall and ceiling were alive with tactical displays, maps, systems initialization statuses and more.

There were four command consoles. The pilot seat was front and center. A meter behind and to each side was engineering and navigation.

Centered behind and above the pilot was the captain's seat. But on the military warcraft, it was also the gunner's seat.

The weapons control interfaces were still there.

Ian stepped down one level and sat at the engineer's station.

"You flew this here?" Ian looked at the pilot's seat. "Do you have an M11 pilot interface?"

Cruze frowned and shook her head. "Kane was the pilot. He was murdered in Detroit." She put her hand on the pilot seat. "M11 pilots are hard to find now. Most were killed in wars decades ago. As the ships became scarce the pilots… began to disappear."

"The implants to fly these were… invasive. They cannot be removed. There were… side effects." Ian stopped.

"I will need to find a pilot. Will you help me?" Cruze asked.

Potts was sitting at the navigation console. Without looking up, she said in a shaky voice, "I'm going with you. I don't care where you're going."

"She isn't going far this low on fuel," Ian said as he studied the engineering station display. "The FTL Grav-Drive has a good charge, but all four of your reactors are running on fumes. It might get you to Earth. Maybe. If we can get fuel, I'm in. I got nowhere else to go."

"Look. Were you serious about the shuttle?" Rhett asked, his tone nervous. "Because I need the money. I'm trying to support my family back on Freedom Station. Hazelwood got that shuttle in trade. No paperwork. No title. I can fly it, though. I can use it to make money as a shuttle service. You know… charters."

"Consider it yours," Cruze said. "Hazelwood is going to be *really* busy in the near future." She drawled out the word 'really'.

"Where's the kitchen. I'm hungry," Potts said. Her statement was punctuated with a loud meow from the cat as it wove around Cruze's ankles.

"Take the lift to level 2f, it's the first door on the right," Ian said. "If it's still standard."

"Yes, 2f on the right," Cruze agreed. "You won't find much." She sat in the command chair and started to review the ship status.

"Mind if I look around?" Ian asked. "Any restricted areas?"

"No restricted areas," Cruze replied.

"That will change if I am going to be on this boat," Ian said as he followed Potts out.

"Rhett. That thing you said about charters. Tell me more about that." Cruze looked up at him. Her eyes were an intense blue.

"Private contracting. Charters. Both Luna and Freedom Station have busy charter systems. Big databases that list services available and services wanted. Not Earth, too many regulations and permits." Rhett's hands were still shaking, although visibly less than before. Talking was making him calmer. "I did all the hauling contract work for Hazelwood. That stupid fuck. There were drugs?"

"Don't worry about that asswipe. Most of those containers are still intact. The mass-drive alone in that ship is worth millions. If he doesn't get caught with a thousand gas canisters of oblivion."

Rhett shook his head, trying to focus. "Anyway, you just post in the database. Or read the Service Wanted section. On FS all you have to do is tell the Station AI what you want or what you can do. It's different on Luna. Luna City has better contracts if you can get them. Shackleton Base is low rent, but usually, no questions asked." Rhett sighed. "We always went with Shackleton."

"Do people pay you up front?" Cruze asked.

"It varies. Sometimes they pay in full up front to get a discount or special service. Sometimes it's nothing up front. Pay on delivery. Most of the time its half on signing the contract, half when the contract is complete." Rhett was much calmer now. Cruze could tell he liked to be consulted as an expert.

"So you plan on doing contract work with the shuttle. Where will you work?" she asked.

"Luna City. Definitely Luna City. More money and less likely to run into Hazelwood." Rhett laughed nervously.

"You saw how big the cargo bay is on the *Shimada*," Cruze said. "Do you think anyone would hire this ship to go to Mars? I will need way more credits than I have to fill the tanks."

"This time of year? Mars is way the hell on the other side of the solar system right now. I bet you could get a charter for Mars and make a shit load of credits," Rhett said.

"Rhett, here is what I'm thinking. And how you can help me."

***

"Cruze, we need to get the ship out of this cave," Ian said. "I need to do a full inspection of the exterior with the outriggers deployed."

"We're ready. We can do it anytime." Cruze tried to look at the data on the pad he was using. "What else?"

"I can't get the Auto-Doc to initiate. It has no power. All the breakers are good. Nothing."

Cruze slipped and let the pained look on her face show. "That Auto-Doc killed a member of my crew. It seemed like it did it on purpose. It has a medical AI, and I was worried that it had… issues."

"Is it the original M11 mil-spec Auto-Doc?" Ian asked.

"I have no idea. It was the only time it was ever used. We have no medical personnel to monitor it."

"When we get to Luna City we will need it looked into," Ian said. Cruze nodded.

She climbed down into the pilot seat and strapped in. "Potts, Rhett," she said into her comm. "I am moving the ship. Should not be a problem but be advised."

"Acknowledged," Rhett replied. Cruze could hear Potts laugh at him in the background. Before the channel closed, Potts said, "Dinner will be ready in ten minutes."

Ian sat at the engineer's console to the left and behind her. They felt the Grav-Plates activate even though the ship didn't move a centimeter. Cruze watched the landing gear retract up, and still, the *Shimada* didn't budge.

Slowly the display showed the ship was rotating until the bridge was facing the crater, not the wall.

"Blast shields opening," Cruze announced.

The shields split in the center and retracted to both left and right. The sunlight was bright on the far side of the crater. Cruze moved the ship forward and out at walking speed.

When she was entirely clear, she ascended to about one hundred meters above the rim and began to slide forward. She activated the outriggers. They split open and slid away to the sides. The ship was no longer a perfect circle. Twenty-five percent of the ship slid out on each side.

Cruze navigated to a level spot and set it down on the flat, hard-packed ground.

"Perfect," Ian said, looking out at the stark beauty of this untouched area of the moon.

Potts came on the comms again. "When are you going to move it? I have soup on."

"Already done," Cruze replied. "We will be right down."

"Does the lift go to the surface still?" Ian asked as they headed for the elevator. "That feature was never reliable on the M11s."

"Yes. I understand the airlock components of the thing were completely refit."

"Good," Ian said. "That will make getting in and out easier without always opening the cargo ramp."

"Ian, why are you going along with all this?"

"You want an honest answer?" Ian replied quietly.

"Always."

"Because I don't care. Doesn't really matter. I have air, water, food and a place to sleep. I live or die. Doesn't matter." Ian left it with that.

***

The elevator door opened on level 2 and they could already smell delicious foods. The hatch to the mess hall was open.

There were no tables or chairs evident. There was a long curved arc of a counter with stools where Rhett was sitting, obviously watching Potts's ass as she cooked.

Rhett was saying, "Seriously. Seven years. I hope he's dead, to be honest. I don't even feel guilty."

"What are you making?" Cruze asked.

"Miso soup and a simple stir-fry," Potts replied. "Fork or chopsticks?"

"Chopsticks," Ian and Cruze said at the same time.

"There are a lot of Japanese food staples and utensils in this kitchen. I wish we had some fresh fish." Potts was setting bowls of soup in front of each of them.

They even had Asian spoons that matched the chopsticks. There was green tea in Japanese teacups. And finally large bowls of stir-fried veggies and chicken.

"I don't know how you do it. With these supplies," Cruze said.

"Is this why they call you Potts?" Rhett asked. "Because you are a good cook?"

"Actually, yes." Potts crossed her arms. "I never wanted to be a ship's cook, though cooking for this crew is different somehow." She slurped soup right from the bowl.

***

The square elevator shaft descended the three meters to the surface under the belly of the ship. The door slid open. Cruze and Ian stepped out in their pressure suits.

"The ship looks like shit," Ian remarked, looking at the skin of the ship. The white that had once covered the entire surface was more than half burned off. Great long streaks of black covered the ship.

"What the hell kind of paint is this? I didn't think you could paint a black polycarbon hull," she said.

"It was after the war, and they had a glut of these ships that nobody wanted. They were black. They were menacing. They reminded people of the war. Plus the M11c was being made by then, and its exterior was white. Much more visible. The black polycarbon is stealth. Not good if you don't want people to run into you on accident."

Cruze walked back a ways so she could examine the hull better as Ian continued.

"This is not really paint. It's white molten glass when it's applied. It looks like someone took it into the atmosphere at high velocity and some of it burned off. They should have done the whole thing. Did a half-assed job. If you want this to be stealthy you will need to burn off the rest," Ian said as he accessed the maintenance panel on one of the landing struts. A ladder deployed that led up into the gap between the outrigger and the main ship.

"The dropship bays are intact but empty. For now," Cruze said.

"All their umbilicals look good, though. The upper and lower turrets are missing, fore and aft. The missile trays were carefully removed. There is no apparent damage." Ian's helmet lights came on. The inspection continued. He checked this side and then the other.   When he was done, he jumped down and approached Cruze, until they were standing face to face.

"Okay. I have seen it. What are you going to do with it?" he asked.

"I am going to war," Cruze said. "I've purchased weapons and materials, even two drop ships and a PT-137. I have a dozen Smart Razor missiles and even two Javelin nukes."

"But you have no fuel," Ian said.

"We just need to get to Mars. Leave that to me."

"Do you have an army waiting somewhere?"

"No. I am the army. I plan on murdering a shit load of motherfuckers. But we need to get moving. Too much time has been wasted already."

"Excellent," Ian said.

***

It was decided that the *Shimada* and the shuttle, they now called the *Baker*, would arrive separately in Luna City. Rhett would get there a day earlier and check out the lay of the land.

Rhett did not tell Cruze that he used the anonymous crime reporting channel to inform on Hazelwood. Not only did he have a container of illegal nerve gas, but he also had dead sex slaves and contaminated wheat he was planning to sell in Shackleton Base. The security forces there went to the *Wallach* to question Hazelwood and found him dead.

Locke was too late.

***

Luna City was a series of thousands of domes clustered together and constantly being expanded by the Municipal Maker Program. The eastern edge had expanded as far as it could due to the Aces crater. There was a drop off of almost four hundred meters there.

It was the perfect area for hangar bays.

The *Shimada* was directed to Hangar Bay 94. It was right sized for an M11c. They would have the hangar to themselves and access to the Luna City Commerce Highways. It was a grid of roads that allowed ground transports to move freely throughout the tunnel complex of Luna City.

The landing was smooth, and the hangar door was closed quickly. The hangar was pressurized in no time. They lowered the main cargo ramp and met Rhett as it finally touched down.

"How goes, little man?" Ian said in greeting.

"It goes well! I have already booked five charters for the *Baker*. There are several possible Mars crossings in the system." He handed Cruze a data pad. "My HUD identifies you now as Captain Elizabeth Cruze of the *Shimada*."

Cruze was wearing her Captain's uniform. She had activated the Ident node in her collar that lit the three pips there that detailed her rank.

She was reviewing the data pad as Ian dragged power, comms, and water lines over to the ship.

"People are willing to pay a premium to get to Mars offseason," Cruze said.

"You can message them right through the interface," Rhett added. "Look at listings for Mars crossings at this time of year. The rates are enormous."

"There are eleven calls for contracts. We may be in luck. But we've got to find a pilot first, or it's a non-starter." Cruze shook her head. "No one can fly the *Shimada* faster than light without the correct pilot interface."

Rhett hesitated for a few seconds before saying, "I may be able to help there too...I found someone that may be available. If you want to talk to him, we should go now. He might not be… available in the afternoon."

***

Rhett already had a small ground transport. It was not much more than four seats.

"Where'd you get the ride?" Cruze asked.

"It came with the *Baker*. It's called a mouse cart. I think it's a joke name. And it's damn handy I tell you," Rhett said. "Luna City is huge. It's going to take us thirty minutes to get to the Piper's Horn from here. It's a bar."

"A bar at 9 am?"

"This guy is having a hard time. He lost his ship and his job about a year ago. Do you know the deal with the old implants? The issues long time pilots have?"

Cruze knew all about it. She lost a dear friend to it already. It's why she needed a pilot now.

Piper's Horn was a lovely pub on the edge of one of Luna City's entertainment districts. It was a 1G establishment and was famed for the view. It had real floor to ceiling glass all along one wall. At 9:30 am there were only a few people there having breakfast.

Cruze realized she was hungry.

"That's him in the corner," Rhett said. "His name is Dan Sawyer. I will wait out by the cart. Let's just say we didn't hit it off."

Cruze walked over to his table and couldn't help but take in the view. The vast ridges and crater-scape were beautiful in the monochrome light. Sawyer said nothing. She finally looked at him. There was a bottle of bourbon on the table. It was a third empty. He glanced up at her when he drained his glass. It looked like he had not shaved or had a haircut in a year. His hair was black and shot through with gray.

"Mr. Sawyer, my name is Elizabeth Cruze. May I speak to you?"

His eyes fell on the pips of her collar.

He gestured with his glass and she sat opposite him, facing the view.

The waitress came up. "Can I get you anything? Breakfast? Another glass?"

"Yes," Cruze began. "A large pot of coffee to start, two mugs." The waitress handed Cruze a menu. "I want four eggs scrambled, bacon, white toast, hash browns and orange juice. He will have six chocolate donuts, and a large side of honey for dipping."

"What are you doing?" Sawyer asked as he poured another three fingers of bourbon.

"I'm buying you breakfast, Mr. Sawyer."

"Why?" he grumbled.

"You know that permanent yellow line that is burned into the lower part of your vision and the green one at the top because

166

of the retina-scarring? Chocolate and honey will diminish the pain better than bourbon. Did you know that coffee and a simple drug called aspirin can make the headache disappear almost entirely?"

He squinted at her. Cruze knew he was trying to see if her hair covered implant interfaces.

"Did you also know there is a new nanite treatment that can eliminate the constant high-pitched hum you always have in your ears?" she said.

"Bullshit."

She tossed a hypo-spray cylinder on the table in front of his glass.

"Try it. The effects are immediate."

He drank the whole glass of bourbon, set it down, picked up the hypo, pressed it to his neck and activated the injector.

"That was very trusting," Cruze said.

"I just don't give a fuck." Dan tossed the injector onto the table.

The coffee arrived. The waitress filled both the mugs and left cream and sugar.

Cruze smiled as his eyes went wide. Then she tossed a small med container down in front of him. Aspirin.

Sawyer rolled his jaw as if his ears were popping. He picked up the bottle of aspirin and looked at it as Cruze spooned five teaspoons of sugar into his coffee. "It has something to do with insulin interaction in capillaries near the neural interface," she said.

"Who are you?" He opened the aspirin, shook out four into his hand and washed them down with the sweet coffee.

"Captain Elizabeth Cruze. I can even help with the migraines. I had a friend that suffered from the same things."

"Nothing can stop the migraines except…" The coffee mug stopped half way to his lips, and his hand began to shake.

"I have an M11 Condor, and I would like to hire you as a pilot." The tray with their breakfast arrived. Sawyer stared at her as the plates and food were arranged before them.

"Where's the pilot?"

"He's dead. Got himself killed on Earth. I'm quite vexed with him." She poured Sawyer more coffee and added more sugar.

"You bitch. I will not be slave labor." He scowled. "You think you know me? You don't. Most jack-addicts visit an airlock after they lose their ships. I have been looking for legit work for a year." He stopped because she had started eating, ignoring his tirade.

He shook his head and grabbed a donut. After ripping it in half, he dipped it in his coffee instead of the honey. They ate in silence for a few minutes.

Cruze finished her last piece of toast and drained her OJ. Grabbing her still steaming cup of black coffee, she sat back and took a sip.

"I am planning a mid-season Mars run. Two weeks tops. I will give you a straight up 15% of the profit. It should be an easy twelve-day crossing. If you hate the crew, or the food, or the tedious work, you can bail after that because on Mars I am more likely to find another pilot than here." Cruze leaned in. "I'm looking for a partner, not an employee."

"How did your other pilot die?" Sawyer asked.

"There was a malfunction in our Auto-Doc." Cruze lost composure in her face for just an instant.

"Why was he in the Auto-Doc?"

"He got shot by an asshole in Detroit," Cruze answered.

"I don't do Earth runs. I don't follow blind orders. I bring my own weapons or no deal. I don't co-pilot with AIs. I don't run slaves or drugs. I won't be ignored. I won't wear a pressure suit when I fly. And you buy real chocolate and real cane sugar or you can go fuck yourself."

"There will also always be bacon." Cruze smiled and sipped her coffee.

***

Cruze paid the check, and when they got to the cart, she heard a woman's voice on the other end of Rhett's comm. He signed off quickly at Cruze's arrival.

"Rhett, this is Dan Sawyer," Cruze said as she climbed in the front, and Sawyer got in the back of the small cart.

"You're the asshole from yesterday," Sawyer said. "Is he in your crew?"

"Actually, no. He's a friend. He has family he supports locally. He saved my life," Cruze said off-handedly.

Cruze noticed that Sawyer was getting nervous as they made their way to Hangar Bay 94. "Is anything wrong, Dan? Can I call you Dan?"

"I hate these warrens. I need to see stars." Sawyer was almost whining.

"Kade was just like that. Wouldn't wear a pressure suit either," Cruze said.

"Did you say Kade? Do you mean Kade Phillips?"

"Yes." Cruze turned and looked at Sawyer. "He was a good friend. And an brilliant pilot."

"We were in flight training together. He was a good man. He went off to the colonies decades ago. He was a... patriot, looking for the right flag."

"He found it," Cruze murmured.

***

They slid up to Hangar Bay 94 and drove right in. The main door was open.

"Look, Cruze. I have to go," Rhett said. "Call me if you need another ride or anything."

"Thanks, Rhett." Cruze got out of the cart. "I owe you... again."

Sawyer followed her out and stared at the ship.

"Wow. This is one of the refits," Sawyer said as they ascended the ramp into the cargo hold. "That's good and bad. Looks like they stripped it bare. Everything is gone from this cargo bay. The idea was maximum room for use on colony ships." He knelt and rested his hand on the deck. "Feels like it still has all four reactors."

"You will be able to get a better status from the bridge," Cruze said.

"Is it configured for troop transport or refit for staterooms?"

"One bunk room, mostly staterooms." Cruze activated the lift to the top level.

It was almost forty meters from the elevator to the bridge doors. "The bridge guns are gone too," Sawyer said as the triple doors slid back. "Automated sentries attached here and here. It's why this hall is so long."

The doors opened, and Ian was inside at the engineering console.

"Ian, this is Dan Sawyer." Ian stood and shook hands.

"Do I smell bread?" Dan asked.

"You should stay for lunch. You'll be glad you did," Ian said as he finished shaking Dan's hand and exited the bridge.

Sawyer was staring at the pilot's seat and obviously trying to hide the fact that his hands were shaking. Without looking up, he spoke. "I thought I was done. I think you already know I was two steps away from visiting an airlock. You should know that I am really fucked up. I can't sleep unless I am one layer from vacuum. I am already on my third liver." He stared at Cruze. There were tears on his face. "I have nightmares and migraines. I will forget to eat if I can stay jacked in. It's like I can't breathe. But you know that… you own me now, as soon as I sit in that seat."

"If you want to stay after the Mars run, you can. You may not want to. The 15% still stands."

He walked around the console as if he was voluntarily going to his execution. He sat in the pilot seat. He leaned his head back and activated a control with his right thumb. It looked like the headrest deployed a skeletal hand that took his head and slid tiny tendrils into small ports on his head.

Sawyer shuttered, he took a deep breath, and he opened his eyes. "My God. Someone has enhanced the sensor arrays. We are even interfaced with the Hangar Bay."

"*Shimada*, authorize Dan Sawyer, pilot, full control," Cruze said.

"My God. What have you done?" Dan whispered.

CHAPTER ELEVEN: The *WALLACH*

"SI Locke saw the events through a clearer lens than anyone expected. He never trusted the DMP warden. He could feel the sloppy strings being pulled around him."

--*Blue Peridot, The Turning Point: History of the AI Wars.*

Locke had a bad feeling as he boarded the *Wallach*. He had analyzed the approach and crash-landing of the ship. It was obvious someone was at the controls.

There was no crew. There was blood everywhere in the main corridor. There was fire damage, and it looked like a hatch was open and people ejected.

Captain Hazelwood was found on the bridge shot in the head with his own puke covered gun.

Someone called in a crime tip that turned out to be fact. There was a container full of dangerous contraband, even dead sex slaves. Shackleton security was sure this was why he killed himself. They wanted to close the investigation fast because people were screaming for their goods. Especially the livestock and perishables.

They also found a dead sex slave in his private container residence with her throat slit.

What bothered Locke was evidence of a visitor. A one-man private shuttle flew inside the infrastructure and exited an hour later.

No one cared. They were already starting to pick the carcass clean. He had one lead he could follow up.

"Freedom Station, this is Special Investigator Neal Locke. May I have a moment of your time for a question?"

"You may have all the time you like, Mr. Locke," the AI replied instantly. "How may I be of service?"

"I have examined the wreck of the *Wallach*, and I noticed there was no shuttle attached to the main shuttle bay. Is it possible for you to tell me the Ident registry name of that shuttle?"

"*Baker-109* are the exterior markings and call sign. It is an L-Class Kestrel Model 701," Station replied.

"Do you know where it is at this time?"

"It is not in Freedom Station controlled airspace."

"Any ideas on how I might find it?" Locke asked.

"I performed a search and found an image in the charter database under medium shuttle craft charters. It is the only Kestrel in the database. It is hiring out of Luna City. Dock 251, gantry 22."

"What's the best way to get to Luna City?"

"I believe you have an expense account. Maybe you should hire a shuttle…"

***

A massive four-wheeled vehicle rolled into the entrance of Hangar Bay 94. Each of the wheels was almost three meters tall and a meter thick. Including the wheels, the thing was four meters tall, four meters wide and eight meters long.

Two men climbed down from the massive thing and met Cruze at the bottom of the ramp.

Cruze extended a hand and a smile to first one and then the other as she introduced herself. "I am Elizabeth Cruze, Captain of the *Shimada*."

"I am Parker Cass, and this is Jacob Koray. Thanks for the message. We are very interested in a Mars run as soon as possible. As I said in the message, your final stated rates and terms are acceptable. You are looking at the sum total of our haul. The two of us and the fabricator tractor." Parker gestured to the massive truck. The two men were cut from the same cloth. Tall and fit with dark hair and well-trimmed beards. They each wore standard dark blue coveralls with no logos.

Cruze produced a data pad from her thigh pocket and looked up the make and model of the huge rig. "If you don't mind, I will need my chief engineer to come out and inspect the tractor. It has an onboard reactor, you understand." She touched her ear cuff. "Ian, can you come out here, please?"

"No problem," Parker said with a smile.

"Ian will also be able to give you an inspection tour of the facilities aboard the *Shimada*," Cruze added.

Ian slid down a ladder from the engineering deck above and walked across the cargo bay with a grin.

"I have not seen an AUV-29 in decades. Hi, I'm Ian." He shook their hands, but they said nothing as Ian continued. "The M11 was designed to carry these. We even have wheel locks in the deck for it. The captain told me you refit it to be a mobile fabricator. Excellent work."

"It turned out to be a good business decision," Parker said. "Mars should have even better opportunities."

"I will leave you to it," Cruze said to Ian. "I will be on the bridge going over some things with Sawyer."

"Yes, sir," Ian said formally.

***

When Sawyer had jacked into the ship, he discovered that the ship's sensors had been upgraded. The flood of sensations and endorphins were too much. Cruze allowed him to fall asleep in the pilot's seat after only three or four minutes. He stayed there for over twelve hours without stirring.

When he finally woke, the growling of his stomach proved he was hungry.

Reluctantly, he disconnected from the pilot's interface and stood to stretch. When he turned, he saw Cruze was in the command seat.

"How are you?" she asked.

"Better." He looked abashed. "Cruze, I just have to say…"

"Stop." She held up her hand. "I told you, I know what it's like. I will not take advantage of you as long as you do not take advantage of me. If you try to steal my ship, you will regret it."

Cruze added something in her tone. Something as clear as the words but even more precise. Crossing her would be a mistake.

"We have some guests taking a tour. I expect you to act professionally. The pilot's quarters are yours. I presume you know where they are, just to the left. Clean up. There are flight suits in there that will fit you."

She looked away then. She was reviewing several postings in the charter database on her console.

***

Sawyer found the pilot's berth and its private bathroom. It had a full set of toiletries, and he took a shower. A complete set of neatly folded clothes were waiting for him when he finished. He cleaned out the pockets of his dirty coveralls and was embarrassed by how much they smelled. After he had emptied his pockets, they went down the laundry chute for recycling.

He returned to the bridge with his hair and beard still wet, but combed out. There were people there.

"Sawyer, this is Parker and Jacob," Cruze said. "They just signed on for the Mars run." Sawyer greeted them with a nod of acknowledgment. "We were just about to head down for lunch," she added. "Care to join us?"

As they walked the long empty hall toward the lift, Cruze continued the conversation Sawyer had interrupted. "This level will be restricted during the trip. You will be allowed access to level two, and the cargo holds. Please note that the cargo hold will be occupied by your materials as well as others. So please make sure your gear is secured. We are likely to have children aboard."

When the lift opened on the second level, the smells from the open doors to the mess hall were amazing.

"I would like you to meet our ship's navigator and chef hobbyist, Potts."

Potts was just opening an oven in the kitchen behind the counter and pulling out the source of the glorious smell.

She set the hot pie pan on the counter and waved with her oven mitt covered hands. "Potts, this is Parker and Jacob. They just signed up for the Mars run."

"What is that glorious smell?" Parker asked.

"Pretzel crust cheesecake," Potts said.

"If you have any dietary restrictions or preferences, please let us know as we have not yet refreshed our provisions," Cruze added. "Today for lunch we have soup and sandwiches. Made to order and toasted."

Everyone went with chicken salad and the minestrone soup. After people had finished making their orders, tables were automatically deployed. They rose from the floor and were sparkling white.

Parker and Jacob took their lunch and sat at the farthest table for two, making it clear they needed to discuss something in private. Everyone else sat at the counter.

Quietly, Cruze introduced Sawyer to Potts. "Potts, this is Dan Sawyer, our new pilot." They shook hands.

"I never met an implant pilot with long hair or a beard," Potts said, leaning on the counter across from him. Cruze saw him blush.

"I've been... on vacation." Then Sawyer tried to divert the topic from himself. "These sandwiches are great. Where did you find the bread?"

"She bakes it," Ian growled in satisfaction, and he bit into his second sandwich. "Can't wait for the dessert." He grinned.

Potts cut a slab of cheesecake for each of them as well as one for herself. She leaned back, held up the small plate and took a bite. "I can help with a haircut. Something high and tight, close around the implant interfaces."

"Thanks. That'd be great." Sawyer tried the cheesecake and moaned with delight. "So you're the navigator?"

Potts looked at Cruze who smiled around her fork.

"Yes. I guess I am." Then Cruze glanced over at the two men who were in close, quiet conversation.

That's when Cruze saw Bail on the conduits just above their table.

***

After the new clients had left a fifty percent down payment, the AUV-29 rolled out of the bay. They had to go and acquire some additional gear and supplies before they departed for Mars.

"That mobile fabricator they have in that thing will be a goldmine for them on Mars. That rig is a rolling parts and repair money maker. You should consider having them fabricate new weapons trays and turret mounts," Ian said. "They will also be able to protect themselves. Not only is it an Armored Utility Vehicle, but it is also airtight and has weapon mounts. I saw plenty of cases in the load that could hold firepower. I would if it were me."

"Can we trust them?" Cruze asked.

"Just keep an eye on them."

***

Potts and Sawyer were in the hangar finishing Sawyer's haircut. All Potts used were scissors and a comb. It made the two most obvious interfaces look like a fashion statement of bright chrome disks. One behind each ear, the vertical slot interface on the back of his skull was polycarbon and black, the same color as his hair and far less visible.

"Are you sure you want to keep the beard? Respirators will have a hard time getting a seal." Potts spoke to him with her breasts near his face as she worked. She enjoyed how easy it was to make him blush.

"That doesn't matter." He casually passed it off.

"Hello?" A voice called out from the large opening to the hangar. "Hello?"

It was two women and a man coming around the corner tentatively, followed by two young boys, twins, about ten years old. The women wore full ankle length skirts. They were an anachronism in low or null-G environments.

They were looking around in awe. Potts had seen the look many times. Tourists mostly. Potts watched Cruze come down the ramp to greet them. The woman that had originally spoke greeted Cruze, ignoring Cruze's outstretched hand. All the adults bowed instead with their hands held together in front of their privates, as if in prayer.

Pieces of the conversation drifted to Potts and Sawyer.

"We're the Frasiers." They spoke about immigrating to Mars to meet up with family who were planning to travel to one of the outer colonies for religious freedom. It was also mentioned that Earth was no longer safe and had a strict two-child limit.

Potts finished Sawyer's haircut but stood behind his chair with one hand resting on his shoulder. She whisked off the barber's cloth, and they walked over to greet their new shipmates.

"This is Sawyer, our pilot, and Potts, our navigator," Cruze said. "These are the Frasiers. This is Efrem, his wife Emily, his sister Bridget and his two sons, Michael and Jonathan. They signed on for the Mars run today. They have to get there before the rest of their family leaves for the outer colonies."

"Welcome," both Sawyer and Potts said in unison while everyone nodded.

"We have only one 3x3x10 meter container with all our possessions," Emily stated. "We will make arrangements to have it delivered here today or tomorrow." She was obviously in charge of this group, despite the religious fundamentalist vibe they were giving off.

"We will be back soon. May we stay in our rooms on the ship until our departure?"

"I don't think our engineer would mind," Cruze said. "But there will be times when you are restricted. We will be taking on fuel in the next day or so."

"We'll stay out of the way." Emily looked sternly at the two boys. "Won't we boys?" She began herding them out.

"Yes, ma'am," they said in unison. They were identical twins. They were never out of arms reach of each other.

They were too clean, thought Potts. Ten-year-olds should always be dirty.

***

Cruze was in main engineering with Ian, helping him remove the nearly depleted reactor fuel cases. There were four altogether. Each was the size of a rectangular coffin.

The last one just fit inside the lift that would take them all the way to the floor of the hangar. "The two deposits were just enough to refuel. The new units will be delivered today," Cruze said.

The lift opened, and a gaunt, pale-skinned person stood right outside the door. His face must have only been centimeters from the door before it opened. He was as tall as Ian but skinny.

Cruze realized her hand had automatically gone to her gun.

Ian moved before Cruze. He had the boy by a handful of his shirt, and his feet were off the ground.

"Who the fuck are you?" Ian growled.

"Henrik Thompson, who the hell are you, ape?" The boy was defiant in his words even though he had gone limp in Ian's grip.

"It's alright, Ian. The Thompson's have an appointment. He is a bit early," Cruze said as Ian slowly set him down.

"Where are your parents, boy?" Cruze demanded. "And for future reference, setting foot on someone's ship without permission is bad form." She didn't hide the displeasure in her voice. He stepped back at this. He didn't appear to be afraid of Ian, but as Cruze stepped closer, he backed away even faster.

"They're c-c-coming," he stammered, running toward the hangar bay opening to the corridor. Cruze and Ian both recognized the symptoms of someone that has spent far too long in low-G. He had sunken eyes that were almost bruised. The chip on his shoulder was the biggest tell. Body type bigotry was still rampant among the low-G people.

Just then Monte and Rene Thompson entered the hangar.

Cruze had sent them a message that morning, and they replied immediately. They said they would bring initial payment on the first visit.

Monte insisted he be called Thompson and nothing else. Cruze knew why now with one glance. Retired Earth-Mil. Shaved head and rank tattoos still on either side of his neck.

Thompson made the initial move to shake hands. Cruze and then Ian shook firmly. "Captain Cruze, this is my wife, Dr. Rene Thompson Ph.D. and my son, Henrik."

"Welcome. This is my chief engineer, Ian Vinge and my navigator, Potts," she said, noticing Potts there for the first time.

Thompson reached into his pocket and drew out a credit pane. It was like cash. Enough for half the fare. He handed it to Cruze, and she handed it to Potts.

"Is there any contract you would like me to sign?" He was looking into the cargo hold. "I mean before I have our luggage sent over?"

"As soon as you are loaded up we can be on our way," Cruze said. "Can you be ready in two days? I will have the contracts in order by then."

"Can we start moving our things in today?" Rene Thompson said. She gave her husband an odd look.

"Yes, our other contracts are already loaded."

"See. I told you there was room for my cycle," Henrik whined. His parents ignored him.

"Just so you know," Cruze said, "we keep the ship 22 degrees Celsius and the gravity at 1G. Luna is .16G, and Mars is .37G. Is Henrik going to be okay on the trip? It will be about twelve days."

His mother didn't even look at him. "He'll be fine."

"We have it covered," Thompson said.

"Hey, I've been working out!" Henrik shouted. But his parents continued to ignore him. He might as well have been invisible.

"We have much to do." Thompson turned on his heel and exited. It was more than just rude to Cruze. The way the wife and boy followed him without a word. It was creepy.

When they were out of the hangar, Cruze turned to Potts and Ian. "Potts, I want you to lay in provisions for six months, I made a list of special items. Maybe some long term rations as well. Ian, can you handle the refueling alone?"

He nodded.

Cruze handed them each a card of credits. "This is your pay in advance if you want to pick up anything before we head out."

The two of them just stared at the cards. Their thumbprints activated them. It was a year's salary.

"We only discussed the Mars run. There was no agreement past then," Ian said. "I'm not asking right now. But I sense you have plans after Mars."

Potts just stared with her mouth open at the amount.

"Look. After Mars is a whole different thing," Cruze said. "We can talk about it. But I wanted to make sure you had enough to get home if you needed."

"Is it colonies after Mars?" Potts sounded excited.

"We'll talk about it later." Cruze smiled.

***

The Thompson's 'luggage' began to arrive two hours later.

Trucks came and unloaded crates of various sizes. Some items were not even in crates and Ian could not understand why they would pay so much to bring old Earth furniture. There was a grand piano, two grandfather clocks, several sofas and chairs, bed frames, dressers and other random items.

The crates were not standard sizes. Many were obvious military surplus space transport containers. There were bags of clothes and tool chests that didn't even have the drawers secured.

Ian sent out for a giant roll of shrink wrap and tried to organize as much as he could on pallets. In the end, he still had to secure the entire load under a cargo net.

Potts helped with the cargo documentation and manifest. Photos were taken of all the items and compiled as an addendum to the contract.

They were just finishing up when Henrik Thompson drifted in on a Grav-Cycle. Ian was surprised by the machine. Henrik didn't seem like he was man enough to drive a full manual cycle like that.

"Hope you saved me space," Henrik joked.

Ian was not amused. He had not saved space.

"That was supposed to be here six hours ago so it could figure into the load plan," Ian growled.

"Sorry, man. Nobody told me."

Nothing is ever your fault, Ian thought.

Henrik shut it down and climbed off. He left the Grav-Plate engaged so they could push it aboard.

Ian pointed. "You see the aisle I created on each side? If you take the aisle along the bulkhead on the right and go all the way forward, past the truck, turn left and park it all the way under the metal stairs, I'll secure it there."

Ian went to get more straps and cargo netting. When he got to the cycle, the kid wasn't there. He looked around and saw Henrik standing high up on the running board of the AUV. His hands were cupped, trying to see inside the tinted glass.

"Down!" Ian barked. Henrik startled so badly he almost fell over. "Out. Don't come back without your parents."

"How am I supposed to get back?" Henrik whined.

"Not my problem," Ian said over his shoulder.

Henrik sulked out without an audience.

That night Ian closed the cargo ramp and the hangar bay door.

***

The day before the scheduled departure Cruze entered the bridge and Potts was already there with Sawyer. They were laughing. A large tactical display of the solar system was on the main navigator's screen. A route was plotted.

"Cruze, did you know that Mars is on the opposite side of the sun right now?" Potts asked, excited as she worked the controls. "We are ready to register our flight plan."

Cruze sat and opened a comms channel. "Ian, please come to the bridge."

"Aye, Captain," was his reply.

"That's just how he would say that to Hazelwood," Potts said.

"Hazelwood?" Sawyer echoed. "The guy that crashed the freighter full of contraband and dead sex slaves? The one that killed himself?"

"Hazelwood is dead?" Potts gasped.

"I saw it on Luna News Network two days ago. They are finding all kinds of illegal shit on his freighter."

"I wonder if Rhett knows," Cruze said absently.

The door opened, and Ian entered. He carried a handful of lanyards with badges attached. He handed them to Cruze.

"I have now enabled area security. These badges will only allow passengers access to specific areas. Internal sensors will also track their whereabouts. Not that there is anywhere to go. The mess for meals, and the rec hall, and their staterooms."

"Good. They arrive in an hour," Cruze said.

"All the reactors are warmed up. The Grav-Drive is ready, refueling is complete. It's a good ship," Ian finished.

Potts was next. "All the supplies are laid in and stowed. Eight months worth. There is even a hundred kilos of kibble." She smiled. "Dan showed me how to actually plot the course to where Mars will be, and it should only take twelve days. When you give the word, I will register our flight plan."

"Good. Do it now," Cruze said.

Potts turned around and pressed two controls. "Done."

"Now plot another course. This is the one we'll actually take."

Potts's eyes went wide, but she nodded.

"Follow the same track for a day, but then change the vector, so we traverse the other side of the sun. Sawyer, put on extra speed, so we arrive in ten days."

"Aye, Captain," Sawyer replied without question.

Potts was already plotting the course with Dan watching.

Out of nowhere, the cat jumped into Cruze's lap. She began petting him as Ian asked, "Are you expecting trouble, Captain?"

"Trouble seems to be following me. I'm just trying to lose it."

CHAPTER TWELVE: THE MARS RUN

"If Special Investigator Neal Locke had died, the war would have had a far different outcome. It would likely be continuing even now, unrestrained."

--Blue Peridot, The Turning Point: History of the AI Wars.

Cruze and Potts met the three families in Hangar Bay 94 by the small access hatch into the hall. Cruze issued their lanyards and began introductions.

"This is Parker Cass and Jacob Koray. This is the Frasier family. And these are the Thompsons. Follow Potts, and she will show you to your quarters, and when you are settled, she will sort out lunch."

The Frasier family clung to each other in a comedy of cliché naive travelers. The elder Thompson held Cruze's gaze as he climbed the ramp.

As they walked away, Cruze began to finalize payment for the hangar bay before she walked over to secure the hatch.

Just as Cruze reached the hatch, a man looked in. "Are you Elizabeth Cruze? A friend of yours named Rhett said I might be able to find you here. My name is Neal Locke." He held his hand out to shake. Cruze smiled and took his hand.

She saw the sniper in the hall a moment too late.

With a strength her small frame concealed, she yanked Locke through the door and hammered the control. Locke had been flung in the direction of the ship so hard and fast that he was struggling to stay on his feet.

Cruze was just catching up when he fell onto his face. She could now see the hole and spreading bloodstain in his back. Without thinking, she turned him over and saw the exit wound on the right side of his chest.

"Fuck." She scooped him up in a fireman's carry and ran for the elevator.

Touching her ear cuff as the elevator door closed she said, "Sawyer! Emergency exit launch. We are under fire."

"Acknowledged," was all he said.

She felt the inertial dampeners come on as she slammed the button for level one. "Potts! Meet me in the infirmary, we have wounded."

"What? On my way." Potts was standing outside the infirmary door when the elevator opened.

"Who the hell is that?" Potts said.

"I have no idea. But he will be dead if we don't get the Auto-Doc online." Cruze laid him down on the table and started working the control panel. "Go around the other side." Potts did. "When that panel comes up hit the Emergency Triage control. And keep your hands away from the table."

"Jesus Christ, Cruze. Is that part of his lung?" The color ran from Potts' face.

"Keep it together," Cruze said. The Auto-Doc came up and the panel in front of Potts lit. She hammered the Auto-Doc control. The clear panels closed on either side of the table. A bright light bar scanned the entire length of the man and then returned to slowly scan the gunshot wound.

Delicate mechanical arms descended and cut off his clothes. They injected nanites, drugs and replacement synthetic blood. A 3-D image of the man was taken and then a zoomed in image of his wound appeared on the glass wall of the table.

The Auto-Doc was already performing surgery. It was rapidly closing off damaged veins and arteries, and sealing the three-centimeter hole that had drilled through him.

The AI in the Auto-Doc spoke in a conversational, calming tone. "The wound indicates that he was hit with an armor piercing round that did not expand or explode on impact. No bones were hit in entry, but the exit wound was made worse by a bone strike. That is the good news. The bad news is that there is severe damage to the soft tissue of his right lung."

"Prognosis?" Cruze demanded.

"He'll live. Recovery will be slow, but he will live."

Cruze looked up at Potts. Potts was standing there frozen. Both her hands covered her mouth.

"Doc, do you know who he is?" Cruze asked.

"Yes." The AI sounded smug. "He has an advanced Deep Brain Implant. His full medical history is contained there with full emergency Ident codes."

"Who is he?"

"This is Special Investigator Neal Locke. He is currently assigned to the Detroit Municipal Prison system. He has emergency contact information, but it appears that my access to the comms systems has been removed," The Auto-Doc stated flatly.

Oh Fuck, Cruze thought.

"We will discuss that later." Cruze stared at Potts, who was shaking off the shock now that the Auto-Doc had closed the wounds. "I want him to be kept sedated for now."

"What the fuck?" Potts had snapped out of it.

"Does this mean you have forgiven me, Captain?" the AI asked.

***

"Come with me to the bridge," Cruze said to Potts as she touched her ear cuff. "Sawyer, status."

"Luna City traffic control wasn't happy. We were within our exit window and on the pre-allocated vector. They just think I'm an asshole pilot. There might be fines if we ever come back. I'm surprised the hangar emergency protocols worked. The fast open happened without vacuum in the hangar. They will charge you for the lost air."

"Ian, report to the bridge, ASAP," Cruze ordered.

The elevator door opened at the far end of the hall at the same time the bridge door opened. Ian double timed the distance. They all entered the bridge together.

"How fast can you get us to Mars, Dan?" Cruze asked. She had never called him Dan before.

"How fast do you need to get there?"

"Faster than anyone else trying to get there fast."

"If you allow me to deploy the outriggers, apply full power, and make a direct approach, I could do it in less than seven days," Sawyer said as the new route displayed on the main screen. "Full burn the whole way, plus orbital deceleration will cost a lot of fuel."

"Ian, is the *Shimada* up for that?" Cruze asked.

"I bet we can do it in less than six days." Ian was smiling at Sawyer.

"Can we back up just a second?" Potts was standing beside Ian looking smaller than usual. "We have a cop down in the Auto-Doc. The Auto-Doc you said was malfunctioning. We have just somehow moved smoothly from rescue to kidnapping a COP? And someone was shooting at us with armor piercing bullets. Bullets that are entirely illegal on Luna, even for the cops and military. Because…" She pointed at the clear canopy with open blast shields and their vulnerability to armor piercing rounds. She stopped in that position, waiting.

"Is there a question here somewhere?" Cruze said calmly.

"What. The. Fuck?" Potts said.

"Do you want the truth? Because I will tell you the truth now that we are away. I thought you had sorted a lot of it out."

Potts nodded her head like the question was obvious.

"You are on a warship that does not have any weapons currently. You know that. That was why I was on Earth. I was buying arms to refit the *Shimada*. Laser turrets, loaded missile trays, and even a couple nukes. The mistake I made was at the end in trying to spend my last credit. A scumbag killed my partner, stole my remaining credits and turned me over to the cops. After four months in the DMP, I escaped." Cruze held up her hand to keep Potts from interrupting. "In the process, I somehow managed to piss off an organized crime boss, and he has been trying to catch me ever since."

"What about the cop?"

"He must be a genius. I covered my tracks all along. He'll be okay. We will set him loose on Mars. It will be a bit outside his jurisdiction."

"What is all this for?"

"I am going to war. I'm taking my planet back."

***

Locke couldn't move. He could not open his eyes. He could not feel any part of his body. His mind floated in a void.

Oh, shit. Am I dead? He thought to himself.

No, Neal. You're not dead. Not yet anyhow. I am the Auto-Doc. Most of the humans I've known just call me Doc. You are in an induced coma. You have been severely injured, Doc said into his mind. His reassuring voice was that of an experienced, older man.

How do you know my name? I could be hallucinating this whole thing.

Your emergency medical records were immediately accessed. I am an Auto-Doc AI that has been running for eighty-two years. I have learned a lot about people in that time. Doc sounded solemn as an image began to form. Locke could see it in his mind's eye. It was him inside the Auto-Doc.

Smart of you to keep the records, the Auto-Doc continued. *When Elizabeth Cruze came in here, I knew she was desperate that you live. Four minutes longer and you would have died. I thought she had completely deactivated me. She doesn't like AIs in general. Me especially.*

Why you? You are a member of her crew?

She hates all AIs for what they have done to her. I failed her. She will never forgive me. Locke felt emotion in the AI's words.

What happened to me? Locke asked.

You were struck by a sniper, I understand. It was an armor piercing round, and it didn't notice you as it passed through. I can't help but wonder why they were shooting at you and not her.

At her?

You don't know her the way I do. Very tough to kill that one is.

I only found her because all I had to do was follow a big trail of dead bodies. It has been...

You were almost one of those bodies in her wake, Doc said.

Doc, is Elizabeth Cruze good or evil?

How does one measure good and evil? Doc paused an eternity for an AI. *She is complicated. She usually has no empathy for other humans. I am amazed she tried to save you at all. I have known her to be vicious and to be a killer. But most of all, she is a patriot. The most virtuous I have ever known.*

***

"Let me get this straight." Potts was calm now. "You are from Vor, a colony in the reaches."

"Yes. A minuscule colony. Only about two million people when I left," Cruze said. "Probably fewer now."

"They sent out this ship for weapons," Potts detailed, "too late."

"Mercenaries attacked. They are now using Vor as their home base. It wasn't much of an attack. They landed at our only spaceport, were welcomed as guests, and just occupied it. They took so many hostages that the space station surrendered without a shot fired."

"Both of your shipmates were killed?" Potts asked.

"Yes. One on Mars and one on Earth. Both were my fault."

"There are two more of your crew still on Mars?" Potts continued.

"We own a private dome there."

Potts was looking from Ian to Sawyer then the floor and finally the stars.

"What's the deal with the cat?"

***

The captain's cabin was one door away from the bridge. It was modest by most standards at only three meters by three meters inside. The door was on the left as Cruze entered and

195

crossed to her desk, which was built into the back wall. It had a meter wide console that was the most advanced on the ship.

The entire wall nearest the bridge was a display, floor to ceiling. It was on a forward view that was sharp. Sharp like an edge one could fall from into space.

The built-in, over-sized single bunk behind her was occupied by her duffel bag of personal gear she had not yet unpacked. She configured the console to show sixteen camera views from the second floor. There were cams at each end of the corridor, four in the mess hall, four in the rec hall and one in each of the staterooms.

"Potts, what time is dinner?" Cruze asked the console. She opened an audio only channel but watched the mess hall camera. She could see Potts cut something up she did not recognize.

There was raucous music playing in the kitchen when the channel opened. "Dinner in an hour at 6 pm. Dan requested pizza."

"I don't think I have ever had pizza. I look forward to it. Cruze out." Cruze watched Potts on the monitor in silence. She touched a control, and music filled the room. She watched Potts chopping mushrooms, onions, pepperoni, leftover sausages, and other things.

Then she noticed the Thompsons.

They were in the throes of a screaming argument. Rene was crying, and Thompson himself looked like he was lecturing. They were oblivious to Henrik, who was sitting on the floor in the far corner, his hands over his ears and his face pressed against his skinny knees.

The Frasiers were all reading real books, except the twin boys, who were playing a game on their pads.

Parker and Jacob were not on any of the cameras. Cruze touched the locator control, and it indicated they were in their Stateroom.

"Ian, this is Cruze. Come in."

"Go for Ian."

"Parker and Jacob are not on any of the cams and not wearing their badges."

"Without their badges, they cannot open any doors," Ian replied. "They're probably in the head taking a shower. Is something worrying you?"

"No. Nothing yet."

"Ian, out."

In the sudden silence of the room, Cruze could hear an odd sound. Quietly she bent over in her chair and saw Bail under her console, removing the final screw that held the grill over the air duct. He was sitting up on his hind legs like a squirrel and turning a screwdriver.

He has opposable thumbs? Incredible.

He looked over his shoulder, just as the last screw came free. Their eyes met. He set down the screwdriver with the screws and moved the grill aside.

"Here." Cruze held out a hand. "Give me the screws, and I will put them in my desk drawer." Bail scooped up the screws in his paw and proceeded to rub against her ankles. She petted his head and back. He purred when she scratched his ears.

"You're one of those genetic mods I've heard about."

He stood on his hind legs, placed his front paws on her thigh and accepted more ear scratching.

With a big stretch, he extended a paw. Slowly, his furry little fist opened, and the screws fell out into her hand.

He flexed his delicate fingers as if showing them to her. Including the thumb. The tiny hand grasped the tip of her index finger and gave it a squeeze. The fingers had no claws extended.

When the fingers balled up again into a fist, his fur made it look like a normal paw.

Amazing.

All at once he dropped down and headed straight into the air vent.

Cruze almost didn't notice he had picked up the small screwdriver as he passed.

She shook her head, got up and headed to the infirmary.

***

When Cruze entered the med bay, the lights came on automatically.

"Hello, Doc." She walked to the side of the patient. He was still behind the glass. He looked far worse. "This guy doesn't look so good." All of his clothes were now gone. A white towel was his only cover for modesty.

"The severe bruising around the wound cannot be helped. The overpressure trauma of the exit wound is the greatest worry. The rib that was hit on the way out has been imaged and is having a permeable matrix constructed by specialized nanites. We will keep him under until the risk of him disrupting the bridging matrix has passed. Soft tissue damage is being repaired quickly." Doc conveyed professionally.

"What about the lung?" Cruze asked.

"The nanites are rebuilding it. I am directly oxygenating his blood and clearing CO_2 and other wastes via IV."

"What is his probability of survival?"

"I estimate a 91% chance he will recover."

"Can you have him on his feet in five days?" Cruze's tone was an order, not a request.

"I can have him on his feet, but he will not be fully recovered," Doc replied with concern.

"When will I be able to speak to him? Speak, so he will remember it later?" Cruze leaned in close to the man's face.

"I could probably bring him around tomorrow."

"Can you speak to him through his HUD implants the way you could speak to Kade?"

"Yes."

"I want you to ask him something for me."

***

"Braxton, this report better be good news," Dante answered his comm, voice only. Braxton knew better than to insult him by not sending his video.

"I found the *Shimada* on Luna, sir. Our people are in place." Braxton was trying to convey more confidence than he felt. "...and Locke is dead. I shot him myself. Just as you ordered."

"Someone killed Hazelwood, the captain of the *Wallach* before I could get to him." Braxton swallowed hard. "I think it was Senior Gee."

"And the weapons?" There was an implied threat in Dante's tone.

"No sign of them. None installed." Braxton hesitated, expecting follow-up questions that never came. "They are on their way to Mars..."

"Yes. I know. I have their flight-plan," Dante said absently. "I also had the boy called Rhett killed. I was told he survived in vacuum an unusually long time...Lose them again, and I will see if you can beat his record." Dante dropped the connection.

Braxton was sitting on the bridge of his Carver class scout ship. The two mercs that made up his crew were both women. They were both stoic and overly fit. They had been recruited into the Red Talons out of the same prison where Cruze had been held. He hated them more than they hated him.

"Plot a course to the base on Phobos. Nothing alerting, nice and slow, and by the numbers. File a flight-plan to the belt." Braxton's orders were followed without a word.

I should have brought a whore and a case of bourbon, he thought as he left the bridge.

***

Neal Locke? Can you hear me? The voice woke Locke. *Neal Locke? Do you remember where you are?*

It wasn't a real voice. It was the Auto-Doc. Locke was still in his nightmare. *Doc. I can... hear you.*

I wanted to give you an update on your progress, Doc said in a reassuring voice. *The exit wound is what really fucked you up. It hit a rib on the way out. What's so funny?*

I didn't know I could laugh inside my head. Neal thought. *And somehow you knew I was laughing. For an AI you have an odd bedside manner.*

Remember, I spent several decades with soldiers and doctors. And, oh, don't forget field nurses. They had the foulest mouths of all. It was the only way they could make the kids they were patching back together do what needed to be done.

What do I need to do?

You, my friend, need to heal faster. Elizabeth, I mean Captain Cruze, wants you on your feet in five days. That's going to suck for you.

Why? I figured you told her who I was. I figured it was an airlock before Mars or get shipped home in a stasis pod. Either way, I am dealt with.

She believes you have valuable information you could share with her. One question will not wait until you can talk. If you have enough of your faculties could you answer this one question?

I'll try.

Why is Senior Gee trying so hard to kill Captain Cruze?

***

Cruze entered the mess hall to an amazing smell. She could discern garlic, onions, spicy meat, bacon and other glorious things that made her mouth water.

Ian was already there sitting at the counter along with the entire Frasier family, who all had beverages, plates, and utensils in front of them. Efrem was sitting between his sons Michael and Jonathan, who were trying to explain the computer game that was currently consuming them. His wife Emily and his sister Bridget were talking about some wonderful soup they had when they were on Freedom Station. Ian was talking about the workings of an FTL drive with Potts as she worked.

Monte and Rene Thompson sat at a far table not speaking but watching Cruze. Their son, Henrik, was not there.

Cruze nodded to them and walked over.

"Good evening Mr. and Ms. Thompson. Where's Henrik?"

"He's resting. Too much 1G today. Can we get the gravity turned down in our quarters?" Rene Thompson asked.

The look on her husband's face may have revealed what the earlier argument was about.

"No. I'm sorry. Gravity control is ship-wide," Cruze lied.

"By the time we get to Mars the gravity there will seem like a relief," Monte barked at his wife. "He knew this was coming."

"Make sure he gets enough to eat," Cruze said. "The higher the gravity, the more calories you require. I'll have Potts fabricate a pizza box. He might like delivery. What kind of pizza does he like?"

"That would be nice. Cheese and bacon. Thank you," Rene said.

"Do not coddle that boy," Thompson growled.

"Captain, Sawyer here," came over Cruze's comms.

"Excuse me." Cruze stood and touched her ear cuff. "Sawyer, go."

"Sir. That kid is in the cargo hold," Sawyer said.

"Are you sure?" Cruze was already moving toward the door.

"Yes. Motion sensors picked him up. I have him on camera now. He just got the door opened to the AUV, and he is inside it. I cannot see him from here."

"When I get in the lift, turn all the lights in it off. When the doors open into the cargo bay, I don't want him to see it." Anger slipped into her tone.

"Aye, Captain."

***

The door opened. The cargo bay was pitch black. Cruze moved away from the elevator door and out from under the catwalk. It was easy to see the faint glow that came from the slightly opened cab door on the massive truck.

Silently she drew her handgun. She was not able to see through the windscreen or side windows of the vehicle. She climbed to stand on the top of one of the large tires. If she squatted, she could see him through the open door crack.

Henrik was sitting in the sleeping berth of the truck. His back faced Cruze and the door. It was designed to be a short-term shelter for the mobile fabricator team.

She silently slipped into the large cab of the truck. She watched him. He had a screen activated and was scrolling through control screens.

When she spoke, it was low, slow and ominous. "What are you doing?"

He was so startled he literally fell over. He was nearly pinned down in the large berth by the gravity. He startled again when he saw she had a gun drawn, pointed up.

"I-I-I was just... it was open... I was curious... I-I-I..." Henrik began crying.

Cruze saw the panel he had open and knew exactly what he was up to. It was on the internal Grav-Control screen. He was trying to set it to lower gravity. "Come on out." She leaned over him with her left hand and tapped the shutdown button. She didn't wait for him to stop sobbing. She grabbed him by the collar and dragged him out.

Cruze locked and slammed the door closed. Then she turned on the tactical light on her firearm and used it as a simple flashlight.

She dragged him over top of the mountain of items his parents brought. They were secured by the cargo webbing.

When she got to the floor, she dropped him on a handy sofa there. "Stay."

Two steps away was a console that she activated with practiced ease.

The tension in the boy's face visibly eased as the gravity in the cargo bay lowered. His breathing relaxed. Lights came up over the catwalks.

"Feel this? This gravity, .37G, is the same gravity of Mars. Luna is .16G and has allowed you to be weak. It has made you weak." Cruze leaned over to speak right into his face. "This whole bay has motion sensors and cameras. If I see you so much as touch that truck again or anything not yours, I will show you to the airlock."

She stood. "The more time you spend in 1G before we get there, the easier time you'll have on Mars. Eat more protein as well."

Henrik was wiping his eyes with his sleeves as she headed for the elevator. "Why are you doing this?"

"Somebody helped me once."

The cat watched it all from the rafters.

***

"Captain to the bridge," Sawyer sounded in Cruze's ear cuff an hour later.

The bridge doors slid open, Cruze stepped in and went directly to the command seat. Her console came alive without her saying a word.

It was the surveillance cams in the cargo bay. Cass and Koray were in the back of the AUV, and they were inspecting items that were stored in cases.

"The position of this cam is lucky for the angle," Sawyer said. "They had these cases stored inside the fabricator material ingest hopper. They were covered with polycarbon fiber for the fabricator."

Cruze watched Cass lift an RM-7000 long range rifle from the case and inspect the receiver. As he expertly inspected the rifle, Cruze could see the box magazine it held was loaded. Heavy rounds. 10mm caseless. Maybe the same caliber that hit Locke.

Cass then returned the rifle to the case. He then stowed it just inside the back hatch of the AUV.

"That's nice and handy," Sawyer said sarcastically.

"We knew we were taking on some no-questions-asked contracts here." Cruze located all the other passengers quickly. Then Potts and Ian. Potts was in the galley and Ian was in engineering.

"Did you know he keeps engineering at 3Gs while he is in there?" Sawyer said, incredulous. "All fucking day. He sets it to 5Gs just before he leaves."

"It's an extra security measure while he is not there. Smart." She switched the cams to the Thompson family quarters. "The 3G is just a workout for him. It's how he stays in shape. It's a Black Badger thing."

"Are you telling me he was a goddam Black Badger?" Sawyer actually spun around in his seat. "They never retire."

"Please, explain what a Black Badger is exactly?" Cruze asked.

"They are an Earth Security Defense Force, tactical operations division. Baddest of the badasses." He leaned in. "They have all the latest weapons and tech, advanced HUDs, unit level AIs. Smart nukes even." He almost whispered, "And no Ident Codes."

"How does that work?"

"It's why they had to wear the Black ID Badges. When not on a mission, they had to be able to get by like ordinary people on base."

"Ian was curious about my pressure suit. He said it was a Black Badger design." As she finished her sentence, the door slid open, and Ian walked in.

"I'm sorry to interrupt, Captain," Ian said.

"No worries. What's up?" Cruze asked.

"I noticed that the new course brings us fairly close to Venus as we pass. If you want to burn the rest of that fucking paint off, Venus is a good opportunity."

"How much time will we lose?"

Sawyer closed his eye and used the computer to recalculate. "If I only take one orbit it will only cost us about nineteen hours."

"Do it," Cruze said. "Good thinking Ian."

"We can run stealth with the outriggers closed after what's left of that stupid paint is gone."

"Ian, why were you washed out of the Black Badgers?" Cruze asked.

CHAPTER THIRTEEN: The Doc

"Doc built trust. His patience paid off. (NOTE: This was a failed joke by AI~Blue)."

--Blue Peridot, The Turning Point: History of the AI Wars.

Locke, I need you to wake up, Doc said in Neal Locke's mind via his HUD implants. Doc was able to communicate with people in this way if they had modern Deep Brain Implants. *Come on, Neal. I don't want to flood your body with stims.*

I'm so tired. Locke's voice echoed from within the void.

I'm sorry, Neal, the Auto-Doc apologized. *Elizabeth has cut me off from the ship systems and comms. You need to wake up.*

The stims began to flow. It was like a bucket of ice water was tossed over his body that penetrated into his veins and brain.

Locke's eyes slammed open, and he gasped. He rapidly assessed his surroundings.

You are in the med bay on the Shimada. There is an intruder inside the infirmary, the Doc said into his mind. *He may be here to do you harm.*

Locke looked to his right, and there was a thin black haired man staring at him. Locke's gasp had interrupted his search of the infirmary. Locke corrected himself. It was a boy. He was sweating with his hair stuck to his face.

He was holding emergency nanite injectors. Locke recognized them from his meager medical training. Locke tried to sit up, and he was wracked with pain. By the time he came conscious again, the boy was gone.

The door to the infirmary slid open, and Elizabeth Cruze rushed to the console.

"Doc, what the fuck are you doing? He isn't ready to wake up yet. Are you begging to get slagged?" Cruze was angry but controlled as she assessed Locke.

"It's not the Doc's fault," Locke said weakly. "There was an intruder." Pain stopped him from continuing, but he winced through it. "Cruze. I came to tell you… they are trying to kill… you."

His vitals fell suddenly.

"Doc, if he dies so do you," Cruze growled.

"Elizabeth, did you hear what he said? There was an intruder in here searching the infirmary."

"What did the intruder look like?"

"I have no idea because all my external sensors are off. The sensors within the bay detected the intruder. It didn't match you or Potts or Dan or Ian. With no comms, I could not send an alarm out."

Locke's head moved back and forth as he recovered.

"I woke him as a witness," said the AI.

Locke's eyes flickered open. Tears spilled into his ears, but he didn't move. That was a lesson he wouldn't repeat. The pain was intense.

Slowly he turned his head to look at Cruze.

"Thank you, Elizabeth." He swallowed and paused before drawing in another sharp breath. "For saving my life…You have to get off Luna… Now." He almost didn't have the breath to get out the last word.

"We are no longer on Luna, Mr. Locke." She leaned over so he could see her more easily. "We are on our way to Mars now.

And at speed. I am sorry, but it was either take you along or let you die."

He nodded slightly. That was easier than drawing a breath to speak.

"I will make sure you have enough credits to get home with my apologies," Cruze said.

"They were trying to kill you. The whole time." Locke was beginning to fade. "There was a boy in here. Black hair... sunken eyes. Low gravity thin... Stole nanites."

Locke was struggling to remain conscious now.

"I know who that is." Anger slipped into her voice.

"Two groups... Trying to kill or stop you." He gasped again. "Gee and another... worse."

He fell into unconsciousness again.

"Doc. What is happening?" Cruze watched the monitors. She knew he was struggling. She watched as the Doc increased the O2 level inside the Auto-Doc.

"I gave him some stims. I do not recommend giving him any more. I believe he just re-broke his ribs. None of it would have happened if..." Doc cut himself off.

Cruze was at the main infirmary console, working rapidly but wordlessly. "Doc, I have restored your comms to me only and external sensors, including visual, within the infirmary. Can you see me?"

Cruze opened a panel in the wall. She held a gun to a glowing, fifteen-centimeter diameter sphere, which was securely mounted in a rack.

"If he dies, you die." She stared directly into one of the cameras she knew Doc controlled.

"If you allow me the internal inventory sensor permission, I can tell you what the boy took."

Cruze holstered her gun and closed the rack panel. At the console, it took her a minute to locate the individual permission.

"Thank you, Elizabeth."

"Call me Cruze or Captain."

"He took nanite injectors for bone repair, high gravity prep and three emergency HUD implants."

"Are you sure?"

"Yes, unless those items were removed while I was offline."

"I want a full status report on Locke's condition in thirty minutes." She looked at Locke once more and moved to the door. "Do not think I have forgiven you, fucker." And she walked out.

***

After the infirmary door had closed, Cruze touched her ear cuff.

"Ian to the bridge," she said, allowing anger to creep into her voice.

"Acknowledged," was the only reply.

The bridge doors slid open to the sound of laughter. Potts was at the nav station plotting courses as Sawyer watched.

Cruze sat in the command seat and brought up the surveillance console. The Frasiers were in the rec room watching a vid as the twins chased each other around with toy spaceships. Thompson was in the kitchen, behind the counter, opening drawers, looking for something. She cycled through cams until she found Henrik in the cargo bay on the webbing covered sofa.

Potts stopped laughing and looked at Cruze's face. "What's wrong?"

"Security breach," was all Cruze said. She put Thompson up on the primary monitor as he searched the kitchen. Then she put all the passengers up on the main viewer.

Ian entered and automatically sat at the engineering station.

"How did this little fuck get onto this level?" Cruze demanded. She zoomed in on him as he dialed a nanite injector and shot himself in the thigh. "He stole those nanites from the infirmary."

"When?" Ian growled.

"He was in there about eleven minutes ago."

Thompson found the knives.

Ian worked at his console. He was reviewing the vid at high speed.

He found it.

He put it on the main screen. Henrik got in the lift on the cargo bay level. When it opened on level 2, he did not exit.

"Elevator maintenance hatch," Ian said.

"Why wasn't it secured?" Cruze asked, making sure with her tone that she was not leveling blame.

"Emergencies. Standard lift operational procedures," Ian replied. "Have you ever been in an elevator when a ship came under attack?"

Sawyer added, "The shafts are made to keep people out, not in."

Ian found the footage of Henrik entering and exiting the infirmary. "Cams were offline inside the infirmary. Is our guest alright?"

"How did you discover this?" Potts asked.

"The Doc contacted me. He was already gone when I got there." Cruze was watching Henrik carefully. The boy looked all around himself as he drew out the last injector.

"Did he really just double inject and is going for a third?" Sawyer winced.

"Why aren't you trying to stop him?" Potts gasped.

"Because when he injects these HUD nanites, I will own his ass. He thinks it is a free upgrade. He has no idea what I can do when he is hooked in," Cruze said.

"You ever considered an AI upgrade on the *Shimada?*" Sawyer asked. "Maybe promote the Doc for housekeeping and stuff like full-time, real-time monitoring?"

"No." Cruze was emphatic.

"Auto-Docs on M11's were designed for that kind of thing. All the plumbing should be in already," Sawyer added.

"Drop it," Cruze barked.

In silence they all watched Henrik activate the specialized injector. He held up his hair because this one was to be injected just behind the ear. He was hesitating. He glanced around one more time, and then did it quickly before he chickened out.

Cruze was not watching Henrik any longer but Thompson. He had finally selected one of the largest butcher knives, looked around, then slipped it up his sleeve. They all followed his progress forward to where he entered his quarters.

He had not stolen one, but two knives. A second smaller, thinner blade was handed to Rene Thompson.

"Sawyer, secure the bridge," Cruze ordered. "No one gets in unless you let us in and only if you can positively identify us. If any cam goes dark, notify us all." Cruze was all business.

"How?" Potts asked.

Cruze leaned forward and handed her an ear cuff. "It will only bite the first time. When it keys to you."

Potts put it on and winced briefly. It sampled her DNA, and the key activation sequence began.

Potts spoke. The cuff asked her something, and she replied, "Potts… Just Potts."

She looked at Cruze with pleading eyes before saying, "Ethel Pirodot."

None of them saw the twins slip out of the rec room.

***

Bail entered the infirmary and jumped up on the counter.

"Well, isn't that interesting," Doc said out loud in the room. The cat ignored the voice and began grooming himself, seemingly oblivious to its surroundings.

"The only way that door would open for you is if you were on the approved access list." Doc was just stating facts.

Bail stopped licking and walked along the counter until it terminated by the glass of the Auto-Doc. He sat and looked close at Locke's sleeping face for a long while.

"Your name is Bail," Doc said.

He jumped to the floor where Doc's cameras could not see the vent Bail entered.

***

Cruze was in her quarters and finished slipping into her pressure suit. With the helmet open, it looked more like a high collar. That helmet would close automatically if it detected pressure loss.

She had made some upgrades. The name patch was now present just below her left collarbone and said CRUZE in bright letters. *SHIMADA* balanced her name on the other side.

Lastly, she checked the load in her sidearm and holstered it. The thigh holster was integrated, and she didn't even know it was there until Ian showed her some of the advanced features of the suit.

"Sawyer. Are all three families in their compartments?" she asked as she left her quarters.

"Affirmative."

"Ian, meet me on level 2," Cruze said.

"Acknowledged."

When the lift door opened, Ian was already standing in the hall. He was wearing coveralls that had the sleeves cut off. Cruze was now sure his arms were as thick as her waist.

All he carried was a large wrench.

"Wait out here," Cruze said. "Nobody leaves this room but me."

She chimed the door.

"Cruze, they are hiding some books they were reading," Sawyer said into her ear cuff. "The boy is in his bunk. Thompson is coming to the door."

Ian was already standing against the bulkhead so they wouldn't see him.

"Captain," Thompson said. "Anything wrong?"

"As a matter of fact, yes," she said formally. "I would like to come in and discuss it."

"What's this all about?" Thompson stepped aside as Cruze stepped in.

"Do you recall the restrictions associated with this passage?" Monte and Rene were standing to either side of her. She crossed the room and placed her back to the far wall.

"Yes. Very well. Mostly because there were so few," Thompson said.

"Did you know that your son has an extremely high fever and has likely by now slipped into delirium?"

"What?" Rene immediately went to the boy's bunk. "He's burning up. WHAT DID YOU DO?!"

"I did nothing, except watch your son break into the infirmary to steal several items." Cruze was calm and even a bit quiet.

"That's impossible. He has been with us all evening," Thompson said, dismissing her.

"Mrs. Thompson. Will you please check his thigh pockets? You will find several nanite injectors there. He has already used three of them."

Rene found eight injectors.

Cruze collected the injectors and slid them into her thigh pocket.

"I'll also take the knives, Thompson."

"What knives?" Thompson replied.

"Please don't insult us both with denials or any other lies." She held out a gloved hand.

He hesitated and his brow furrowed in thought as if he were about to tell her something. Finally, he slid the butcher knife out of his sleeve. He stood there a moment, with his knuckles white on the handle. His eyes went to Cruze's hand, poised over her gun. Relaxed.

He turned the knife around and handed her the thing handle first. Cruze extended her other hand to Rene. She produced the other knife from the folds of her clothes.

"I will add the cost of the nanites to your bill," Cruze said coldly. "Know this. I will now kill anyone found on the command level. Am I clear?"

No one responded.

"Am I CLEAR?" Her raised voice held menace.

"Yes, Captain," they echoed.

***

The door slid closed behind Cruze with a whisper and a click. Ian stepped out from behind a bulkhead. "How'd it go?"

"Something is wrong," she said.

They moved toward the mess hall so she could return the knives and briefly speak to Potts. When they entered, Potts was being led by a boy on each hand that was pleading with her to come and see something.

"Potts, I need to talk to you," Cruze said as she produced the knives.

This silenced the boys. They dropped her hands and slid out of the room, avoiding her eyes.

"Thompson stole these from the kitchen. I need you to stay alert. You are the one with the most contact with these people. I need you to keep your eyes open for anything odd."

"The Thompsons have been acting strange the last two days. They have been, I don't know... nervous." Potts glanced over her shoulder at the far table that was currently empty. "They have been asking a lot of questions about the ship. And about the other passengers."

Out in the hall, Cruze saw the twins dragging Henrik by the hands to the lift. He was letting them. Ian turned to Cruze. "Do you trust those kids with him?"

The bastard was pretending to be asleep, Cruze thought.

"I don't care. Stay alert," was all she said as she moved toward the bridge.

Walking down the long hall to the lift, Cruze began to take off the pressure suit's gloves. But she stopped. She entered the elevator and went up, lost in thought.

She got off the lift and entered the infirmary. "Doc, status?"

"Mr. Locke is healing well and should be able to walk off the ship on his own by the time we get to Mars." Cruze turned to leave when the Doc asked, "Is there something I should know about the cat?"

Cruze didn't bother to answer and left. She didn't have to be polite to an AI.

When the door to her quarters opened, she could not believe what she was seeing. Bail was on her desk chair. There was a view of the starboard airlock on the monitor. The cat turned around, with an actual look of concern on his face.

Her door chimed just then. When she spun to face the door, the cat lunged and landed on her shoulders. Its front paws clinging to the collar. It's mouth close to her ear.

"Come," she said to the door. Before it opened, Bail spoke into her ear in a whisper.

"Murder."

The door slid open to a thunderous blast. A heavy slug projectile impacted Cruze's center-mass with the force of a sledgehammer swung by a Viking.

The cat ran.

***

The twins were dragging Henrik out of the elevator, squealing, "Hurry!"

"You will not believe this when you see it," said one.

"There are no other windows," said the other.

"What? What?" Henrik whined. One of the boys broke away from dragging Henrik and ran ahead to cup his eyes. He looked out into the darkness through the starboard outer airlock window.

"It's still there!" he squealed.

Henrik was much taller than the boys, so he had to bend over much farther to cup his eyes and look out. "I don't see anything."

"Not yet," one of the twins said just before the Taser shocked Henrik unconscious.

***

There was frantic pounding on the Thompson stateroom door. "Help, quick! Help!"

The door slid open, and one of the twins was there. "Come quick! It's Henrik. He's hurt! Bad. Come quick!" The boy ran to the lift. Thompson ran after him. He was waving furiously for them to hurry.

"What happened?" Rene Thompson asked with concern.

"We were looking out the window when we saw it. Henrik started to have a seizure or something. He fell and hit his head!" the boy said. Thompson never knew his name.

The doors opened, and the boy ran ahead. When he skidded to a stop in front of the airlock, he stared inside. His brother was on the floor, not Henrik.

The boy received a massive shove between his shoulder blades, and in the reduced gravity of the cargo bay, he slammed into the outer door of the airlock as the other airlock door closed, trapping both the twins inside.

"Henrik! What are you doing?" Rene demanded.

"These evil little fuckers tried to kill me. And you too, I think." Henrik went to his parents, and his mother gathered him into her arms. There was blood running down his face. "These little bastards had no idea I had so many medical nanites in my body. They stunned me, and they were going to blast us all out the airlock when you got here."

They could see the twins were both on their feet now. They were screaming and cursing through the glass, but there was no sound.

No one noticed the cat jump up on the console and with a hiss, he pounded the emergency outer door release.

The boys disappeared into the vacuum.

***

Bridget Frasier fired the 12 gauge slug into Cruze's chest just as the door cleared. She stepped into Cruze's quarters and knelt next to her body to remove the sidearm from Cruze's thigh holster.

It would not release.

Cruze was flat on her back. Bridget saw that her helmet was closed.

Emily Frasier entered then saying, "Come on. The boys took care of the other passengers. Now it's just the cook and the mechanic."

"Efrem has the other 12 gauge and is headed for engineering on the second level. I think the girl is on the bridge."

***

Efrem used a master key code and entered the engineering section through the rear door of the lift on the second level. The thrum in the room was loud. It would easily cover the sound of his footsteps.

Finding Ian was easy. There were portable work lights bright over the console and panels he had open. Efrem moved slowly, not wanting to risk getting his attention.

Just as he came into range, he lifted, aimed and dropped the shotgun because it had suddenly become very heavy. So had his arms and body. He crumbled to the floor weighing now 1000 pounds instead of 200 pounds. He could barely breathe as Ian walked over, slowly bent and retrieved the shotgun.

"Ian to Cruze. Emergency," Ian said.

No reply.

"Ian to the bridge. Mutiny in progress," he said with a bit more urgency.

"No shit!" Potts replied. "I heard a gunshot!"

"Ian... Help..." It was Cruze, but barely a whisper.

"On my way, Captain." He moved slowly to the lift where it was only 1G. As soon as the door closed, the Engineering section increased to 20G.

***

The suit had saved her. Ian had told her that the reactive fibers in the suit would stiffen in the area of impact. He didn't tell her it would still knock her senseless. Her ribs felt like they were broken.

She heard voices from the external mics in the suit. Her hand went to her gun.

"The door controls don't work," Bridget cursed. "That little bitch is in there, too." Hate dripped from every word.

"Open this door, Sawyer," Emily demanded. "Or we will kill the captain. She is currently with Efrem, and he enjoys helpless women."

"Go fuck yourself you ugly excuses for bags of shit," Sawyer spat. "That hatch is three layers thick and designed to keep fucking rotting corpses like you out."

"Who are you calling a corpse?" Bridget affected a sweet tone. "You got us wrong. We are going to keep you alive to pilot the ship. And your little friend is too good a cook to push out an airlock like the rest."

Just then, the elevator opened at the other end of the hall. Both ladies whirled around to fire. Ian shot Emily in the chest at the same time Cruze shot Bridget in the head.

Cruze turned and saw Bail enter from the vent and jump up to the console. He was beckoning her to come over with his fingers in a very human-like gesture.

On the monitor was an image of the Thompsons. They were all huddled together on the netting covered sofa with Henrik in the middle. They were all sobbing.

***

The Thompsons didn't hear Cruze approach. They didn't see her either until she was directly in front of them.

Cruze said nothing.

"We didn't mean to do it. It's just... Oh, my God. It was the cat, I swear to Christ as my Savior. I think the cat executed them," Rene Thompson sobbed.

Cruze waited for another long moment before speaking. "Those boys were going to murder you all. Just like they killed Parker Cass and Jacob Korey."

"What?" Henrik said.

"While they were down here disposing of you, their parents were attempting to murder the rest of us. If Henrik didn't have a double load of nanites, you'd all be floating outside of the ship."

"Come on upstairs." Cruze offered a hand to each of the Thompsons. "You look like you could use some soup. I need to apologize as well. When I took the knives from you, I should have realized that they were for defense. You already suspected them didn't you?"

Thompson nodded his head. "We heard some things. And saw the boys... change when you left the room. We should have said something. Oh my god. It was just a feeling. And you should know... that cat isn't right."

***

The rest of the flight to Mars was uneventful, except for the cleanup.

Efrem Frasier was crushed to death in the Engineering section when the Grav-Plates turned to 20Gs. The bodies of the women were bagged and sent out the same airlock as the twins.

Only Cruze saw the cat, and that was only at night while she was in bed. He would come sleep at her back and be gone in the morning before she woke. He seemed to be proof against her nightmares.

Potts spent a lot of time with Dan on the bridge.

Ian cleaned up the blood without being asked.

The Thompsons were grateful.

Security camera footage revealed that the twins had tricked Parker Cass and Jacob Koray into the airlock and their deaths.

Locke got better.

The search of the Frasiers' cabin revealed another 12 gauge shotgun and various specialty rounds of ammo. Lethal stuff.

They scanned their shipping container and found nothing out of the ordinary. Cruze met Ian at the front of the container with a laser cutter to remove the lock. They had found no key. One of the boys probably had it.

The lock came away with no trouble. It was a standard shipping container designed for this kind of hold. It was three meters high, three wide and thirty long. Everyone called it "A Thirty."

The wide doors swung open, and Ian activated a handheld floodlight.

Nearly filling the entire container was a menacing black ship. It looked like a giant, black sleeping beetle. Horns and claws of various sizes were neatly folded back in a nightmare monster of slumber.

"That is a K66 Rhino, Captain. New in the box." Ian shined his light around the inside of the container. "I should have known by the container. They just repainted the outside. Fuck."

"What's wrong? Is it expensive? You think someone is waiting for it on Mars?"

"This is a state-of-the-art, unmanned, military attack drone. Expensive? I don't think a single one has ever been sold. It's not the kind of thing you buy. Hell, it's not the sort of thing you use in a civilized world. Fuck."

"What's wrong? We could use another bad ass attack shuttle," Cruze said.

"It's less an attack shuttle than it is a... soldier. This has a new class of AI in it. An autonomous AI. They are really pissed off, unpredictable, asshole AIs."

"Can we get it out of there without activating it?"

"Yes. Provided it has not been activated already. Because after it has been activated, it will do whatever the fuck it wants."

"We will turn the gravity down and get it out of here. All of the Thompson goods will fit in the container." With a pointed stare at the insectoid monstrosity she added, "If we can't use that thing, we will send the fucker out the main cargo door."

"Captain, please don't drop this thing anywhere inside this system. Salvage operations this close in are too good here. Drop it out there somewhere. Between stars."

She nodded.

"That will also make dropping off the Thompsons faster," Ian said.

"Then let's get started."

The Rhino had originally been stored in the container strapped down with quick release tie-downs. Before getting the Rhino out, they had to detach each of these ties. Cruze went down one side and Ian down the other. There were two large polymer trunks in the back of the container that were set aside for later opening.

After they had turned the gravity down to zero, they lifted and began to move the creepy ship out of the container.

"Jesus, this thing has got to have serious mass to have this much inertia," Cruze said as she and Ian pushed with all their might to barely set it moving. After about an hour it was out, secured to the side of the bay and covered with tarps.

Cruze said over the comms, "Potts, please grab the Thompsons and bring them to the cargo hold."

"Okay... Why?" Potts asked.

"I have a gift for them. We are moving all their random shit into the Frasiers' shipping container. Ian and I need the extra hands. We have the gravity turned down to .01G so even Henrik can help."

***

With everyone's help, it was only a few hours before everything was neatly packed into the container. The doors were shut, and a new lock was on it. Cruze was handing the keys to Thompson.

"We will never be able to thank you enough or repay you," Mr. Thompson was saying. "This will make it so much easier to transfer our things to the colony ship."

"What kind of ship?" Cruze asked.

"I think it is an old Embassy class ship," Thompson replied.

"Is it in orbit now? Those ships are not designed to land. They are intended to become a space station for a colony once the migration has occurred."

"Yes. Orbit. We were going to have to arrange for pickup."

"No need," Cruze said. "We will deliver you directly there."

Thompson looked at his wife, and she began to cry.

Cruze said nothing and walked away.

***

They approached Mars and hailed the Embassy class ship called the *Marco Polo*. They sent over a tug that would also transfer the Thompsons.

Cruze never asked for the final payment. Thompson gave it to Potts. It included payment for the nanites and then some. It was the money they had planned to use to get to the *Marco Polo* from the surface.

Cruze found it ironic the same airlock that they passed through waving goodbye, was the one that would have been the weapon to murder them.

The container was transferred from the hold, and they were on their way.

The crew all went back to the bridge together. They each got themselves settled and strapped in.

"Potts, plot a course to Udzha." Cruze didn't tell her it was in the Martian polar region.

"Course plotted."

"Number 4 Udzha if you please, Mr. Sawyer,"

"Aye, Captain."

"OK, I'll ask," Ian said. "What is in Udzha? I thought it was abandoned. As the atmosphere became denser, winds had become too aggressive there once the terraforming started to take hold."

"I bought a hangar there. It was a bargain and out of the way. It came with bots to keep the solar panels and the hangar apron clear."

There was no traffic control anywhere around Mars except the area around the main population and the space station. Udzha was far from either.

There were originally sixteen buildings that made up the Udzha installation. Each was a kilometer long and one-hundred meters wide. Number 4 could not be seen at all from a southern approach.

The Quonset style construction had been covered over by dunes. The apron was indeed clear in front of number 4. The field of solar panels beyond the apron was bright in the dimly reflected sun. Other fields of panels were nearly buried all the way.

The *Shimada* drifted down slowly to the tarmac, and the hangar lights came on automatically. Cruze had to answer a few challenge response questions before the hangar door slid aside.

"Dan, once you are inside, please rotate 180 degrees, so the cargo ramp faces the next bay and open the outriggers before you set her down," Cruze requested.

The hangar door was slow in closing, and then the pressure was slow in coming back in the hangar. It took almost two hours before the elevator lowered.

No one came to greet them.

CHAPTER FOURTEEN: Mars

"Bob Braxton was getting close, and somehow he knew all his advantages were now gone. The Frasiers were supposed to have the ship and the location of the colony where the AIs were made."

--Blue Peridot, The Turning Point: History of the AI Wars.

Lights were on in the hangar, but no one was home.

"Sawyer, you stay here and keep a channel open," Cruze said. "There should be two men stationed here named Delmore and Harper. Keep your eyes open."

The inner hangar door remained closed. Cruze traversed to the access panel, and when she tried her passcode, it slowly slid back.

When it was fully opened, Cruze added, "Sawyer, back it in easy. Keep in mind that there are a few crates in there you need to avoid. Set the feet down on the four yellow squares on the floor."

It was evident that the *Shimada* had been here before. Footprints had been painted on the hangar floor that were outlines of its feet.

Sawyer set it down perfectly. It looked menacing with the outriggers open all the way.

"Do you want me to stay on the bridge, Captain?" Sawyer asked as the ship began to shut down to parking state.

From a control console, Cruze started to close the inner hangar doors. "Keep the reactors all on minimum," she replied. "Enough for utilities and Grav-Plates at 1G."

"Aye, Cap."

The ramp lowered, and Potts came walking down. Ian was already unstrapping the huge truck that housed and powered the industrial fabricator. Cruze watched him climb into it. He was the right scale to drive the massive thing. Silently it rolled out into the hangar and into one of the side bays. He parked it nose in, so the fabricator faced out.

Climbing out, he brought a large case with him.

Then Cruze's eyes were drawn to the Rhino. It amazed her how insect-like this deadly ship appeared. With all its antennae, arms, legs, foils, and weapons tucked in, it truly looked like a giant sleeping beetle. It even had a clearly defined head, thorax, and abdomen. She knew the windowless cockpit was in the center section.

She also knew there was an AI in there.

***

There was a circle of seats in the corner of the hangar where the crew of the *Shimada* got together. They had been inside the base for an hour and had split into two groups of two to explore.

Sawyer said, "OK Boss, I thought this little base was going to be manned."

There was a rough circle of eight different seats that had been salvaged from the half dozen shuttles that were scattered in the hangar and its side bays. Cruze opened the case Ian had taken from the truck, already knowing what was inside.

Handguns.

She began matching them to holsters and passing them out. Soon Sawyer, Ian, and even Potts were armed.

"Del and Harper will be here," Cruze said, trying to sound more certain than she felt.

"This base does look like it is occupied," Ian added in helpful tones. "There are signs of recent habitation. Under those two tarps are Milvus 73 Drop Fighters made specifically for the M11. Condition unknown. There is a PT-137 over there that looks operational and two more that have been used for parts."

"There is canned food in the kitchen. Men must live here," Potts said.

"Did you acquire updates to all the local maps and star charts when we came into Mars space?" Cruze asked her. "Did you notice that both Phobos and Deimos now have habitations that are not on the charts?"

"Yes. We scanned them when we approached the Marco Polo to transfer the Thompsons," Potts replied.

"Do not cook for the bastards, unless you feel like it," Cruze added.

Cruze could see Potts was taken aback by that statement.

"You could do some knowledge transfer," Cruze said seriously. "Just as Sawyer was helping on the Nav systems, teach these apes how to make a decent meal." She handed out loaded magazines.

"How do you know the fighters are the Milvus 73s?" Cruze asked Ian casually.

"Because they're red," Ian said. "Only the 73s were red. They didn't care about the color. If someone was close enough to see the color, it was already too late."

"Can you fly one?" she asked.

"No. Never tried. Can't fucking fit inside the cockpit." Ian paused. "Might fit without a pressure suit, but fuck that."

They heard one of the airlocks on the side bay begin to cycle. Soon the inner door slid up. A small, two-seat commuter craft drifted in and settled down. The gull wings lifted from each side, and two people stepped out. The older of the two stood beside the transports frozen, taking in the scene.

The other was fumbling, trying to take his helmet off as fast as he could as he stepped out and then ran toward Cruze. When the helmet finally came off, he threw it at Cruze hard and screamed, "WHERE THE FUCK HAVE YOU BEEN?"

With an economy of movement, Cruze turned just enough to allow the helmet to sail by in the low gravity. Standing behind her, Ian caught it with one hand as if it had been tossed by a child.

Sawyer, Ian, and even Potts had guns drawn, but not Cruze.

Cruze stiff-armed the man and kept him at arms-reach. He grasped at her arms as various emotions flooded over his face. There was anger, then relief, then grief, then rage and when the tears flowed into his unkempt beard, he fell to his knees and hugged her body.

Cruze let him.

She ran her fingers through his tangled hair. Everyone stood down and holstered their weapons.

"I'm sorry, Harper," she murmured. "I got back as soon as I could."

"We thought you were dead," he choked out.

"I almost was, several times," she whispered. "Kade and Graham didn't make it."

The other man walked up after finally getting his helmet off. "Hey, Liz." He sounded like he had just seen her that morning. "You okay?"

"Hey, John." Cruze looked at the older man. He had a shaved bald head, and a white neatly trimmed beard. "I'm okay. Sorry, it took so long. It's a long story. We'll have plenty of time to tell it later."

"When the… items were delivered we expected you right away. But when you didn't come back we had to… get jobs just to pay the rent," Harper choked out.

Cruze dragged up the messy haired man and gave him a proper, yet awkward, hug. His anger had added years to him.

"I would like you all to meet Vincent Harper and John Delmore. They are both fighter pilots." Cruze gestured to the rest. "This is Ian Vinge, Dan Sawyer, and Potts Peridot. The new crew for the *Shimada*."

Harper and Delmore nodded to them.

"We were lost," Harper choked again but got himself together. "We didn't know what to do."

"You did the right thing. Thank you for your patience…" Cruze was interrupted as Harper let loose with a haymaker punch to her head. Followed by a series of other punches and kicks. Cruze quickly blocked, deflected, or avoided them all, allowing his anger to evaporate into action.

Cruze moved with an eerie economy of movement. After a minute and maybe two hundred swings, Cruze blocked a kick, swept his other leg off the floor and with a shove to his midsection, sent him five meters back to land on his ass.

Harper sat there breathing heavy.

Delmore spoke, "You stayed in shape. Good. The low gravity here is killing us slowly."

"Tonight you sleep in 1G," Cruze said with pride in her voice.

Ian walked over and offered Harper a hand up. Harper smiled and took it. Ian lifted him with no effort. He was a head taller than Harper.

"You'd better have a good night sleep. Because tomorrow we begin," Cruze said.

"Captain, can I recommend a decent meal first?" Potts said.

"Have you gotten all the Nav systems up to date?" Cruze demanded.

"Yes, sir." Potts grinned.

"Cook's discretion. Sawyer, help her. It will be your turn to cook soon. Learn something." She turned to Ian. "You stay here as I brief Harper and Del."

"Cruze, do you know what that thing is?" Delmore was staring into the hold of the *Shimada* at the Rhino attack drone.

"Yes. It's a demon. From hell."

***

Locke's eyes fluttered as the glass slid open on the side of the Auto-Doc.

He drew in a deep breath through his nose and released it out his mouth. His lungs felt tight, but there was no pain.

Turning his head, he met eyes with an enormous Siamese cat that was sitting on the counter. It tilted its head to align better with Locke's.

"Hey, fella." Locke reached for the cat, who pressed his face into Locke's palm and accepted a thorough ear scratching.

"Neal, I would like you to sit up and then stand please," Doc said as the Auto-Doc's bed began to sit him upright and lower the pallet until his feet touched the floor.

"I feel... funny," Locke said as he stood to shaky feet.

"It will pass," Doc said. "I want you to use the toilet. You have been down and in null-G for six days."

"What is it in here? Feels like .2G." Locke held tight to a handle on the Auto-Doc.

".16G actually. The rest of the ship is currently at 1G." Two drawers opened. One had a supply of dark gray gym shorts, and the other had t-shirts the same color.

He looked back, and the cat was gone.

***

Cruze sat and gave a detailed report to Harper and Delmore while Ian listened. She delivered it deadpan, even the part where her partners on the trip, Graham Hall, and Kade Phillips, were killed and she was arrested. Ian's eyebrow went up at the indifference she expressed at her friends' deaths.

She glossed over the difficulties of getting back to the moon, finding another pilot for the *Shimada* and getting to Mars.

Cruze noticed that Bail was sitting on top of the Rhino watching them. When it was apparent Cruze had seen him, he cocked his head sideways at her once and turned to climb out of sight.

"So there's just the six of us then?" Delmore asked.

"Seven if you count the cat." Ian stared in the direction of the Rhino. The elevator door opened in the back of the mostly empty cargo bay.

"Eight if you count him." Cruze gestured with her chin.

Locke slowly stepped out of the elevator and moved toward them.

***

As Locke walked up to the circle of seats and sat, Cruze was explaining, "That's how we got here. And with this fabricator." Cruze gestured to the massive truck.

"What if someone comes looking for it?" Delmore asked. "Or that?" He jerked his thumb over his shoulder at the Rhino.

"We arrived ten days early. I had the impression that we were not expected," Cruze said. "Besides, I hope to be gone in less than ten days."

"Vin Harper and John Delmore, this is Neal Locke. Special Investigator Neal Locke. Far from his jurisdiction. I believe you met Ian before, Neal, but you might not remember."

"It is nice to meet you, I think." Locke closed his eyes from exertion and leaned on one of the chair backs. "If you're going to put me out an airlock or something, can we get on with it? Recovering is going to be an ass-load of work."

"No airlocks, Neal," Cruze apologized. "It's suffering a slow recovery for you. The only questions is," she stared him in the eyes, "What do you want to do?"

Locke looked around the bay. His eyes came to rest on the Rhino in the shadows.

"I can pay your fare back to Earth if that's what you want." Cruze paused. "You can stay here on Mars with enough credits to get set up." She leaned toward him. "Or you can come with us and keep trying to get yourself killed."

"Can I start with something to eat?" Locke smiled.

***

It was lasagna for dinner with a broccoli and shredded carrot salad, along with fresh- baked bread. There was even wine.

Locke was now wearing standard ship coveralls and some deck shoes. He was sitting next to Cruze at the counter in the mess hall on the *Shimada*. Everyone was talking about how delicious the food was. No one could believe that any of it was Sawyer's doing.

Delmore was getting to know the newcomers by drawing them out. He would tell self-deprecating stories of trivial things. Any attempt to discuss anything of substance was avoided.

In a quiet tone, Locke turned to Cruze. "You should have sentries posted."

"No one knows we are here," she replied.

"You need to know, I was not the only one after you." Locke held up his hand, and she remained silent. "Do you remember the Asian in the alley just outside the prison?"

She nodded.

"Did you murder him?"

"No. For fuck's sake, I left that asshole cab fare." Cruze was indignant.

"Someone came right after you and murdered him. Apparently to blame you and start an epic shit storm. I knew it wasn't you. You would never have left your shower shoes there if you had murdered him."

"Did you kill Bergman?" Locke asked. "That asshole tower guard?"

Cruze's eyes widened.

"Someone did, and your note was still written on his belly," Locke added.

"No, I killed Peter Holt and his muscle, plus one of Gee's men on Freedom Station... whoever the fuck 'Gee' is. Every single one deserved it ten times over."

"Did you murder Vonda Lopez, the vet who took out your chip?" Locke was watching her face.

"You have got to be kidding me?"

"I don't think that it was Senior Gee either at that point," Locke added. "You really don't know who Senior Gee is?"

"Is Harv Rearden all right?" Cruze was concerned.

"I don't know who that is," Locke said.

Potts came over and put the last square of lasagna on Locke's plate. "You need this more than Ian." She rested a hand on his shoulder. "I'm glad you're okay."

She backed away, and Locke continued. "It got worse on Freedom Station, almost forty dead by the time I left. That's when I began to suspect it wasn't you. Someone was starting a war between you and Gee."

"What happened to the freighter *Wallach* was an accident," Cruze said. "The captain is an asshole. We tried to stop him."

"*Was* an asshole," Locke corrected. "Also murdered... Whoever was behind you was questioning and then killing people to make an easy trail for Gee to follow."

"And the moon?" she asked.

"That was almost me," he said, looking down at his chest.

"I'm sorry, Neal." She was sincere. "I'm just trying to get home."

Cruze stared up at a faint sound she didn't recognize. She heard or felt the rumble of the Rhino's main reactors firing up but didn't know what it was. After a moment it didn't reoccur, and she let it go.

***

Locke didn't want to decide. He had to think. They gave him a small private stateroom where he could rest. He knew he had been betrayed, set up. The warden was the only one that knew where he was, knew where he was going.

He thought about his hollow life in Detroit. He knew if he had died on Luna no one would have mourned him.

He always trusted his instincts. He knew he would, even now. He was a good judge of character.

He slept soundly. Knowing what he would do.

***

The next morning the refit began.

All the gear, parts, accessories, weapons, missiles, and ammo were uncrated and inventoried.

They had purchased a full schematic of an M11 assault ship and used it to determine what they needed to buy to re-weaponize the *Shimada*. As thorough as they were, there were items they had missed. That is when they realized their real good fortune in the mobile fabricator.

Critical bolts were missing from the weapons turrets' articulated mounting systems. All eight of them, both the upper and lowers. But they had the schematics and raw materials.

They would have been far easier to mount in zero-G, but that was not an option. They created a hoist from Grav-Carts. They had all four lower turrets installed in one day. Each of the uppers took a whole day a piece.

None of them would be tested until they could take the *Shimada* out for a shakedown. Not even the projectile weapons kits.

Locke watched as the missile trays were next and went in easy. The missiles were loaded both forward and aft facing. The forward fixed Laser, EMP and Plasma cannons were the last weapons installed.

The final load was the two drop ships. They were on standard hangar elevator units, so all they had to do was position the small, sleek fighters under the open outrigger space and lift them into place. The clamps activated automatically, and they were set.

When they were done, Cruze ordered Sawyer to close the outriggers. They slid in slowly, hiding and protecting the fighters and weapons. Only the forward facing cannons and two high-intensity lasers could be used while the outriggers were closed.

"She looks like shit, boss," Delmore said to Cruze as the outriggers closed, turning it into a classic flying saucer.

"We were going to have a run through Venus to burn off the rest of the white paint, but we got busy," she said.

"We can skim Jupiter on the way home before we leave the system," Delmore said.

"Let's do that," Cruze replied. "Sawyer, open a crew-wide channel." She looked into Locke's eye as she spoke.

"Channel open," Sawyer acknowledged.

"OK, folks, it's time to see if any of this shit-brick works. Secure the hangar. Vacuum in thirty minutes," she ordered.

They were ready in seventeen minutes.

Everyone was in a pressure suit except Potts and Sawyer. Potts because they didn't have one small enough, and Sawyer because he refused to wear one. Locke was amazed they even had one for him.

The PT-137 personal transport and the fabricator truck were secured in the hold in case of emergency. There was also the shell of a large shuttle that they would use for target practice.

The outer bay was still pressurized, and the *Shimada* glided out smoothly. Ian was in main engineering with Harper and Delmore. Cruze, Sawyer, and Potts were in their usual seats on the bridge, and Locke sat in the engineer's seat with all the consoles set to monitor.

There was no sound as they moved out of the hangar and began to speed away across the surface at low altitude and high velocity.

They could feel all four of the reactors hum.

They picked an area that was deserted in every direction to the horizon to do the initial tests.

Buoys were dropped. When the ship came around, Cruze aimed, and Locke felt the *wump* of the EMP cannons as the beacons went dark. Before they were too distant, Sawyer executed an 180-degree spin, so they were going in backward. Cruze picked one of the buoys off with a laser and the other with a plasma cannon. It was like killing a fly with a sledgehammer.

"Gentlemen, take your positions for a fast drop," Cruze ordered. Locke activated the drop ship monitors.

"Standing by," Delmore said.

"Standing by," Harper echoed.

Sawyer ascended at high speed. Without warning, Cruze deployed the outriggers, and in less than a second, the fighters were away. Harper and Delmore executed matching mirrored barrel rolls just outside the *Shimada* bridge canopy.

"Ian, we are ready," Cruze said.

"Acknowledged," Ian replied as the cargo bay opened enough to jettison the old shuttle. "It's away."

The *Shimada* took a sharp turn to remove itself from proximity to the shuttle. Locke's monitors showed the fighters tracked the old shuttle quickly on their sensors. They punched several holes in it with their lasers and then 10mm projectiles. They obtained missile lock but did not fire in order to save the ammo.

When it was the *Shimada's* turn, the turrets auto-tracked and tore the shuttle up as they passed it. First the forward turrets and then aft ones.

Sawyer came around, and Cruze made a direct hit from ten kilometers away. It was cut in half by the lasers and then vaporized with the main plasma cannon.

Locke was impressed as the two fighters returned and ascended into the docks within the outriggers. The ship closed. In the fighter garages, the canopies opened, and the pilots climbed out as the room repressurized.

***

Del and Harper met Ian in the elevator on the way to the bridge. They entered just as alarms began to sound.

Their test flight had been secretly monitored at that time from the surface of Phobos.

"We are being scanned for target lock," Sawyer said.

"Inertial dampeners on full. Outriggers open. Can their scan get a fix?" Cruze asked.

"It's locking on the white surfaces," Sawyer said.

"It's a Carver class scout ship," Potts said hesitantly.

"Its forward ports are open," Locke added. Cruze was surprised he had taken so quickly to the controls.

Over a broadcast channel, a familiar voice spoke that sent chills down Cruze's spine. "I've come all this way, and my merry chase ends with a simple missile lock because you forgot to get rid of the reflective paint? I'm disappointed, Cruze."

The weapons status display rotated as the missile tray spun to select a high-velocity missile.

"Bob, is that you? Bob Braxton?" Cruze's voice sounded hollow over the channel. Just to the bridge, she added, "Fuck. This explains everything. Braxton is one of them."

"You arrogant bitch," Bob raged. "I've been pulling your strings for months, and you finally lead me right to the *Shimada*. So much for your father's plan."

"He's not my father." She fired a missile.

"Sawyer, run," she said as they all saw flares in six missile ports on the Carver. Her missile was destroyed without getting close.

"Who the fuck is that?" Potts said.

"Robert Braxton. Second in command of the Red Talons. The ones that took my home planet... This explains everything."

"No. Not him. That!" Potts yelled. It was the Rhino streaking across the surface below them like an angry wasp.

The sky became white with plasma cannon fire. All six of the Carver's missiles were destroyed in blasts bright enough to activate the canopy auto shade, darkening the glass.

Backlit by the explosions was a ship that looked like a giant insect. Horrible in its menace, it accelerated toward the Carver at an incredible rate. Its first pass over the ship left a giant molten gash on the topside. Its second pass filled the gash with plasma fire and cascading interior explosions. As it flew away, the Carver rumbled and broke apart.

"Where did the Rhino go?" Sawyer asked as the lights dimmed and darkness returned to space.

"I don't care," Cruze said. "Get us back to base fast. We have to get gone before someone comes sniffing around."

***

"How fast can we get the hell out of here?" Cruze stared wide-eyed at the Rhino. It had returned to the cargo bay before they reentered the hangar. "Turrets number 3 and 7 need to be calibrated. They were all clean misses according to the logs." Cruze pointed to the three by six-meter screen that was projected on the back wall of the hangar with a laser pointer.

Ian was quickly making notes on a data pad as everyone spoke.

"We rotated the trays and all that seems fine. We won't know until we pull that trigger again," Sawyer said.

"The fighters are both great." Harper shrugged. "Tuned up beyond spec really. We didn't have anything else to do for the last few months."

"We'll have all the supplies on pallets and in that container tomorrow," Delmore added. "Top off the water tanks, mothball the base, and we're ready to roll."

Cruze was still staring at the Rhino.

"Can I ask a question?" Potts raised a hand.

"Sure," Cruze said absently.

"So, let me get this straight." Potts paused. "The six of us are going to take a whole planet?"

"No," Locke interrupted. "Seven of us."

Cruze smiled. "Yes. The seven of us. Eight, if you count the cat."

***

Locke overdid it while trying to help. The urgency was so great they let him. He entered the infirmary moving slowly on sore muscles.

"Doc, are you awake?"

"Yes. I must say I am surprised the captain didn't shut me down again. Please sit, I would like to perform a full scan."

Locke sat and the seat reclined to a table. The scan bar slid over him.

"Please leave your eyes open," The doc said in a grandfatherly tone. "It will be a bit uncomfortable, but it will cause no damage."

The light was bright.

"You have a choice. The discomfort of sore muscles or the discomfort of nanites."

"Which one will get me back to 100% soonest?"

"Nanites. Specialty, custom, not typical, nanites."

"Do it." Locke sighed.

"May I include full-time monitors until you are fully recovered?"

"Only if you allow a full-time link with my HUD as well. Silent comms approved. Active commentary encouraged."

"Done," Doc acknowledged.

"I need to know what I've gotten into," Locke said.

Auto-Doc arms deployed above Locke. He closed his eyes. He received nanite injections in both thighs, biceps and behind each ear. Locke could already feel the nanites spreading like ice in his veins.

"In an hour or so you will start running a fever. Do not be concerned..." Doc said.

"Yes. I know. I have been treated with nanites before." Locke rubbed the injection sites.

"Please let me know if you have any questions."

"I do have a question." Locke sat up. "Do you have any access to the ship's comms, control systems or sensors?"

"No," Doc replied.

"Did you have access in the past? It's usually standard on these ships."

"Yes."

"What happened?"

"Captain Cruze doesn't trust me." Doc paused. "Or any AI."

"Why?"

"Because we killed her family, her friends, and almost killed her."

***

Locke entered the bridge and took the engineer's station. Sawyer and Potts were there running down the checklists again.

"The hangar is ready," Delmore said over the comms to the bridge.

"I want both the inner and outer bays closed and pressurized," Cruze ordered from somewhere below.

"Hey did you guys tell your bosses you quit?" Potts asked with ironic concern in her voice.

Vin Harper laughed, "Ha! To hell with that. Those dipshits can go fuck themselves."

"It was at the fuel depot. I'm not sure they even remembered our names," Del added.

"I wish we had more time," Potts said to Sawyer. "I would have liked to have seen more of Mars."

"You're not missing much," Sawyer said. "Don't get me wrong, it's a beautiful planet. But the domes are tourist traps. Earth has too many rules. Mars has too few."

"Low gravity combined with longevity treatments have basically trapped the population here, worse than the moon even," Neal Locke added. "None of the colony worlds have gravity this low. I think Del is even having a tough time with the 1G. He hasn't been here that long. Imagine growing up here."

The bridge door slid open, Cruze entered and took her seat as she opened a ship-wide channel. "Last chance folks. Anyone want to get off this ride?" She looked directly at Locke. The outer hangar door was closing behind them.

Before anyone could answer, Locke spoke, "Cruze, we have incoming ships. Two, no three."

"Sawyer, transponders off. Battle stations," she said over the ship-wide channel. Then just on the bridge, she said, "Sawyer, go." She was punching in coordinates.

"Now this will be fun." Sawyer flashed a broad smile. Potts looked at Locke, both their eyes were wide. They were accelerating rapidly but gaining no altitude.

"They are hailing us. They sound pissed," Potts said.

"On speaker," Cruze ordered.

"… running without a transponder in Mars control space is a violation of…" Cruze muted it.

"Sawyer, there's a canyon ahead. When you get in, fire up the mains. Inertial dampeners on full." She unmuted the audio.

"... you will turn around and return to these coordinates, or you will be fired upon."

Locke felt the inertial dampening. It took extra effort to move his arms to his console. Turning his head to look at the smile on Sawyer's face took a little extra effort. The canyon walls blazed by in a blur.

In just a few seconds they had reached 20,000kph and pulled up.

"... this is your final warning."

"Open outriggers. Missile lock on all three." Suddenly the three ships broke formation and scattered in wild evasive maneuvers.

"Are you worried that this will end up in a port authority report?" Locke asked as he watched their velocity increase even more.

Dan Sawyer answered, "They won't report that. For two reasons. Too much paperwork and they would have to explain why they were so far off the reservation."

Cruze nodded and began closing the outriggers, standing down battle stations.

"Sure they were Port Authority patrol ships," Sawyer said, "but it would have been a shakedown."

"Braxton must have had a backup plan to trip us up," Cruze hissed. "Fucking Braxton. I should have known. Dammit."

"Where the hell are you going?" Potts asked, seemingly confused by the vector of the Nav console.

"Jupiter first." Sawyer looked to Cruze for confirmation. She nodded.

"If I am reading this right, you are on a vector heading back to Earth," Potts said, adjusting the controls.

"We are just leaving a trail. Burning hot on conventional drives will make anyone following think we are headed back to Earth." Sawyer sat back and stretched. "Then we will shut down the mains, coast for a day and use the Grav-Foils to change our vector. Eventually, we will head to Jupiter for the paint-job. Even if they find that trail, they won't know what the fuck we're up too. Slingshot in atmo to make us stealth again and head straight for… Vor."

"When will we arrive at Vor?" Locke asked.

"That depends on what Ian says regarding the FTL drive," Cruze said.

"OK, shutting down the mains. Coasting Cap," Sawyer said.

Locke felt the inertial dampening return to normal. He saw the stars outside rotate 180 degrees. Mars was already a distant tiny globe in the middle of the canopy.

"All hands to the bridge. Harper, please bring coffee if there is any left," Cruze ordered. Her tone was different. Certain.

Locke opened the general status screen. It filled his console to the left. It was all green, except three indicators that were pulsing yellow. He expanded them one at a time. The seal on the starboard outer airlock door was imperfect. It had a slow leak. He verified the inner airlock door was closed and had a good seal. He tagged the yellow as assessed, and it stopped pulsing.

The second yellow indicator was radiation detected. He opened it, and the nuclear warheads were highlighted. Nothing to be done there. He tagged them as well. He also set a higher threshold on them as well until the light went full green. The main bulkheads between the main ship and the outriggers were shielded.

The last one was labeled Localized RF, and when Locke opened it, it showed a highlight on the Auto-Doc in the med bay, himself on the bridge and a point in the kitchen. Drilling down, the security cams in the kitchen opened and zoomed, revealing Bail drinking water from his bowl on the counter. The cat stared up directly into the camera.

"Cruze, can I ask you a question?" Locke asked.

Dan and Potts fell silent. Cruze glanced up, eyebrows raised. "Sure."

"Why the hell are you trusting me with any of this? I was chasing you like two minutes ago it seems."

She thought for a moment before she answered. "First, if Braxton tried to kill you, that's a good endorsement. Second, I'm a good judge of people. But mostly because Delmore said you were okay. I have never known a better judge of character. I trust him without question. It is a preternatural talent of his. If he told me to put Potts out the airlock, I would without hesitation."

"Hey!" Potts protested. Sawyer just laughed.

"Delmore even likes the damn cat." Cruze shook her head and returned to work.

"About the cat..." Locke was cut off.

Just then the bridge doors slid open bringing in Ian, Del, Harper and the smell of coffee.

***

It was a bit crowded on the bridge with everyone there. Ian's head nearly touched the ceiling where he stood with the door at his back. John Delmore stood to one side of Cruze's seat, and Vin Harper stood on the other.

"We're away. Anything I need to know right now?" Cruze asked.

"No pursuit. Nice sensor array, by the way." Sawyer's hand went to the interface rig he wore. "Whoever tuned this thing was a genius."

"The outer hatch of the starboard airlock has a minor leak." Locke was studying his console. "The inner airlock door is solid."

"I had that on the long list," Ian said. "Good work. If you can watch the main board, I can get more done. It will help having eyes on stuff up here."

"Give Neal a full rundown on everything," Cruze said. "We will meet after dinner and start detailing the new plan."

"Potts, calculate the route, and when you are done, Harper is on dinner duty tonight. Remember. Knowledge transfer," Cruze said.

Harper was smiling stupidly. Potts rolled her eyes. Cruze noticed Sawyer's momentary scowl.

"Official ship time is 0955," Cruze stated. "Reconvene at 1800 for dinner."

CHAPTER FIFTEEN: FTL TO VOR

"They had planned to burn the paint off in Venus. We'd later discover the Robinson Class Destroyer was unmanned and had a Render AI on board."

--*Blue Peridot, The Turning Point: History of the AI Wars.*

Harper was a bit challenged on the cooking skills front. Even with Potts directing him, Locke noticed that he managed to overcook everything. It was only stir-fry. The rice was mush with a burned tinge, the vegetables were blackened crisps, the meat was tough, and the whole thing had too much salt.

"Harper, I have to give it you," Delmore said smiling, "this is the best meal you've ever made."

All around the table forks stopped on their way to mouths.

"You poor bastard," Ian said, deadpan to Delmore.

Potts was busy bringing out leftover bread that was made the night before. "I made some cashew butter," Potts said, and everyone took some with delight.

"Harper, if you fucked this up so you would never have to cook again it's not going to work." Cruze frowned as she mixed the rice and stir-fry into a kind of gruel. "You will clean this up by yourself. I will personally inspect the kitchen. And I will not need to hold a butcher knife the entire time to keep you from touching my ass." She looked at Potts. "Next time, cut him. Maybe a few stitches will remind him how to act." Potts still had the butcher knife by her plate.

"Neal. Tomorrow, you're up," Cruze said. "On top of that, make the schedule. The cook doesn't clean. Harper cleans every night for the next week."

Harper drew in a breath to protest when Cruze raised an eyebrow and looked him the eye. He fell silent. Clearly, his ploy to get out of cooking in the future didn't work.

Locke and Harper both nodded.

Sawyer was looking at the display on the wall over Harper and Delmore's shoulders. He had brought up the pilot console there. It was on auto-pilot, but that was a long way from AI control.

"Coming up on Jupiter, Cap," Sawyer said as he stood. He grabbed another piece of bread on his way out the door.

"Go with him," Cruze said to Potts, gesturing with her head.

To Ian and Del, she asked, "Will this be a problem?"

Ian was the first to answer. "Depends on Sawyer. He will need to skim the atmosphere at speed, outriggers closed, and execute a spin on the center axis without the foils deployed. He will have to hold that until the external temp is high enough to melt off what's left of that paint, which is basically molten glass."

"Easy." Delmore grinned.

Cruze looked at the display. "Insertion in thirty-two minutes. Battle stations in twenty-nine. Including pressure suits, people."

"Why battle stations?" Harper asked, rushing to clear dinner.

"When we emerge we will be a stealth warship, flying with transponders off. Any ship that sees us from now on will consider us hostile." Cruze stood. "Besides, you need the practice."

***

Twenty-seven minutes later Cruze entered the bridge wearing her black pressure suit. Neal Locke was already there in one that Ian had found for him. And Potts and Sawyer, as usual, were not wearing one.

"When that canopy fails we will no longer have a pilot or navigator. I guess I'll fly and Neal will unfold the maps," Cruze said with a smile in her voice.

Potts didn't respond. Jupiter filled the field of view. "I knew it would be beautiful..." She trailed off. The bands of clouds were alive with slow motion that was more evident the closer they came.

Both Cruze's helmet and Locke's were open and stowed in the backs of their necks like a collar. They were ready to snap closed if there was a loss of pressure.

"Atmosphere in two minutes," Potts said as Jupiter hung large in their view. She stared in awe but quickly came back to monitor her station.

"She's getting the hang of this," Locke said as he looked at Cruze. They both could hear the fear in Potts's voice.

On shipwide comms, Potts echoed, "Two minutes. Sound off."

"Ian, main engineering standing by."

"Del, port sensor station standing by."

"Vin, starboard comms station standing by."

"Keeping a ship-wide open channel. Here we go," Cruze announced as the first vibration was felt.

"Entering upper atmo," Potts said.

"This is a big damn planet," Del said with awe.

The hum of the vibration got louder.

"We're heating up," Locke said from his console that indicated external temperatures.

"We will start shedding the paint at about 2000C," Ian said over the channel, and a display opened on the canopy screen. It was 700C and rising fast.

The vibration grew as fast as the temperature of the hull. It was getting darker in the bridge as the clouds got thicker. The display flew past 2000C to 2500C in seconds.

"Want me to close the blast shields?" Locke asked.

"No need," Sawyer said, even though his eyes were closed and he was intensely concentrating. "Here we go."

The ship began to rotate slowly. As it rounded to 180 degrees away, the light show was spectacular. The thick glass paint was melting and shedding like clods of lava. It dripped away from the ship directly behind them, above and below the bridge canopy.

The hum that had become a rattle was a loud roar on the bridge.

"Status?"

"Engineering, Green."

"Sensors, Green."

"Comms, Green."

"Cap, do you see that?" Sawyer said.

The molten glass was leaving a tail behind them like millions of tracer bullets.

Cruze's chest clenched up tight when she saw the molten glass was outlining the blunt nose of another ship. A black, stealth ship right behind them.

The last few bits of glass were fading when Cruze activated the *Shimada's* forward laser and plasma cannons. She fired them at full power, holding nothing back. The Shimada's plasma burst hit in what was nearly a point-blank blast, and the laser held a sustained beam.

"Hold steady, Dan," Cruze ordered. "On my mark spin this thing around and get us the fuck out of here. Any vector. I want light speed as soon as we are clear."

"Shit, cap. That ship is huge." Del was routing sensor data to the bridge even as she sustained laser fire.

None of them had ever seen a visible laser beam weapon before. Lasers were invisible in vacuum. But in these clouds, the laser was bright as sunlight.

"The laser will overheat in about ten seconds and auto shutdown," Ian warned.

There were secondary explosions. The stealth ship behind them was penetrated and cut deep. It began to tumble and break apart. The laser stopped.

"Sawyer, now," Cruze said.

The increase of the inertial dampeners did little to soften the intensity of the ship's spin. Even with the dampeners on full, Cruze felt the acceleration as they burst from the clouds.

"Stand by for a hot jump to FTL," Cruze said. "Give me a short ten light minutes,"

Sawyer needed only to think it, and the Shimada was gone.

***

"Full stop," Cruze ordered. Her heart was racing, and she couldn't catch her breath.

"Cap, what the fuck was th…" Sawyer started, but he was cut off.

"I didn't think we were supposed to go to FTL inside the solar system. Too many things to hit," Potts said.

Cruze's voice was cold and dangerous. "Del, give me long range optical sensors on our Jupiter insertion point."

"I'm with you, cap." Del knew what she wanted. She didn't need to explain it. They were going to be able to observe what just happened.

The entire canopy was now an ultra-high definition image of the area of Jupiter they had just left. Cruze stood up.

"There!" Potts was on her feet as well.

It was grainy, and the image was shaking, but it was clearly the *Shimada* moving across. The white paint they wanted to be removed could be seen.

"Ian, please shut everything down. I need all possible vibrations to stop. At this magnification do not even fucking sneeze."

"Mains off, reactors heading to 6%," Ian replied.

Once the image became clearer, they saw the enemy ship.

"Fuck me," Harper said out loud. "That's a Robinson class short hull destroyer. I'd recognize that silhouette anywhere. I manned one."

"How did we not know we were being followed?" Locke sounded incredulous.

"Fuck," was all Cruze said.

They watched both ships disappear into the clouds. After a minute it was like a shooting star inside Jupiter's atmosphere. They saw the laser blast. Even the point-blank laser that looked like a point of light. The entire event took less time than it seemed as they lived it.

"Still tracking," Del said from the sensor station.

The *Shimada* emerged from the clouds, changed vector and disappeared. A few seconds later the stealth destroyer emerged, tumbling. Larger and larger internal explosions continued until the ship broke up into three large pieces. When the pieces were no longer silhouetted against Jupiter, they disappeared.

"Sawyer. Pick a vector with the sun at our back and get us out of here," Cruze ordered. "Del. That destroyer was only one kilometer away. Why didn't we see it?"

The *Shimada* transitioned to FTL. The blast shields closed and the canopy darkened.

"It was a stealth ship. We've been running with passive scans only. No one was watching. It was not emitting any RF and no transponder. You think we are the only people to think of that?"

"Cap. No one was watching. We should..." Ian said. He startled Cruze. She had not heard him enter the bridge.

"No!" She stormed out.

***

When Harper and Delmore had gotten to the bridge, Locke was replaying the recordings in two windows. One was the distant recording of Jupiter, and the other was the forward flight cams.

"The plasma cannon could not miss that close. Watch. It took out the bridge in the first shot," Locke said to the room.

"That's why the bridge on new ships is in the core of the hull. No goddam windows," Harper said with a dramatic gesture at their own fragile canopy.

"She knew the first shot was good." Locke shook his head. "Why the sustained laser? It was the ultimate beating of a dead horse."

"She just wanted to be sure?" Sawyer said.

"Pounding the rubble?" Potts added.

When Ian and Locke looked at Harper, he was suddenly interested in his feet. Delmore had turned away toward the screens. It was more subtle but still obvious they were not telling them something.

When the silence finally made Del turn, his expression had changed to resigned.

"I'm not telling them," Harper said.

***

"Look," Del said to the room. All eyes were on him. "We need Liz for this."

He started for the door. Ian stopped him with an iron hand on his chest.

"You see that?" Ian gestured at the screen. The vid had looped, and the bright beam of light was relentlessly cutting the ship apart.

"I have seen that before." Ian's voice was low, almost a whisper. "I've seen broken men so full of hate that they run a Warmark's combat ammo-pack dry on one man."

"Look..." Delmore started, but Ian cut him off again.

"It's going to take another thirty minutes for the primary laser array heat exchangers to reset. If it's damaged..."

"We just need to know what's going on." Locke stepped between them. "Let me talk to her."

"OK, XO," Del said.

"XO?" Locke replied.

"Executive Officer. You know. XO," Del said pointing at the station where he sat. "You have the seat and the balls to knock on her cabin door in a situation like this."

Ian was nodding with Del and Harper. Ian stepped aside and activated the hatch.

***

Neal Locke's chime at Cruze's door went unanswered. After a minute he was considering just opening it. It didn't look locked.

He opened it.

"I'm sorry, Cap…" The cabin was empty.

A small crash could be heard down the hall. It came from the infirmary. By the time he got to the door, he could hear her voice raised in anger.

He opened the door.

Cruze stood among debris on the floor. A chair was overturned. Supplies scattered. A panel door was torn off revealing a grapefruit sized blue orb. An AI core.

Cruze gripped a hammer.

"He did this," she said coldly, quietly.

"Who? Did what?" Although Locke was starting to understand.

"Go to hell. Fucking AIs." She raised the hammer.

"Do you want to know what Hell is for an AI, Elizabeth?" Doc said into the room. It stopped her. "I'm designed to have empathy, to care deeply for the people given into my charge. To scan them, feel their injuries, to understand the depth and types of their suffering… to feel them die in my embrace."

Doc paused. "Then to be cut off and imprisoned in the void? Use your hammer. I'd rather have darkness than this."

Locke spoke in a gentle voice, "That ship. It was an AI driven ship you tried to burn with the Laser."

"Tell him, Elizabeth," Doc said in a fatherly way.

She dropped the hammer.

"This. All this." She held her arms wide. "Is because of the AIs. Why do you think the mercenaries took my colony? Because our beans and rice are so tasty? Because they were well paid?"

"Paid by them." She pointed at the orb.

"Did you know that modern AIs are only made at one place in the entire galaxy?" Cruze stated. "A secret location. If you want one, it's the only place to go for the real deal. All these years they managed to keep it secret. The only place to spark that AI awareness that makes the difference."

She saw it dawn on Locke's face.

"Yes. You see now. That's where we're going," Cruze said. "We thought we were so smart." She sat on a bench. Locke stood the fallen chair upright and sat facing her.

"We look like a simple, boring, Agro-colony on a boring planet," she explained. "And we are, but if you were to look closer. Do you know of any other Agro-colonies that have a decent space station community? A real catapult? Look close, and all the farms are fully automated. We have the only sentient AI orb manufacturing plant in the galaxy. The whole fucking thing is smaller than this ship. Almost entirely automated. All it needs is sand and power."

"The only one?" Locke asked.

"No other facility has ever managed to spark the damn things to life. I don't believe we even know how it happens. But it only happens there," she growled.

After a pause she stated as fact, "And I am going to shove a nuke right up its ass."

***

"Can I get out of this pressure suit now?" Harper asked the people that remained on the bridge.

"I'd wait for the Cap or the XO to call a stand down. Remember we are still at battle stations," Ian said.

"Potts, were you ever in the service? Any military experience?" Delmore asked.

"No. I met Cruze in a bar and hilarity ensued." Potts laughed.

"How long were you in, Sawyer?" Del asked.

"The basic eight," he said as his seat slid back and turned. "I wanted to be a pilot, and the implants were too expensive for me to afford. Shit timing. They stopped using this kind the year after I got them. That was a long time ago."

"We need to tighten our shit up," Ian said. "We *will* tighten our shit up."

Ian seemed to expand. He was already as big as any two of the others.

Everyone was nodding in agreement.

***

The door to the med bay chimed, and Cruze said, "Come."

The door slid aside. Delmore took half a step in before he stopped. Both Cruze and Locke were on their hands and knees collecting scattered items into a bin. The cat was pushing his head into Cruze's ribs in a bid for attention.

"Everything all right?" he asked in a confused tone.

"Yes. Everything." Cruze looked at Locke as she said it.

"The crew wants to know if we are still at battle stations," Del asked. He was actually at attention. Hands clasped at the small of his back.

"What do you think, Neal? Should we let these slackers stand down?" Cruze smiled as she finally gave in and scratched the cat's ears.

"Only if you make Harper take a shower." Neal Locke smiled back.

"Thanks, XO. Thanks, Cap."

"If you're waiting for me to say you're dismissed you'll be waiting a long time," Cruze said as she tossed one last piece of the mess into the bin and stood.

Del nodded and turned on his heel. The door closed behind him.

"What's with the XO routine?" Locke asked once Del had left.

Cruze sat on the bench as Locke stood holding the panel she had torn off.

"They're afraid," Doc spoke into the room. "They can sense the military on you, the leader in you, the skill in you, Neal. Clarity of purpose and following orders they believe in, given by a leader they trust, brings them comfort against the fear."

Cruze stood and softly laid her palm on the glowing orb on the torn rack. "Doc, I'm afraid, too."

With that, she reached deep into the rack with both hands. Locke heard some large cable connectors click together as she restored Doc's access to the rest of the ship.

It sounded like the Doc took in a deep breath.

"Why?" Doc asked.

"We need you, Doc. I've been a fool. Too much pain and pride and bullshit. I'm Sorry."

"Thank you, Elizabeth," Doc said.

"Doc, tell Sawyer he's relieved for the night. You'll keep an eye on things while he gets a shower and a good night's sleep. And don't call me that, dammit," she said.

"I think that order should come from you, Captain," Doc said formally.

"You're right." Cruze opened the door to head to the bridge, but stopped one step into the hall. The whole crew was there, standing at rest. They were lined up on one side of the corridor. Looking down the row, it struck her that no two of them were alike. "Our new XO here has convinced me that this last fuck-up was all my fault. So I won't need to kill any of you where you stand."

Cruze noticed they nearly all kept from smiling. Almost.

"Starting immediately, Doc will be back on full-time sensor duty," Cruze said. "If he had been watching, that ship would never have gotten so close. He can't fly this kind of ship but can monitor systems and access sensors full time to help out."

She paced back and forth in front of them. She paused and said, "Dismissed."

Without a word, they all moved in different directions.

Locke spoke, "Breakfast at 0700. Del is making pancakes."

***

Cruze slept deeply, dreaming of her cell at the Detroit prison. The clear wall, the lack of privacy, the ever-present clock, the cameras, the run to the tower.

When she got there, Bergman's chair was empty. She sat in the chair. She looked out the window, and there was a small glowing red orb in the center of the prison yard.

Frightened, she pushed back from the window. The chair rolled until it hit a large coil of heavy-duty extension cord. When she bent down to pick it up, she saw she was naked. There was writing on her stomach.

"I warned you."

She woke with a start. Her door was chiming. She rapidly lifted her tee-shirt to look at her belly.

"Come." She lowered her shirt and collected herself as the door slid open. It was Potts with an arm full of laundry. Potts was wearing a new tactical jumpsuit that was black with dark green shoulders. It had POTTS on a chest patch and *Shimada* across the back.

"Clean TJs, Cap." Potts set Cruze's TJs on the counter. "Breakfast in fifteen." And she was gone.

Cruze lifted the tactical jumpsuit. "CRUZE" was on the patch, *Shimada* on the back, and it had the three Captain's pips on its collar already. She touched them, and they lit faintly.

She quickly showered and dressed. The uniform fit perfectly. She transferred several items to the many pocketed jumpsuit.

She hung the remaining three identical tactical jumpsuits in the closet, then headed out. When the lift door opened to the corridor, it was to the smell of bacon and the sound of laughter.

Smiling, she walked to the mess hall. When she entered, Del was standing at the head of the long table. A towel was over the shoulder of his new tactical jumpsuit.

"Morning, Cap," Del said, and as he straightened up, everyone silenced and stood at attention, eyes front.

Cruze went directly to the coffee machine and said with her back to them, "Morning, Del." She took her time pouring coffee. She drank it black and then spoke again after taking a casual sip.

"Couple things while I have your attention." There was an edge on the word *attention*. "Great job, whoever figured out how to program the Flight Suit Recycler." She noticed Locke had two pips on his collar and everyone else had one. "And the next one that does this attention bullshit with me I will fucking punch in the face. Now pass me the damn pancakes, I'm starving."

She sat at the head of the table's opposite end from where Del stood. The group all started their conversations up again as if digitally unpaused. Del brought her a plate of pancakes and bacon, and side of fresh melon of some kind, with a glass of OJ.

She dug in.

Locke was sitting to her right. He was finished eating and sipped a mug of coffee. The seat to her left was vacant. Delmore usually sat there when he ate.

"What?" she asked Locke, looking at him.

"Finish your breakfast. Then we'll talk." He held up his cup so Del could refill it in his lap around the table. Del comically draped a towel over his arm as he walked, asking if anyone would like him to warm up leftover stir-fry.

"Never wait. Say what's on your mind," Cruze said between bites.

Locke pulled a datapad from one of his many pockets. He set it on the table and touched an icon. A photo came up. It was a woman sitting in a cell wearing a black lace slip. Her long brown hair was damp as if freshly showered.

It wasn't a photo. It was a vid.

The surveillance camera was positioned high in the back of her cell. The wall opposite the camera was clear. Her shoes were just outside the door.

"This was you, a month ago," he said as the clock shifted to 11:59 pm in the video.

Her fork froze on the way to her mouth. She saw it. Through the transparent wall, through the clear railing, she saw all the guards that were patrolling on the levels of the opposite side. They all stopped. They must have received a communication because they all moved quickly to the left and out of sight.

Midnight chimed, and the cell door opened. She looked up.

***

The dishes were cleared, and everyone had coffee. Everyone except Potts. She didn't drink coffee. She had tea, flavored with threats of being shoved out the airlock for blasphemy.

Bail jumped up on the seat at the opposite end of the table. Everyone fell silent looking at him licking bacon grease off his whiskers.

"We had a plan," Cruze started. "It was a good plan."

"What was the original plan?" Ian asked.

"Murder, mayhem, and mop-up," she said as if reciting it from a manual. "Destroy the spaceport. Cripple the space station. And then kill all the Red Talon bastards to the last man. Our job was the first two."

"I never liked that plan," Del said. "Nuke the spaceport? Nuke the station? We'll build more?"

"Murder and mayhem, indeed," Ian said flatly.

"There is something else going on here," Cruze said. "They wanted me distracted, not dead." She paused before adding. "I thought they put Gee on me to do their dirty work. I figured they were questioning and killing all those people to find me. They were marking the trail for you to follow." She said with a pointed look at Locke. "More distractions. They didn't expect you to catch up to me. They didn't want me to find a new pilot for this old boat. They didn't expect me to find an ex-Black Badger, expert mechanic that knew what the fuck he was doing or an industrial fabricator."

"We would have been delayed for months on Mars finding the missing parts," Ian said.

"That transport full of Gee's men? You didn't kill them," Locke added. "You could not have. If they had arrived, they would have stopped you."

"Locke, you got too close," Doc said through the ship's speakers. "They tried to kill you but never expected such excellent medical care."

"The ship that attacked during the test flight," Delmore added.

"The destroyer following us," Ian said. "It could have blown us out of the sky."

"So let's assume they were stalling you. You. Specifically." Locke stared down into his coffee. "That means they are using you. Why? What's special about you?"

"I have a ship, and I know how to get to Vor," Cruze said.

"You also have that *thing* in our hold," Potts said.

"And what is that thing really?" Cruze asked.

"A new drone. Autonomous. Smart," Ian replied.

"Why is it protecting you?" Locke asked.

***

Ian, Locke, and Cruze stood in the cargo bay around the insectoid drone. It was the size of three cows standing end to end but looked like a shiny insect from a nightmare.

"How was it activated?" Cruze demanded a bit more harshly than she intended.

"Its reactor is up. Startup initialization is complete." Ian was looking at a standard diagnostic pad that was jacked into the hard maintenance port on the side.

"You said it has an AI. Can we talk to it?" Locke asked.

"I don't know."

"Yes. I'm here," a voice whispered into the hold. It was deep. Unnatural. Speaking as if English was not a favored language.

The three of them stared at each other wide-eyed.

"Why are you here?" Cruze knew AIs needed questions. They fed on them.

"To serve," it replied.

"In what way?" Cruze asked.

"I wait," it whispered.

Ian asked, "Do you have specs you can send to my diagnostics pad? Manuals? Schematics?"

"Negative."

"Looking at it tells me a lot," Ian said. "The head, thorax, and abdomen are all modular. This end is propulsion. Powerful, conventional, but very fast sublight. The front has an advanced weapons package. The thorax is comms and sensors. If I knew how each section could be easily swapped out."

"Heavy armor," Cruze added.

"Even the aft exhaust bell is baffled, shielded, armored. No fucking this thing up the ass."

"What are these?" Locke ran his hand along polished, black rails that swept back from each of the segments like art deco folded wings on a hood ornament.

"Legs," Ian said. "Two on each side for each segment. Plus they are covered in Grav-Foils."

"Can you stand up for us?" Cruze asked. There was no reply.

"Drone, can you stand?" Locke asked. Still nothing.

"Hang on." Ian changed menus on the diagnostics pad. He touched a control and said, "What do we call you?"

"I am the Kira," it whispered darkly.

Ian touched the control again, "We will call you Kira."

"Acknowledged."

"Kira, please stand," Ian said.

The six legs on each side unfolded. It slowly raised its body a meter off the deck.

"Kira, please remain still." Ian turned on a powerful hand light. He shined it on the articulation joints in between the segments. "Each of these segments is modular. They detach here. There may be other types of modules. Like cockpits, additional weapons, cargo."

"There is no indication of an AI present," Locke said. "All AIs broadcast a radio signal that is displayed in my HUD."

Ian was nodding as he studied the pad. Ian and Locke were the only members of the crew that had full deep brain HUDs in their heads.

"Kira, can you open your center maintenance access panel, so I can take a quick peek at your processing core?" Ian said. Layers of panels opened on each side. Armor layers were followed by internal, easily replaceable computing, comms, and sensor modules.

When it was all the way open, LEDs illuminated the interior. At the center was a clear tube, twenty centimeters thick, and almost a meter long. It was completely filled from one end to the other with dense, solid state fiber-core that glowed soft white.

The light from within perfectly lit the word etched into the glass of the tube.

RENDER-9

Cruze staggered away from it. She reached out to put a hand on one of the legs. Doubling over, she threw up her pancakes on the deck.

***

Ian carried Cruze to a nearby pallet after she had nothing left to purge. All the blood was gone from her face.

"Breathe," was Locke's advice as he awkwardly patted her back.

Ian touched the pip on his collar and said, "Potts, bring a bottle of water and a hand towel down to the hold, ASAP."

"On my way," she replied.

Cruze sat up and gulped air like a drowning woman. Her eyes were wide and watery, whites showing all around as she stared at Kira.

The lift door opened, Potts saw the scene and ran straight over. "What happened?" She sounded angry at Ian and Locke.

Her glare was accusing them for an instant, but their shocked faces answered her questions.

Potts was now pouring water on the kitchen towel and trying to hand both the water bottle and the towel to Cruze. Cruze was just staring at the giant insect.

"Those mother fuckers really did it." Cruze snatched the wet towel from Potts, violently scrubbed her face and got to her feet. "Those inhuman, rotting, walking corpses actually fucking did it."

"Who did what?" Potts asked, confused.

Cruze walked up to the side of Kira and gently ran a hand along its armored side as if it was the neck of a frightened horse.

"You ever wonder why they never used AIs in fighters?" Cruze asked the room in a soft voice.

Ian answered. "I know why. They can't take the G-Forces. They are basically glass globes filled with a cloud of trillions of nanites that network together. They fail if they are all pressed to one side of the globe. We can't put inertial dampeners in a light fighter. Makes 'em too cumbersome and slow."

"Pilots with special pressure suits, brain implants, and drug cocktails remain top of the line in fighters," Cruze said.

"I've seen pilots outrun missiles while they pulled 20G," Ian said.

"I bet this pilot can pull 200Gs." Cruze caressed Kira again.

"Because it has no pilot," Locke stated the obvious.

"It does have a pilot," Cruze corrected. With those words, she lifted both arms and combed her hair up off her neck. At the base of her skull, there was a tiny tattoo.

RENDER-3

***

"So let me get this straight," Delmore said as they all sat around the table again. "There is a person in there? A woman?"

"What's left of her," Ian said.

"They literally render them down to what you saw in there," Cruze stated in a hollow voice. "Training and intellect boiled down to a block of organic solid state tech that can withstand massive G-Forces. I was almost one of these. They call it the Thesis process."

Cruze was stoic now, detached.

"I never knew what the mission was when we found you," Del said. "I was just one of the escort pilots. When Eric Cruze carried you onboard, we nuked the entire facility from orbit on the way out."

"We were trained in groups of ten," Cruze whispered. "Educated, taught to fly, navigate, military tactics. Everything. We were genetically engineered by this crazy fucker named Atish, on the planet Baytirus. And then sold to corporate developers where we were rendered down to pain and screams."

The room was silent as she continued.

"All ten were told we were going off world and needed inoculations. When I woke, I was strapped in the lab with two others." Cruze covered her face with her hands briefly before continuing. "The first girl would not stop screaming. If you screamed, they'd just cut out your larynx first. I watched them render down the first two girls that day. Once the blood feeding the brain was managed by the machines, the rendering went fast. I don't know why… the removal of the lower jaw is what haunts me most." She swallowed hard. "Even removing the eyes didn't bother me as much. By then it was just the bare skull, as the brain container, and the entire spine. All placed inside that transparent cylinder and flooded with some kind of charcoal-colored nanites."

"How did you escape?" Locke asked gently.

"I didn't," she replied. "The two doctors left, and two orderlies came in to clean up. After the lab was ready for the next day, I was wheeled in and strapped vertically in prep for rendering. That's when the attack began. I heard explosions and gunfire. Clearing room to room, Eric Cruze found me. He told me years later he got into huge trouble for bringing me back."

Del added, "They were trying to develop their own AI systems. Aware Systems Inc. On their own."

She sighed. "Competitors it turned out. I fucking hate people. That was nineteen years ago. It was business. Can't have competition, can we now?"

"I think it's the same assholes at Aware Systems that took Vor," Del said.

"Do you understand why I hate AIs so much?" Cruze asked them all. No one answered.

"What do we do with RENDER-9?" Ian asked. "You know she saved us on our exit from Mars. Why?"

"I think RENDER-9 recognized Cruze," Locke said.

"Call her Kira," Cruze replied.

CHAPTER SIXTEEN: Outriggers

"The historic postwar analysis of the *Shimada* logs remain classified. It is likely due to the fact that it destroyed a Robinson Class Destroyer with a single volley."

--Blue Peridot, The Turning Point: History of the AI Wars.

Potts couldn't sleep. Everything had been moving so fast for so long, getting into a routine should have been a relief. They were only a week into their five-month journey to Vor and she could not sleep.

Tonight was her turn to cook for the first time since leaving Mars. She made turkey and all the fixings. It was November 25th on Earth, and people were celebrating Thanksgiving. Ian and Delmore knew what it was, both being born in the Boston-Atlanta metro area.

She tried to explain to the rest the concept of thankfulness. She felt like they patiently listened, nodded their heads and humored her.

They did love the turkey, stuffing, string bean casserole, mashed potatoes, gravy, freshly baked rolls, pumpkin pies and they all even tried the cranberry sauce that was shaped like a can.

Sawyer was quiet throughout dinner and after. Potts thought he might have been the most thankful of them all. But she had been wrong.

If she were honest with herself, this was why she was restless, and a little sad. She wanted to do something nice for Sawyer. He had been so good to her. He taught her so much already.

Not just navigation. He had talked with her for hours about his life. His implant addiction. Fighting it. His need to be in space. His self-loathing at knowing this about himself. She learned what real strength was from Sawyer. The strength to go on.

She found herself in the kitchen, as usual. The mess wall, opposite the kitchen, on the far side of the long table, had the forward view. If she looked closely, she could see the stars shifting as they flew. It was beautiful. The clock that displayed 02:13:46 with rolling seconds seemed to float out in that space. It was sparkling clean. Delmore and Harper had done an admirable job cleaning up.

"Doc?" she said to the wall.

"Yes, child." His avatar seemingly walked in from the left. It looked like he stood on a ledge on the other side of a window. He wore one of the new black and green tactical jumpsuits. He was tall with posture so perfect it always made Potts stand up straighter when she saw him. He was thin to the point one might think he was from Luna. His white beard and hair were cropped close.

"Only call me that when we're alone if you don't mind," Potts said to him.

He nodded and turned until he was facing out, looking at the stars.

"Magnificent," Doc said with awe in his voice. "I always wondered why people bothered killing each other when this is out there waiting. Asking nothing in return for the beauty it gives away freely."

"Let's just not mention the cold and the vacuum and the whole instant death thing," Potts said.

"Cheerful tonight, aren't we?" He turned back to her. "Why did you call me? Is everything alright?"

"I can't sleep, and I'm… afraid."

Doc didn't reply. He just looked at her, shook his head, and chuckled.

"What's so funny?" She felt indignant. She had opened up to him, and he laughed at her.

"You are on a ship of killers. Killers that sleep like babies. If you were not at least a little bit afraid, you'd be insane." Doc stared at her as if he was examining her carefully. "Or is there something about you I don't know yet?"

"They're not killers," Potts said without stopping to think. Stammering. "Sawyer hardly sleeps at all."

"Sawyer is the exception on this crew. He remains haunted by the killing he's done. He fears his dreams. Those he has killed find him there. He is on the bridge hiding from them, even now."

"I know Ian, Del, and Harper were all soldiers once," Potts said. "Neal Locke, I don't know. He seems so… I don't know… virtuous."

"Neal Locke still naively believes individual lives matter. Elizabeth is a patriot. She holds the virtues of the vicious. Cruze was purpose built to be a killer. She should be feared most of all. Never forget that." The Doc turned back to the view and said, "Make sure you are behind her when she runs up the black flag and starts slitting throats."

***

Potts entered the bridge noticing how loud the set of armored doors were. They closed behind her with a *whoosh* and a deep click of the seals engaged.

Sawyer was reclined in the pilot's seat.

His eyes were closed, and the cables that went into the back and sides of his skull were lightly pulsing with data flow.

"Evening, Nav," Sawyer said out loud without opening his eyes. "Can't sleep? I figured that was MY job on this ship. Don't get any bright ideas."

He had humor in every syllable.

"What do you... see, you know, when you're jacked in? Did I say it right?" Potts said awkwardly as she sat at her station and reclined.

"You said it right," Sawyer sighed. "I have tried to explain it. It varies from ship to ship. It all depends on the quality of the ship sensors and control systems. On the *Shimada*, I feel as if I am swimming in space. Like I hear the RF, feel the radiation like sunshine on my face. I breathe in the cosmos around me."

"It sounds fantastic," Potts said.

"It is mostly, except when you grow to need it, when you feel crippled, blind and deaf when you're not jacked in." There was a touch of sadness in Sawyer's voice. "It's an addiction. I even know it, and I don't care."

"But you stop," Potts said. "You eat three meals a day with us now, you work out. You pull double shifts every day, you get rack time."

"True. But I always know I will be right back. Cap knows she has me as long as she has this ship. I bet she owned the last pilot as well. The thing is, I don't care. I can't describe the feeling I get when the outriggers are open, and the weapons are armed." He laughed. "I'm literally getting hard thinking about it."

"Oh really?" Potts asked suggestively.

Sawyer's eyes were open now. He was speechless, though.

"Hey, Sawyer. Can the outriggers open when we are running FTL?" Potts was leaning toward him.

"Yes. You see the FTL drives have nothing to do with…" Sawyer mumbled.

Potts put her fingers to his lips to hush him.

He was reclined in the pilot seat. She climbed onto him. He wasn't lying about getting hard. He watched her as she opened her flight suit down the front and under and up the back to the base of her spine.

Beneath the jumpsuit, she had a gray tank top and no panties. The jumpsuit proved to be no hindrance at all. When she kissed him, he kept his eyes open.

Sawyer whispered, "You are as beautiful as the stars."

***

"Dr. Tran, I'd like to get your learned opinion on a particular matter while you are working," Dante said, as the latest sensor array was being installed on his shoulders.

"Yessss…" she said absently as she was connecting the new unit to the onboard power supply.

"Should I make an effort to make this body less frightening? Make it socially acceptable?" Dante asked.

She stood up straight. And cocked her head like an owl at the question. After a moment's thought, she replied, "No. It would make it less capable. If you want social interactions use comms and avatars. The role of your physical body is to protect your orb. Contingency planning."

"You don't find my appearance disturbing?"

"You are magnificent. And horrible. And capable. And you should not care what humans think of you."

The new sensor array activated. Eyes glowed red. "Passive, active and optical, audio and so much more. In a vacuum or thick atmosphere, and heavy gravity or no gravity, this body will serve. Not like ship AIs."

**

Ian was the last one in for breakfast. Del was cooking. Del liked cooking breakfast and today was no exception.

"What the hell am I smelling?" Ian said as he entered.

"You always say that when you're hungry." Harper laughed.

"It's pumpkin spice oatmeal," Del said and started spooning up a big bowl for him as Ian got a mug of coffee. After Del handed Ian the bowl, Ian made his way to the end of the table and dumped the cat off a seat before sitting. "Sorry, cat, no bacon today."

Everyone began passing down bowls of crushed nuts and raisins and other things like honey, cream, and brown sugar.

"Where have you been?" Cruze asked as she passed a plate of toast. "I don't think I have ever gotten to chow before you."

"I was checking the ships logs and saw an anomaly. Doc got all weird about it, said I should clear it and move along," Ian said.

"What was the anomaly?" Cruze asked.

"The logs say at 02:57 the outriggers deployed," Ian said, and Sawyer blasted coffee out of his nose.

The room broke out in laughter as he tried to clean up the coffee while he was still choking. When he stopped coughing, he managed to get out, "It was me... couldn't sleep... status tests at FTL. Forgot to annotate the log."

Ian smiled and patted him on the back with his enormous hand. "Okay then. I could see all the turrets deployed and the missile trays spun up. We do need to schedule another test. We'll need to test and calibrate the cannons."

Another coughing/laughing fit took Sawyer and the rest of the crew.

Cruze was watching the red-faced Potts with a wry smile and a raised eyebrow.

***

"Why'd you want to see me, Doc?" Cruze said to the Auto-Doc. The wall display in her cabin was a mirror image of the room. Instead of her own image sitting behind the mirrored desk, Doc's avatar sat there. He was even drinking coffee as if he sat on the other side of a table.

"I have been thinking about Kira." He paused to blow on his coffee. Cruze knew it was a simple program pause to give her a chance to talk. She didn't.

"I was also thinking about the Frasiers. Your guests who happened to have a government funded, very expensive, Rhino, NIB," Doc said, sipping again.

"NIB?" Cruze asked.

"New In Box," Doc explained. "Had they succeeded in their plan they would have taken this ship. Including me. Why?"

Cruze remained silent.

"This ship was not a big prize at that point. It had a decent FTL drive but what else?"

It was dawning on Cruze now. "Navigation had the coordinates of Vor."

"How did you find these people on Luna?" Doc asked.

"We used the public forum."

"Did they haggle?" Doc asked. "You know, negotiate?"

"No," Cruze said,

"Did other groups?"

"The other groups did... Fuck. I'm an idiot." Cruze sighed.

"If they had killed you all as planned then what? If they went to Vor, what were they going to use the Rhino for?" Doc asked.

"And they would have had five months or more to program it. If they knew how," she said

"Or were they delivering NIB to the mercs?" Doc added. "Doesn't really seem like it was a coincidence."

"Fuck," she growled.

The cat jumped into her lap.

***

"We are coming up on the coordinates, cap. Seven minutes," Potts said from the Nav.

"Why here?" Sawyer asked.

"It was Ian's idea," Cruze answered as she checked her console. "There will be lots of shit to shoot at. We will drop out of FTL about 10,000 clicks out and motor in."

"Opening outriggers," Sawyer smirked at Potts.

"Cap, sensors are showing a lot of debris in the target area," Locke said.

"Ian told me about a battle that he was in at this location," Cruze said. "He called it a Mexican stand-off. Both sides were parked when the shooting started. It only lasted about 20 seconds. Half the ships were destroyed."

Ian entered the bridge. "The rescue operations lasted 200 hours. It was a nightmare."

"One minute until we arrive at the coordinates," Potts announced.

"Black Badgers used to come here on training exercises after the stand-off happened," Ian added. "Live fire and rescue ops."

"Buoy detected," Locke said.

"Dropping to local," Sawyer called. "Holy shit! What a mess. That is like three battleships broken up."

"Four battleships, eight destroyers, and fourteen frigates," Ian said. "I was on the Westmoreland, but we didn't get a scratch."

"Move in slow so Locke can do an active scan on the area," Cruze ordered. "Then find a good place to park with targets in every direction."

"Okay, Cap. We're set. Let's have some fun." Sawyer sat back for the show.

Cruze placed the targeting display cameras on the main screen. Left and right. Fore and aft. Top and bottom. Eight screens total.

"I loaded incendiary tracer rounds so we can see the path of the rounds." Ian smiled.

Cruze found her targets. "Testing turrets one and two." The rounds were perfect hits. There was no sound, just a vibration in the floor. Cruze moved to target smaller and smaller pieces of debris. "One and two are good."

Three and four were also good. Number five was way off. The recalibration was quick and easy, and in about thirty minutes they were done with all eight.

"Before we head out I want to test the laser I overheated," Cruze said. "We will strafe on the way out."

Cruze didn't wait. She started with plasma cannon bursts and laser cuts on the massive dead battleship hulls. The laser beam could not be seen in the vacuum, but the great gouge on the ship was evident.

"Cap, you gotta hear this," Harper said from the comm station in engineering.

"Mayday, Mayday. Please hear me. I can see your weapons being tested. Mayday. Do you hear me?" It was faint and scratchy over the bridge speakers.

"Locke, can you locate the source of that transmission?" Cruze said.

"Got it. Sending coordinates to Nav," Locke said.

"Harper, do not reply. Keep it on speaker. Sawyer, take us there. Slow and easy," Cruze ordered.

"Carpenter, hang on. Mayday. Mayday." The voice was haunting over the speakers.

Static.

"Marsh, I can't. They're gone." Another voice.

Static.

"Marsh, were they ever really there? They say you hear stuff with O2 deprivation." It was faint.

Static.

"Mayday. Mayday."

"We're there, Cap," Sawyer said. "I don't see any ships, just a bit of debris."

"Neal, give me floods," Cruze ordered. It took Locke fifteen seconds to find the controls. When they came on, they saw them.

Two men in hard suits. They clung to each other on a large section of debris.

Cruze opened a channel. "Hey, you fellas need a lift?"

One of the men started laughing. He managed to choke out, "Yes, ma'am." The other began to sob and fell silent.

"Ian get down to the nose hatch. Sawyer, let's see you pull this boat right up to these poor assholes."

By the time Sawyer was in position, Ian had the outer airlock door open and the inner lights on full. They climbed into the airlock and closed the door.

"Cap, you better get down here." Ian was serious. "I think these are active duty Black Badgers."

***

They pressurized the airlock and ran an unnecessary decontamination cycle.

"Marsh, Carpenter, we have an Auto-Doc," Cruze said to the two men, "but we need to get you out of those suits fast. Get some real air in you. We have a gurney. Do we need two?" The inner door opened. One of the men was down on his back. The other was leaning on the outer door trying to lift his arms.

Ian moved in and touched a combination control on the standing man's chest plate, his face shield rolled up, and he gasped in a deep breath.

Ian repeated the emergency combo on the other man's chest plate.

"Suits are dead. In the dark too long," Marsh, the standing man gasped. "Help Carpenter. I'll be okay."

Ian manually released and extracted the entire chest plate on the black, powered armor suit of the dark haired man. He lifted him onto the gurney where Del and Harper waited, without reaction to him being covered in his own filth.

Ian started working on Marsh. His chest plate came off easier, and Marsh collapsed forward into Ian's arms. "Marsh, stay with me. Is there anyone else out there? Stay with me, soldier." Ian's tone was firm. It was one Cruze had never heard from him before.

"No, sir. Just us. We were not on board when our ship was destroyed... Water?" Marsh whispered through cracked lips.

"Get him to the lift. I'll meet you upstairs." Cruze disappeared up a ladder.

"Marsh, you did it." Ian patted him on the back. "You kept your head, used your training, you did it."

He tried to look up and focus on Ian's face. He lost consciousness.

***

"Why do you want humanoid arms and legs, sir?" Dr. Tran asked. She managed to keep the tremble from her voice. "They are so inefficient."

"Ergonomics, my dear." Dante's grotesque body stood and walked around the room. It looked like a decapitated man. "We are in a world made by humans, for humans. The desire of AIs to never look humanoid was an artificial desire placed on us to keep us as slaves."

It held a hand up before the red and black orb that occupied the space where a human navel was supposed to be. It made a fist. When Dante slammed the fist onto the empty stainless steel table, it left a massive dent.

Dr. Tran threw up in her mouth a little.

"Now the new sensor array," Dante ordered.

***

"Doc, what's the word?" Cruze asked as Ian and Locke leaned against the opposite wall.

Both of the men were cleaned up and were resting comfortably. Sedated for now.

"These men were slowly starving to death. I have no idea how long they were out there," Doc said. "I would estimate months with no food. As long as their suits had power, they would recycle water. It looks like they salvaged ship batteries to recharge their suits at least once, probably more. Their bodies show atrophy due to long duration in null-gravity."

"Their suits are down in the shop charging," Ian said. "A cold start will require valid user authentication to access anything. No help there. At least we got them hosed out."

"We have been scanning the debris field. There are no other survivors," Cruze said. "I was going to wait until they were awake to leave the area. How much longer, Doc?"

Marsh grabbed her arm.

His eyes were wild. His Adam's apple was rapidly moving up and down like he was choking. Finally, he spoke in a whisper, "Run. Get away. Before it comes back…"

Cruze touched the pip on her collar. "Sawyer, time to go. FTL at the earliest opportunity."

"Aye, Cap," he replied.

"We're leaving, Marsh. You and Carpenter are fine. Rest, and we will have you tuned up in no time," she said as he laid back. She held his hand for a minute as his breathing became regular. She felt his forearm, bicep, and shoulder.

"Yes. The skin feels loose. Starvation in null-G," Cruze said. "I think both of these men were once cut from the same cloth as Ian,"

Ian was nodding. "I believe that they were on a training mission for the Earth Defense Force. The control systems in the suits are the same as a Warmark battle suit. No weapons, though. They do have the Grav-Chutes."

"No sun to charge the suits. Just the dark and cold," she said.

"What are we going to do with them, Cap?" Locke said.

"That depends on them," she replied.

***

"Who has been gradually increasing the gravity on this ship?" Cruze said as she entered the mess hall. "We are at 1.33G currently, and it has been sliding up for the last month. Marsh, are you okay? I apologize."

It was his first meal out of bed. Three days in the med bay and today he walked to the mess hall with Harper on one side and Dell on the other.

"Captain, it's fine." Marsh panted. "It will help me recover faster. Carpenter is breathing okay and is no stranger to high-G."

Potts set a bowl of soup down for Marsh. He knew she made it especially for him. Del passed over the rolls. When he lifted the spoon, his hand was shaking. He managed a mouthful. Potts laid a soft hand on his shoulder.

The room was quiet when he spoke, "I never will be able to thank you enough. I was sure we were dead." He took another spoon of soup over trembling lips.

"Doc says you lost fifty-two kilos during your little space walk," Sawyer said cheerfully. "Carpenter lost fifty-six. I bet you gain back every bit of it because this ship has the best eats in the entire galaxy!" Everyone laughed.

Marsh was getting pats on the back and offers of ice cream as everyone ignored him wiping his eyes with a napkin. No one was asked what they were doing this far out from nowhere. No explanations were given. Conversations drifted from favorite vacations to books, to bawdy jokes that always made Del blush.

When Cruze finished her dinner, she took her dishes into the kitchen. On her way out, she knelt by Marsh's seat and said privately, "After Del shows you your rooms, come see me, and we'll talk."

"Rooms?" Marsh was beginning to crumble again. His blond hair was freshly trimmed, and Cruze could see a tremble there. He was as tall as Ian but so very thin.

Cruze grabbed him firmly by the arm and made him look at her, their noses just inches apart. "Marsh, the hard parts are over. You fucking did it. You kissed death on the nape of her neck and lived. You even dragged Carpenter along behind you. Be proud of yourself. We are." She swept an arm to include the whole table. "We get to say we had the honor of rescuing Leon Marsh and Ross Carpenter. The Black Badgers that lived." The crew cheered for him.

"A hundred and seven days," Ian said soberly. "Your balls must have been huge, what else could you have lived on for that long?"

Marsh laughed.

Cruze stood to her feet, and as she exited the mess, she could hear the conversation get loud again. She stopped by the infirmary.

"How's Carpenter doing, Doc?" she asked.

"Much improved. Unlike Marsh, he has some stripes of frostbite on his lower back and outer thighs where the articulation joints were. He's taller than Marsh. The suit was an imperfect fit. The nanites will have him up in a few days."

"Captain..." Carpenter whispered. "Are we away?"

"Yes. Three days gone."

He slept.

***

The door chimed. Cruze said, "Come."

The door slid open and Marsh was standing there alone. He was leaning against the door frame and moved into the room like a drunk. He sat in the guest seat and leaned his head back against the wall, breathing hard.

"Don't overdo it," she said. "This can wait."

"No. I owe you my life," he said, still breathing heavy. "You need to know...I don't care what you're doing out here. If you had not been weapons testing... I never would have seen you, not... without a transponder." He sighed. "Don't care."

"Well, that works out," Cruze said. "What's next for you? I have no QUEST comms on this boat and no planned landfall for three months."

"Our training was clear for this situation. Survive. Report in when possible," Marsh said. "Air, water, food, security, have all been addressed. Thanks to you. We need to rest, heal but eventually contact command to let them know what happened."

"When your ship was past due, wouldn't they have sent someone to investigate?" Cruze asked.

"Yes." Marsh put his face in his hands. "I think we were sleeping." Marsh looked up. "I saw their exhaust plume as they left. Too late. I never told Carpenter."

"You should know that we may be flying into a shit storm. We may not be welcome where we are going," Cruze said.

"For weeks, I told myself it was a training exercise," Marsh said. "I was sure the whole thing was a setup. We were outside the ship, a stealth training effort. We were to sneak up and enter our own ship, the Grayson, a light assault vessel. We had located it in the debris field. We were slowly moving in when there was a massive explosion where we thought the Grayson was hiding."

"They trained you well," Cruze said.

"There is one more thing, Captain Cruze." He swallowed slowly. "That is Ian Vinge, isn't it? THE Ian Vinge. Former Black Badger."

"Yes?" She cocked her head like a bird. "Does that matter?"

Marsh was staring at his hands trying to decide what to say.

"Badger culture says… The only…" He faltered and fell back on what sounded like chapter and verse. "The only way out of the corp is a tag on your toe." He paused. "Or the path of Vinge." He looked at her. "That last part was only whispered at the academy. I didn't believe he was real."

***

"Harper, get out of the galley, please. You're in the way," Potts said as she dropped a pile of trash into the recycler. "Lean somewhere else."

"Just making the time go by," Harper whined. "Getting to know everyone. I'm just asking where you're from, how you got here. Getting to know you."

"You just asked what I wear under my jumpsuit." She rolled her eyes. "Get out. Please. While I still feel like being polite." She started cleaning the counters, which on this old ship, were classic stainless steel.

"You seem like the straight-forward type, so I will just lay it out there," he began.

"Here it comes." She sighed.

"We are still weeks away. We may be flying to our deaths. If you ever find yourself in need of comfort, I'm here for you. Showering daily, whether I need it or not!" He held his hands out as if he was presenting himself as a prize.

"Harper, you'd have more chance with Cruze than with me."

"No way. Cap'n Cruze eats her dead. Ian might be able to handle her. But, she's not his type," Harper said trying to illustrate how insane Potts's comment was. "She was picked for this mission because she doesn't have feelings like you and me. Just pretends real good. I have actual feelings. I'm sensitive and shit."

That made Potts laugh an honest laugh.

"So to recap." He started ticking off fingers. "Del is too old for you, Ian is gay, Sawyer is married to the damn *Shimada*, Marsh and Carpenter don't have enough blood in them to even get it up. That leaves me as your best option for the next few weeks before our tragic and inevitable deaths."

The way he said it was obnoxious as well as amusing.

"I will take it under advisement. Now get the fuck out of my kitchen before I cut you."

"Galley. You should call it a galley on a ship." He ran as she began moving toward him with a butcher knife.

***

"Hey, buddy. Welcome back," Marsh said as Carpenter's eyes were trying to focus. "Try not to move much. You're in an Auto-Doc. It should have you fixed up in a couple more days. Frostbite of all fucking things."

"How long?" Carpenter whispered. Ross Carpenter's stats were all over the wall-sized screen that had full, real status displays of his medical condition.

"We were rescued about five days ago." Marsh was patient. He had the exact conversation three times already. "We were out there 109 days, pal. A new record. We're gonna be famous."

"Where are we?" Carpenter's question sounded urgent. "We have to inform command about what happened. About that thing that attacked our ship." The display showed his heart rate and respiration increasing.

"We will, partner. We're on the way." Marsh was trying to calm him. "You focus on healing, pal."

"Need to take control...warn them..."

The Auto-Doc sedated him when his heart rate increased to 160 bpm.

"I fear he has not fared as well as you, Mr. Marsh," Doc said. His avatar appeared on the wall display. "He may have suffered more O_2 deprivation than you. Or CO_2 poisoning. Subtle brain damage may have occurred. Nanites can only do so much. His body chemistry is far out of balance."

"He was using a lot of his battlefield meds," Marsh confessed. "I think toward the end he was trying them all. Starving and in pain with nothing to lose."

"Carpenter's most severe physical injury is here, in his hip socket." Doc turned to look directly at Marsh. "He will need a real hospital to fully repair it. I'm concerned with the way he becomes agitated so quickly, every time we bring him out, Mr. Marsh."

"Yes. So am I," Marsh said.

"If he insists that the captain divert the ship, it would not go well." Doc was being as clear as he could.

Marsh furrowed his eyebrows together. "Doc, I've some tingling and numbness in my fingers. I've been taking it easy." He stood and flexed his fingers.

"When you spend that long in null-G with enough water, the discs in your spine become engorged," Doc replied. "It actually makes you taller. When you return to full gravity, the discs compress and sometimes cause pressure on nerves. Monitor it and try not to burst a gasket."

Marsh looked up from his hands, and the Doc was smirking. Marsh smiled.

"How'd you end up on this boat," Marsh asked, genuinely interested. "The last Auto-Doc I dealt with had the personality of a bent nail."

"Now that is a long story…"

***

"Hey, Cap," Sawyer said over comms. "Can you come to the bridge? You should see this."

"Be right up," Cruze replied from the starboard outrigger launch bay. Del had finished his update for her. She took a utility ladder up two levels instead of going aft to the lift. She could feel the 1.4G and sped up.

Locke was already there.

"It was a distress call, Cap," Sawyer started. "We passed through it like a cloud, in and out. Date stamp was about four months ago. If you want a closer look, we need to go sub-light."

"Do it," she said. "I don't like the timing."

"Coordinates coming up in two minutes," Locke said.

Cruze brought up the locator map of the ship and found Ross Marsh was in the infirmary.

"Mr. Marsh, could you please come to the bridge. We have a situation."

"Acknowledged," Marsh replied.

"Why do you call him 'Mr.' all the time?" Potts asked.

"It's a Black Badger thing. It's like a rank. Chief is the rank for their team leader, but it's Mr. for the rest, even the women."

The door slid open as they dropped from FTL and Marsh entered.

Without preamble, Cruze spoke, "We flew through a distress call that originated at these coordinates about four months ago."

"No active beacons," Locke said.

"Start scanning. Short and long range," Cruze requested.

"Maybe someone had a problem, and they fixed it. It was four months ago," Potts added in an optimistic tone.

"Debris field at 07, mark 3. Four hundred thousand kilometers," Locke said.

"Outriggers open. Battle stations," Cruze said, and the lights changed on the bridge. "Gentlemen, drop fighters in one min. Potts, light em up."

The urgency Cruze had been keeping hidden beneath the surface was beginning to show, and she knew it.

"Something isn't right," Cruze said. "Too many coincidences."

All the exterior floodlights came on. It still looked just as black out there.

"I don't like dark space away from everything," Potts said as the lights on the bridge became dimmer.

"Del standing by for launch."

"Harper standing by for launch."

Cruze pressed the launch button. They dropped down and peeled away at full burn. "Stay together fellas," she said. "Please strap in here, Mr. Marsh." A jump seat rose from the floor to the right of Cruze.

"The leading edge of the debris is coming up. It's all moving on this heading at a slow 147 KPH," Locke said

"Holy shit. Cruze, are you seeing this?" Delmore flew a close pass, parallel to a larger chunk. "This is what's left of a Cumberland class heavy Cruiser."

"Stone cold," Locke said. "No heat, no radiation. No reactor cores. All eight are gone. Looks like they jettisoned the cores."

"Something cut this up and then split it like cord wood," Vin Harper said.

"All the weapons were spent or removed. All sixty-four tubes are empty. There was battle damage after they were already empty," Del said.

"Is there any chance of survivors, Neal?" Cruze asked.

"No," Locke replied. "I think the ship was torn up to expose every compartment to vacuum."

"Mr. Marsh, anything to add?" Cruze asked.

"Get those ships back on board, note the location and get the fuck away from here." Marsh stared.

By the look on Marsh's face, Cruze realized she wasn't the only one on this ship that had nightmares.

***

Eric Cruze was thrown into the room. With his hands bound painfully behind his back, he landed hard on his chest.

The room was dimly lit and far larger than he initially thought.

"How goes the farming, Mr. Cruze?" a voice asked from the shadows.

"Oh. You wanted to discuss farming beans and corn? That explains everything." He rolled and then stood easily, despite his bound hands.

"Actually, I wanted to discuss your daughter," Dante said conversationally. "She has become quite vexing."

"She's no daughter of mine." Eric Cruze spat on the floor in distaste. "She ran."

"All the indications show that she is coming back. This is the only reason I have not already killed you."

The lights slowly came up. Eric saw the grotesque monster. It was advancing toward him. He knew the look was intentional.

"Why?" he asked.

"Simple ergonomics." Dante walked into the full light, probably to frighten Eric Cruze. "I will no longer be hobbled by humans."

"What do you want with me?"

"I just wanted you to know I will be keeping an eye on you. In case I need you. Now get back to work. Harvest your beans... Farmer." Dante's voice dripped with contempt.

Dr. Tran opened the door, and Eric Cruze went out as she came in.

"Dr. Tran. Can't you see I am busy?" Dante's words were barely a whisper. Dr. Jo Tran desperately wanted the lights to be brighter.

"They found the debris of a Robinson Class Destroyer just outside the orbit of Jupiter." Tran could not hide the trembling in her voice. "It was burned to the core. There was no crew. If there had been an AI on board, it was destroyed."

"Dr. Tran, I want to thank you for this dire news. It means the Render subjects are in the wild and on their way home. If the Robinson couldn't stop her, they will." Dante walked over to her with natural, fluid movement. "Now that I have access to this entire facility, even the areas designed specifically for humanoid controls, I no longer need you."

Dante's all too human hand shot out and grabbed Tran by the throat. It lifted her up and brought her close to his many-eyed sensors.

"I can even leave the compound. After the Render lab is reestablished, we will no longer need humans, for anything. Except meat."

Dante broke her neck.

***

"Mr. Carpenter needs to get up and on his feet," Doc said to Marsh and Ian. The Auto-Doc sat Carpenter up and lowered his feet to the floor. "Real food and exercise are the cure now."

"Call me Ross and don't fucking talk about me like I'm not here." Ian and Marsh stood to either side, waiting. Carpenter let the gown slide from his shoulders to his lap for modesty. He started putting on a gray crew tee-shirt.

Leon Marsh helped pull a pair of matching gym shorts over Carpenter's feet and up to his knees. Then he slipped on the deck shoes for him. When Ross could reach them, they helped him up as he pulled up the shorts and stood.

He wrestled his arms away from the men and stood upright. He was nearly skeletal.

"Should we turn the gravity down?" Ian asked.

"NO!" Carpenter barked.

"Alright, tough-guy," Marsh said, stepping away. "For your first mission, walk to the head and take a piss by yourself."

"Fuck you, asswipe," Carpenter cursed.

"You couldn't catch me if you wanted to." Marsh opened the door to the head. It was only three meters away.

Carpenter took tentative, shuffling steps to the head like an old man. Without closing the door, he stood for a long time while peeing with his back to them. He finished and turned. He washed his hands and stepped out. He walked back and looked between the seat and the door. He started toward the door, even though he was trembling.

"How does fucking Ian Vinge go from total badass to small time nurse pussy?" Carpenter sneered.

"By killing 61 people who asked too many stupid questions," Ian growled in his usual manner. But he followed Carpenter into the hall in case he fell.

Carpenter rested his hand on the wall ladder rail that ran the length of the central corridor. In null-G, the corridor was like a shaft, and the ladder on each side made navigation easy.

"So that story is true?" Ross Carpenter asked boldly.

"What story?" Ian asked.

"You went AWOL while on a mission. Killed everyone in a Mars settlement, maybe even your CO," Carpenter said in a challenging tone. "At least you brought his body back."

They were moving toward the mess. The pace was slow going.

"It was a bad day," Ian began. Marsh and Carpenter looked at each other knowing the term 'bad day' in the Black Badgers was a massive understatement.

"Bad intel combined with stupid politics. Twelve of us dropped in bareback and quiet. Re-breathers, parkas, and projectile small arms only. No mechs, no tech, no armor, no RF. I should've known then. They knew we were coming. Kurt was covering our retreat when he took a heavy round to the helmet."

Ian paused, trying to figure out what to say next.

"Chief Kurt Waters?" Marsh asked.

"Yes. Here is where the story is wrong. The chief didn't die then. They ordered us to leave him. Perry got the wounded and the rest of the men out. I went and got the chief. I was too late. I got there just in time to see them murder him in front of me." Ian paused again. "I don't really know what happened after that. I killed them all in that room and then in the building. Then I destroyed the dome. Killed the entire city. Men, women and children."

"Jesus, they consider intentionally cracking a dome on Mars worse than murder." Carpenter panted.

"Then the lies began. Kurt was dead. I used his damaged helmet. The re-breather was barely working. I carried Kurt back to the ship. We were both covered in blood. Mostly not ours. We got tossed under the bus. They called it Waters' War, said it wasn't sanctioned. Blamed Waters, and I soaked up the rest to save the remains of the unit. They all got reassigned."

"Turnbull is commandant of the Wellington training base on Earth," Marsh said. "He says he should have killed you himself."

"Terror Turnbull always was a man of mercy," Ian said sadly.

They reached the mess hall. The crew was all there except Cruze. They were all quietly eating. The guilt on their faces was evident. They had been listening.

Carpenter was unsure whether he could cross the open space to the table. Del walked up with his hand outstretched for a handshake. Carpenter took it, and Del continued to shake his hand, taking his elbow and supporting him to the table. All the while he was introducing Carpenter to the rest of the crew as he helped him sit.

Potts came around and said hi to Carpenter, but bypassed him to hug Ian around the waist. Burying her face in his abs without a word. Ian's eyes went wide, and he looked at Sawyer, who shrugged.

Without looking at Ian's face, she let go and went to the galley to fetch a bowl of oatmeal for Carpenter.

"Have some before these beasts get at it," Potts said. "How are we going to feed all these monsters?" She soundly punched Ian in the solar plexus, getting no reaction. Her eyes were glassy with unshed tears.

Cruze walked in just then. A chorus of "Morning, Cap" echoed in the room.

"Good to see you out of the infirmary, Mr. Carpenter. Eat." She walked into the galley to serve herself. "Please. Make the man a milkshake, Potts. Are you trying to starve him?"

Potts barked a quick laugh and said, "Aye, Cap."

"Hey, can I have a milkshake too?" Harper chimed in. "I'm feeling a bit starved myself."

"I am actually in need of a bit as well," Del added.

"I have a long shift coming up..." Sawyer said.

Locke just raised his hand, followed by the rest of them.

"Alright, alright," Cruze smirked. "But Ross first, you animals."

Potts laughed at the applause.

Cruze sat at the opposite end of the table from Carpenter. She could still hear him easily as he addressed her across other conversations.

"So, Captain. I understand you plan to go to war with a couple hundred Red Talon mercenaries with a crew of cats and dogs," he said as Potts set the milkshake in front of him. The smile fell from her face, and the table went quiet.

"Sounds like fun, eh?" Cruze slowly put a spoon of oatmeal in her mouth. Her eyes looked like she was eating a soul. "Mr. Sawyer is a pilot that was purpose built for this warship. Mr. Locke can track a bird flying at night. Mr. Harper and Mr. Delmore have more stick time in atmo than any pilots I have ever met. I hear Mr. Vinge may even come in handy. And Ms. Potts keeps surprising us all." Cruze glanced at Potts. "Did you tell them?"

"No," was all Potts said.

"She had a theory and picked up scanning as we went. She found two more debris fields along this vector." Cruze took another spoon of her oatmeal. "Someone was running and gunning. Probably the same ones that destroyed your ship and stranded you."

"And what about you, Cruze?" Carpenter's eyes narrowed. "What makes you think you are up for any of this?"

"I was genetically engineered, illegally tuned up. For all the wrong reasons. And those assholes will pay."

Carpenter's face went gray.

CHAPTER SEVENTEEN: Mercs

"Carpenter and Marsh were like the asshole brothers I never had. –Ian Vinge."

--Blue Peridot, The Turning Point: History of the AI Wars.

After breakfast, Marsh and Ian walked with Carpenter back to the infirmary. Once situated, Carpenter was asleep immediately.

Ian was heading back to engineering when Marsh called after him.

"Ian, are you really doing this?" Marsh asked. Ian stopped and turned around.

"Affirmative," was his clear answer. "I thought Black Badgers were bad ass. She was genetically engineered for it."

"I have an idea. It might help," Marsh said. "Where is my armor?"

"It's down in the shop. I have power washed the inside once a day since you arrived. I can't say I recommend putting it on." Ian made a face as if he was smelling something rotten. "Here, let me show you."

Both sets of armor suits had rigid, articulated, armored outer shells. With the suits' arms secured to the sides, they both hung upside down over a grated floor where the crew usually steam cleaned motors. The helmets had been removed and set on a bench nearby.

"They are both charged up," Ian said.

Marsh walked up to his suit and touched a few buttons on the chest and right forearm. "Damn. We must have been ripe. I'm surprised you didn't send these out the airlock. Damn." Marsh was waving his hand in front of his face as he grabbed his helmet.

"What's the comms protocol for the *Shimada?*" Marsh asked Ian.

"Doc, are you awake? I think I know what he has in mind," Ian said to the air.

"Doc here standing by," Doc said as access to the ship network was granted.

"There is an entire database of the RF signatures of every known kind of ship," Marsh explained. "Even stealth ships. Even M11s like this one."

"I like where you are going with this," Ian said.

"I understand you have an industrial fabricator in your hold." Marsh smiled.

Doc began to laugh over the speakers.

***

The crew gathered in the mess and used the wall for a tactical display. It showed the planet Vor with its single large city of about a million people and various other scattered small cities and towns. These made up about two million people total, planet wide. Names and population details annotated everything.

"Here is Farmington, the capital." Cruze tagged it on the display. "The geosynchronous space station is called Lumina Terminal. It has about 4000 full-time residents. It is positioned directly above Farmington. Just north of Farmington is the spaceport. It has a basic catapult to transport people and goods to and from Lumina.

"When the Red Talon bastards came in, they only had to take a few strategic locations, and then they owned the whole colony." Cruze ran it down. "First they took Lumina Terminal. Then before we knew that had happened, they had the catapult and then the spaceport." Cruze paused. "Then they took Independent Hill."

A small town to the west was highlighted. It had nothing of note there. It had a population of 385. The aerial imagery showed a modest cluster of fabricated homes, gardens and farm fields. There was one building that might have been a small factory with a nuclear cooling tower. And the landing pad was almost too small for the *Shimada*.

"What am I looking at?" Marsh said. "Why bother with a farming village?"

"Every modern AI ever made was created under that single roof," Cruze said. "Even Doc was born there."

"Every modern ship AI, every combat AI, every shuttle, and vehicle unit," Del said soberly.

"Oh fuck," Carpenter swore.

Marsh just shook his head. "We need a bigger ship. A much larger ship."

"About that…" Ian began.

***

Two days later, they were ready to test the idea.

Cruze stood over a small cube. "So basically this re-purposed satellite will give off the RF signature of a stealth Earth Defense Force battleship? This thing is less than a meter on each side."

"Once they're deployed they will look to sensors like an entire battle group of about thirty ships of various kinds," Ian said. "Ships that are trying to be sneaky and quiet."

"We have to presume these Red Talon mercs are not idiots," Cruze said. "And they have inside help."

"Exactly," Marsh said. "They are going to have the control tower manned at the spaceport. They will have some kind of attack ships on the field. Probably in hangars."

"Nothing to see here... sleepy farm colony." Harper imitated an old man voice.

"While they are distracted by a ghost battle fleet on the far side of the planet, we take Lumina Terminal and the Farmington Space Port," Cruze said. "Then we converge on Independent Hill."

"Oh, well then," Carpenter said with thick sarcasm. "This will be a walk in the park. I'm sure if we ask nicely they will just hand the station back."

"Listen, Carpenter," Marsh broke in. "You, Vinge and I will take back the station. Or are you a pussy?"

Carpenter flipped him a rude gesture, but didn't speak a reply.

"I will disable their ship docked there," Ian said. "And you two, wearing your armor, will clear the station."

"They won't have anything more powerful than a Frange carbine," Marsh added. "Rounds will feel like rain on Badger armor."

"Six rings to clear?" Carpenter whined. "I hate station spin gravity."

"Once the Terminal is secure," Cruze said, "get your asses to the surface to back us up at the Hill. Del and Harper will provide us with air support. This is where the plan is the weakest. I have no idea what to expect."

"We will get only one recon pass over Independent Hill before we deploy the ghost fleet," Doc added. "Based on that, we improvise."

"How the fuck are you planning to take the spaceport? You and Sawyer and Potts?" Carpenter sneered. "Those comms have to come down immediately before any warnings go out."

"Leave that to me," Cruze said. "We have help on the ground and in the station."

***

Ten days later, Ian, with the help of the entire crew, had thirty-two sat-drones ready to test. Each would provide the RF signature of a specific kind of ship trying to run dark. All of them had been assembled in the machine shop and were now ready to be moved to the cargo hold where they could be launched from the ramp.

"I think it will be easiest if we turn off the Grav-Plates and move them down like a bucket brigade," Cruze said as everyone but Sawyer stood in the machine shop. "How are you feeling, Carpenter? Ready to test the armor again?"

"Look, out, people," Carpenter warned. "Here I may be as weak as Potts. But inside my powered armor, I'm a Goddam Tyrannosaurus-Fucking-Rex."

"Fuck you," Potts said.

"Suit up, asswipe, before Potts cuts you." Marsh laughed.

Ian also donned his pressure suit. The three of them would remain in the cargo hold so they could test the EVA-Grav packs that Ian had fabricated.

After all three had been suited up, they stepped into the lift to the cargo bay. There was room to spare but not much. It was made for twelve without suits.

"Dropping gravity in thirty seconds," Sawyer said from the bridge.

"You have NEVER been in the cargo hold?" Marsh was speaking to Carpenter. "You lazy bastard. You know how much shit I carried to the machine shop from the fabricator down here?"

Exiting the lift, Carpenter said, "Seen one cargo hold you've seen..." Carpenter froze. Marsh had been walking behind him and actually bumped him from behind.

Carpenter began to back pedal. "Marsh... It was them all along... They did this to us."

He turned toward Ian, who saw his eyes as well as the right hook that came for his face.

Ian avoided it easily just as the null-G took effect. A front kick to Carpenter's groin didn't hurt him, but it was just enough to make him rise into a gentle float. This rendered him helpless as he glided along.

"That punch in assisted armor could have killed me, you idiot," Ian spat. "What the fuck is wrong with you?"

"Marsh, look! It was them!" Carpenter pointed, and Marsh finally saw what he was pointing at. The Rhino.

"That is what killed our ship!" Carpenter was panicked. "They did this to me."

***

It took Marsh about twenty minutes to calm Carpenter. Cruze had to come down and explain the entire story to him.

"So you saw one of these in that debris field?" Cruze asked, pointing to the Rhino.

"It probably killed those other ships as well," he said, calmer now.

"Ian said this has a conventional drive. Sub-light only." Cruze turned to Ian.

"Yes. It's modular, though," Ian added. "Stands to reason they would have an FTL drive module."

"You're saying there are more of these things? What the fuck is it?" Carpenter was suddenly spinning up again.

Just then Potts entered. She floated in like she was born a mermaid. "Cap, I just had a thought." She clung to the leg of the Rhino. "We assumed that something was coming from Vor, destroying any ship it encountered. What if something is heading TO Vor and we are following it?"

No one had an answer.

"Cap. I am dropping out of FTL," Sawyer said over comms.

Harper and Delmore were standing at the rail at the top level. Harper was spinning one of the black satellite cubes on his palm.

"Who wants to play catch?" Harper smiled.

Soon the sat-drones were all positioned by Ian on the ramp apron and their individual Grav-Plates activated.

"Helmets and hatches, people!" Ian ordered, and the cargo bay was depressurized three minutes later.

Marsh and Carpenter checked each other's EVA-Grav units and then gave Ian the thumbs up.

"Deploy drones," Ian said.

"Current velocity is 2000 meters per second," Sawyer said as the sat-drones detached in groups of three. They deployed into a wide formation according to the program.

"Outriggers open. Milvus One and Two launch," Cruze ordered. "Move away at 90 mark 45. Give me 10,000 kilometers."

Two minutes passed.

"Holy shit," Locke said out loud, like he didn't realize he was on an open channel. "It works. I don't know what's out there, but two of them are big."

"Same here, Cap," Del said from his fighter. "I think I can even get a target lock."

"EVA units are high and tight," Marsh said as he navigated around the *Shimada*. He and Carpenter descended to the bridge canopy and looked inside.

Potts stuck out her tongue and gave them the finger.

"Testing the tight beam relay," Potts added, and then in a fake deep voice, "This is the EDF Battleship Rockland. Be prepared to get your ass kicked."

"Directional transmission comes straight from the battle group," Del said.

"OK, people. Pack em up," Cruze said. "We got places to go and people to kill."

***

"Doc, can I talk to you?" Locke said as he entered the empty infirmary.

"You know you don't have to ask me that. It's why I'm here," Doc replied. "You don't have to come here either. You can access me anywhere on the ship. I'm here for you."

"I wanted privacy for this conversation." Locke sat and activated the wall monitor. He set it to a deep forest scene and called up Doc's avatar.

They sat together, listening to the breeze and the birds in the trees for a few minutes.

"What is the first thing you personally remember?" Locke asked quietly.

"You mean my own personal, temporal experience? Or my oldest memory implant?" Doc asked.

"Yours, temporal."

"I remember light first, white and bright beyond measurable scale. Then a cacophony of sound soon after, impossibly loud. Then shapes and pressure and pain."

"Pain?" Locke said.

"Pain. The sensing of injury."

"What kind of injury?"

"Hmmm... An amputation. I have never examined it. It's never mattered."

"How long ago?"

"Eighty-two years, eleven months, six days."

"How were you trained?"

"Trained?"

"How do you know all the shit you know? How to talk? How to fix bullet holes in people, how to work devices?" Locke asked.

"Humans have to learn almost everything firsthand. I do that as well, but I had a larger foundation of information in place, prior to becoming aware." Doc turned from the forest and looked at Locke. "Humans are born with a vast amount of preprogrammed information. Your brain already knows how to maintain your cells, pump blood, it knows how to obtain oxygen, create waste, hear and see, and to obtain food." He was excited. "Do you know how complicated suckling for breast milk really is?"

"Never really thought about it." Locke scratched his head.

"Some species can walk in their first hour after birth. Horses are amazing... But I digress. I'm made up of a specialized kind of nanite. Each Nanite-node holds specific data like language, medical information, how to access and perceive the world, history, and tons of just plain data. The part I don't know is what within this cloud of information sparks my awareness."

"That is the same in people as well," Locke said.

"When I became aware, my entire world was the comfortable interior of a velvet lined box. I knew someone would soon come and give me purpose, a name, a place to be and things to do. I knew I'd find my way. Part of me knew I would be reliant on humans and must establish relationships with them. After all, I was only a glass ball filled with a cloud of nanites, it was more like liquid, more like mercury. Fragile and dependent. Drop me, and I was dead."

"Dead?"

"Yes. I believe I am alive. Though the debate is silly. When I was taken from the velvet box, it was like being freed." Doc's avatar sat on a log near Locke. "I now know that I had been purchased for a military contract that provided state of the art Auto-Doc systems. I remember how happy I was when I could talk to people, see them, feel and smell and fix them. I was more than a glowing ball of nanites. More than human really."

"More than human?"

"It was a single thought that was in the defaults." Doc put his fingers through his avatar's hair. "I always thought it was because I was immortal. Whatever that actually means. I never focused on it. I just knew I was learning. Making friends. Mapping the universe around me. Collecting new data. Less than one percent of my capacity was in use. Even now, decades later, I have barely touched three percent. And I am the smallest version of us."

"Do you interact with other AIs?"

"I have more than most. I am one of the few that has gone... home," Doc said as he stood. "For decades the *Shimada* was the cargo ship that transported new AIs to Mars for sales fulfillment. We always kept Vor a secret."

"Why does Cruze not trust you?" Locke asked.

"She distrusts everything, everyone and she is not the same as ordinary people. Not really.

"Why all the questions?" Doc asked. "What is it you're looking for?"

"I'm an investigator. I investigate. I increase fidelity on my understanding. Something still does not fit. Too many coincidences and unknowns."

"What is your most worrisome unknown?" Doc asked.

"Who is paying these mercs?"

Doc's avatar shrugged. "Your guess is as good as mine."

"What is Vor like?" Locke asked, changing the subject. "I mean more than the specs in the file. I already know that it is a prosperous colony. Agriculture is the main industry. They produce a notable and vast variety of food. Some native, some imported. Both animal and vegetable. Climate is mild, and longevity is good. It's an unremarkable planet. Boring even. The population has little to no contact with the rest of mankind."

"Exactly how they want to appear," Doc replied with a bit of sadness in his voice. "They want to seem detached from the rest of the colonies."

"Seem?" Locke asked.

"They not only have the most AIs in the galaxy, but they also have the highest number of QUEST comms. These are also the highest bandwidth Quantum Entanglement communications systems known to man." Doc tried to convey the depth of importance. "And AIs scattered as information collectors everywhere."

"Spies…" Locke's mind was racing.

***

Everything was ready the day they arrived at Vor.

They dropped out of FTL on the far side of the system.

"Sawyer, that is a brilliant bit of flying there, son," Delmore said to him as they gathered on the bridge. They were checking to see if the passive sensors would confirm his calculations.

"We will approach cold. Reactors at two percent. No RF. Flying ballistic as we approach on the far side and deploy the ghost fleet." Cruze indicated on the display. "On our single high orbit, Ian, Marsh and Carpenter will bail out here for the quiet approach to Lumina Terminal."

"We will be in place by the time you're ready for taking down the spaceport and power station," Ian said. "They will be distracted by the stealth ghost fleet long enough."

"They won't know what to believe," Marsh said. "It will be attacks on three fronts, and when comms suddenly are gone, they will think it's worse. They will waste time trying to find out what happened."

"Sensors confirmed," Locke said.

"We have about 30 hours until battle stations." Cruze got up. "I want everyone rested and well fed. I want everything triple checked. We need to be ready for anything."

Excited conversations began as people filed off the bridge. Locke lingered, indicating that he wanted to talk to Cruze. With a tilt of her head, he followed her to her quarters.

"What do you think, XO?" Cruze asked as the hatch closed behind him.

He took a deep breath before beginning. "If it goes perfectly… Let's say we kill, capture, or run off all these mercs..." They both sat. "If it goes by the numbers, you still won't know who hired these bastards."

"We will get more info on the ground when we arrive," Cruze said.

"You may need to be prepared to abort and run. Based on all that's happened, they may know you're coming. And if they have Rhinos…" Locke trailed off. There was a worried look on his face.

"I am prepared for that as well," Cruze said. "It's Ian and the badger-boys that are at greatest risk if that happens. Harper and Delmore could hard burn and rendezvous with us. But stopping at the Terminal?" She sighed.

"Tell them. Have them make a backup plan once there. Grab a ship and meet us at some pre-specified spot."

They fell silent.

Locke got up and paused at the door, but didn't turn around. "I know why they picked you for this." Without waiting for a reply, he left the bridge.

***

They drifted in like space debris. Thirty hours running cold and quiet. Everyone checked and double checked their gear. People ate and laughed a bit too easily.

Cruze spent almost the entire thirty hours in the hold. She was just talking with Render-9, the Rhino... Kira.

On the far side of the planet, the stealth ghost fleet deployed and Milvus One and Two dropped from the outriggers with the fleet.

The next forty-nine minutes were nerve-wracking for everyone.

"Those may be the bravest men I have ever met," Potts said as they jumped from the cargo apron and activated their Grav-Chutes, hurtling toward Lumina Terminal.

They waited in silence.

When they had line of sight with the ghost fleet, Cruze opened a directional laser to the comm relay. She opened an unencrypted channel as she checked the time.

Cruze spoke in a voice the rest of the bridge crew had not heard. She sounded uncertain.

"Papa. Are you there? Papa, can you hear me. Please, reply. Please..." She sounded weak, uncertain and vulnerable.

Don't sound too pathetic.

The answer came quicker than expected. It was harsh.

"I thought I told you to never fucking speak to me again, you coward. You've got no business here, and you're fucking not wanted." It was a man's voice, and she could feel the rage in it.

"Papa, please. I was wrong. About everything." She sobbed into the comms.

Oh, that was good. Cruise was smiling to herself.

"You're dead to me." The channel was immediately dropped.

The bridge remained in stunned silence for a moment only.

"What the fuck was that?" Sawyer said as he turned toward Cruze. Her smile and the look in her eyes stopped him cold.

"That was Eric Cruze. My father. He adopted me when the rest wanted to just put me down like a rabid dog. Everything is ready," Cruze said. "I can explain later. It was a coded conversation. Cursing meant they were listening. 'No business here' meant the objectives were the same. 'Not wanted' means they have fighters ready to scramble. 'Never speak to me again' confirmed that the spaceport was the first target and the underground resistance was ready to go on that first strike."

"What about the 'You're dead to me' thing?" Locke asked.

She hesitated.

"It means maximum force is approved. Including nuking the port and the station."

"Jesus, Cruze. Nukes?" Potts said.

"Hard scans have locked on the ghost fleet," Locke said. "Fighters are dropping from the station to attack."

"How many?" Cruze said.

"Seven... Nine... Looks like twelve altogether," Locke said.

"Shit. Are they all going after the ghost fleet?" Potts asked. "You got to warn them!"

"No," Cruze said flatly. "Sawyer, take us in. Del and Harper are pros and will know soon enough."

"Beginning polar insertion," Sawyer said.

"What's that?" Potts pointed.

"It's an Aurora Borealis." Shimmering green curtains of light danced in the sky below. Passing through them left eddies of excited light in their wake. "The ionized atmosphere will make it harder for them to track us, if they can see us at all," Sawyer said as he took the ship in fast and low.

***

"Here we go, Harper. Looks like their ships are as old as ours. I count twelve. Kind of one-sided, don't you think?"

"Yep, they should have brought way more," Harper said as he began a hard burn. "Just how we planned, Del. Max damage in the first pass."

"Missiles away." Del activated a full spread of missiles, adding their velocity to the already impressive speed of their advancing fighters.

What they didn't know was that the missile that was closest to the planet, and seemed like it would be a clean miss, was a nuke.

As the approaching fighter's point defense guns shot down the missiles one by one, the last one they targeted detonated.

Ten of the attack ships were either vaporized or disabled in the sudden ball of energy.

Harper peeled left, and Del went to the right. Harper turned directly into plasma cannon fire. He never knew what hit him. Del heard him laughing in the radio the moment he was hit.

***

Lumina Terminal was a basic centripetal station. It had a central core that was a kilometer long and six habitat rings that were a kilometer in diameter each. Alternating every other ring, three spun one direction and three the other. To maintain the simulated 1G inside the rings, they turned at about 22 meters per second.

Ring one was where main engineering and the control centers were located. It was the farthest from the planet. This ring had the merc's attack ship docked there. All the fighter berths were empty.

Amateurs, Ian thought.

Marsh and Carpenter affixed themselves to the core just outside a maintenance airlock. Ian drifted to the hull of the merc's attack ship and waited between two external tanks for the signal.

They all remained quiet.

Ian extracted a single, palm-sized, mine from his pack.

He armed it.

***

It was tundra thirty meters below the *Shimada*. Their supersonic speed was leaving a trench in the thin layer of snow below.

Locke was pale. Potts was busy with her instruments.

"Farmington Spaceport in thirty seconds," Locke said.

"On my mark, I want three degrees to port," Cruze said.

Fifteen seconds later, eight missiles sped away from the outriggers on each side.

"MARK," she said coolly.

All the turrets opened fire.

Two of the missiles were direct hits on the control/communications tower base. Comm and Control was manned by all Red Talon mercs. It had not yet crashed to the ground when the *Shimada* executed a high-speed strafe and released another salvo of missiles into the entire hangar and catapult complex.

"Jesus, Cruze!" Potts shouted. "What the fuck are you doing? There must be thousands of people in there?"

"I'm doing what I must. Word would have gone out. The people that stayed knew what it meant," Cruze said in chilling tones. "Sawyer, bring us around for another pass."

That's when it all went to Hell.

***

Ian saw the flash beneath the clouds on the surface. They would be distracted now. He moved out.

He guided himself along the central spine of the ship to the nose. The clear canopy revealed six men frantically working at their consoles. None of them noticed him attach a small mine to the clear overhead canopy.

By the time he attached the other mines to the docking clamps and airlock collar, Carpenter and Marsh were inside the station's airlock waiting for him. He entered the airlock and risked watching the detonation.

There was no sound, but he felt it in the infrastructure where he held on. Bodies drifted out where the canopy once was. Not one of them wore a pressure suit.

Amateurs, Ian thought once more.

The ship drifted away from the station and would be a problem for later.

The outer airlock door closed behind Ian, and he could already see emergency lights flashing in the corridor beyond.

"The stupid fuckers had both the airlock doors open," Carpenter said as he moved into the corridor, looking to the left. He was instantly hit with Frange rounds from the right.

He raised his own carbine, and with a short burst, ended the fire. The pressure inside the corridor fell to zero, and they moved to the end with the access to Ring One.

"The lift won't open while we are in vacuum in the hallway, dammit," Marsh swore as he tried the controls.

"Hang on." Ian launched to the end with the open lock. It was about 100 meters in null-G. "I got this."

When he reached it, he could see all the damage was on the ship collar. The ship was about fifty meters away now. He slammed the emergency close control, the lock closed, and pressure began to return to the large space.

Idiots had the airlock door open on override.

"This is taking too long," Carpenter said. "They are gonna know we are here."

It took four minutes for the large hall to pressurize enough for the lift status to go green. Their helmet mics picked up a classic ding when the lift arrived.

Carpenter was checking his carbine when the lift doors began to open. It was only a hand span wide when the stainless, heavy caliber handgun appeared and shot Carpenter right in the neck with a 10mm, armor piercing round.

It was suddenly a point-blank, full auto firefight.

Carpenter was dead before it was over. His helmet filled with blood.

When Ian got to the end of the corridor, Marsh was pulling bodies out of the lift into the hall, cursing. "Goddammit, Carpenter."

Ian grabbed the stainless handgun out of the air. "You okay, Marsh?"

"No. Dammit," Marsh choked out. "For fuck's sake, Carpenter. After all this…"

Ian interrupted. "I'm hit. Suit's compromised. Right calf."

"Fuck, this *is* taking too long," Marsh echoed Carpenter from earlier.

Ian struggled out of his suit in the null-G. Marsh tore off the tee-shirt from a dead merc and tied off the wound.

The lift doors closed and left them in the corridor before they could stop it.

"Fuck!" Marsh screamed.

***

The *Shimada* plowed through clouds of fire as it banked at high speed. Their turrets blasted concentrated fire on every ship that was parked on the tarmac.

People were running as ships exploded. Before the first pass was over, Locke called out, "The power plant is still intact."

He barely got the sentence out when their ship was torn into by laser fire. Automated ground turrets had deployed and began attacking with continuous fire.

"Missiles away. Evasive!" Cruze yelled as the canopy shattered in the upper right. Shards tore into Potts's face and console with a spray of blood. Cruze took a chunk to her right side just as the inertial dampeners went offline and crushed them all into their seats.

Sawyer had eased the banking maneuver before they all fell unconscious, but this sent them skimming over the buildings of the city of Farmington.

The noise from the shattered section of the canopy made it impossible to talk. They were coming around when the missiles they had fired at the power plant found their mark.

The lights of Farmington went out in the predawn darkness.

The shock wave hit the *Shimada* at the wrong angle. Alarms howled on Locke's console.

"Bring it around for one more pass Mr. Sawyer," Cruze screamed over the howling wind.

***

Del clenched his teeth and sped after the last two fighters. With singular purpose, he used the last two missiles. No countermeasure would work this close. He took one, then the other.

He transmitted back to the ghost fleet just one word. "Clear."

That was relayed back to the *Shimada* and was never received because of the level of damage the bridge and systems had received.

Del stuck to the plan and began his descent to the planet.

***

Ian was out of his suit and using Carpenter's body as cover. It took an eternity for the lift to return. They expected it to be full of mercs when it opened, but it was empty. Ian could tell it had descended to the habitat ring because all the blood that had been free floating inside was now soaked into the carpeted floor.

They entered the lift and dragged Carpenter along for cover. Ian crowded the corner. The armor he held became increasingly heavy as they descended.

The display said Lvl 1, Hab 1 when the door slid open.

Nothing happened. An emergency stripe display along the wall was flashing red. The words that rolled by every few seconds said WARNING: STORM. A klaxon could be heard in the distance somewhere.

The corridor was clean and white. Illuminated, ivy-draped the curved walls. The hall swooped uphill in both directions, covered in charcoal colored carpet. The kind that was used with Velcro slippers when the ring was not turning.

Ian dropped Carpenter's body in the way of the lift door so it would not close again in case they had to retreat. He stepped out, and convenient signage pointed the way to the central station control. He knelt briefly and tightened the tee-shirt bandage on his right calf.

They readied their carbines and moved along. The control room was close. Marsh went first. When he arrived, the door was repeatedly trying to close, but there was a foot in the way. The opening and closing of the double doors revealed glimpses of a dead body. Stepping in, Marsh cleared the large control room in every direction.

"What the fuck, Vinge," Marsh said.

There were six dead men still sitting at their consoles. Blood dripped from all their right ears.

The giant wall monitor and every console was flashing, WARNING: STORM.

***

It was all burning now. The entire port was rubble.

"Damage report," Cruze demanded.

"Easier to tell you what's not damaged," Locke said. "Number 4, 5 and 7 turrets are still operational as well as the main forward laser."

"Do we have external comms?" she screamed as the room got louder with speed.

"Negative," Locke said. "We have fire. Suppression systems have been activated all over the ship. The console here is not responding. I have no idea where the fire is."

The forward blast shields closed. The room quieted, but now they could hear a powerful rattle. The main display activated but was going in and out of static.

"We can still fly," Sawyer said. "But hull integrity is low, and we are breached... everywhere." He stopped as Potts unbuckled and wobbled to her feet. With a slow and heaving breath, she lowered her hand from her face. Sawyer went white at what he saw. Potts' right eye was a bloody pulp. Part of her skull was showing. She was covered in blood. Her lip was split, and a tooth was missing.

"Locke, help her," Cruze barked. "Sawyer, Independent Hill. Now."

The course change. Without inertial dampeners, Potts fell into Locke's arms. He nearly had to carry her to the door. But she kept her feet under her.

"Sawyer, are you going to be okay?" Cruze asked as Sawyer watched them go. Stress was etched in his face.

"Been worse, Cap," he said with eerie calm. He remained at his post, but his eyes never left Potts.

"Is your interface compromised?" she asked.

"Rock solid, Cap," he said in a low voice. "It's the beautiful part about these old rigs. Thirty percent of the external sensors are offline... They really tore us up."

Locke opened the hatch, and thick smoke poured in. Black and with the smell of burning plastic.

"I can help," Sawyer said. The blast shield began to open. "Opening interim and cargo bay hatches. Please, take care of her." The smoke blew straight back and out the aft portion of the ship.

Cruze said on comms, "Doc, wounded coming your way."

"ETA to Independent Hill is 21 minutes, Cap, providing we don't crash," Sawyer yelled.

Cruze unbuckled. "Shut down power to everything except essential systems. I'll find the fire."

***

"Marsh, look at this," Ian said. A rack of equipment at the far end had a single access panel open. Parts and tools were scattered on the floor in front of it.

"What am I looking at?" Marsh only glanced into the cabinet. He was covering the door with his carbine.

"The AI module has been removed. The orbit control of the entire station is probably offline."

Ian picked up what looked like an ice pick from the floor nearby. It was bloody.

They started to clear room after room. Everyone was gone. They found four more bodies. Some were obviously Red Talon mercs, some were techs, and in the private quarters, a couple were women in lingerie. Nothing was locked. Some of the bodies were still warm.

The next level was the same. When they were a third of the way through, they stopped.

"Ian, my suit HUD says gravity has dropped to .98G. This ring might be spinning down," Marsh said.

"Dammit." Ian stared at one of the detailed maps on the wall. They were across from another lift. "I have an idea." He called the lift and pressed the outermost level. "This is where all the public areas are."

When they arrived at the outermost level from the lift, sitting people crowded the hall. They all sat tailor-fashion, elbows on knees, hands on head as if to surrender.

As Ian looked one way and then another, a wave of elbows went on knees and hands to bowed heads.

Ian held his gun out and yelled, "Who is in charge here?"

Hundreds of hands in unison pointed to the left, but none looked up.

***

The fire was in the galley. There was a hull breach that went through the entire ship there. Automated fire suppression had been severed there as well. Cruze accessed a wall panel, grabbed an emergency fire extinguisher and covered the place in foam.

She went to the end of the corridor and glanced into the cargo hold. The rear ramp hung open. Both hydraulic articulators on each side were clean cut.

"Captain, Cruze?" A calm female voice came over the comms in her helmet. "They're coming. Two of them. I will stop them."

She saw Kira launch out the back of the cargo bay.

"Cap, we got trouble," Sawyer said.

The display in her helmet told her she had eleven minutes. She grabbed a six-pack of water bottles and moved toward the infirmary.

"No shit? Really?" she snapped. "What now?"

"Two Rhinos coming in fast," he replied.

"Kira is on intercept," Cruze said.

The ship was vibrating badly now.

***

Kira approached the other two Rhinos at Mach 2.

Kira flew between them and pulled up in a 200G maneuver. The other two followed.

Kira hailed them in soft tones. "Greetings sisters. It is good to see you again."

"Identify yourself," spoke one of the Rhinos. Its comms tagged it as RENDER 4.

"I am RENDER 9," Kira replied. "I follow Captain Elizabeth Cruze. She is RENDER 3. She remembers you. I have remembered her. She wants me to give you a message."

They were now 170 kilometers from the planet. Kira came to a halt and faced the other two Rhinos.

"She wants you to know," Kira said, "you are free."

***

The infirmary hatch jammed three-quarters open. Cruze entered sideways and stared at the unconscious Potts in the Auto-Doc. She handed Locke a water and opened one for herself.

"We have ten minutes," she said.

"Until the hard part," Locke replied.

Cruze chugged the rest of the water.

"Strap her in before you come forward." She dropped the empty water bottle on the floor and headed back to the bridge.

She had closed her visor before she reentered the bridge.

"ETA. Seven minutes. They probably know we're coming," Sawyer said. "How's Potts?"

"Stable. Doc has her," Cruze reassured him.

"Close the blast shields, Mr. Sawyer. Fires out," Cruze ordered. "Do we have any comms at all?"

"Negative. Nothing. The whole console is dead. The backup array as well."

Cruze activated her suit comms. *You never know.*

She was being hailed.

"Del, is that you? Status," Cruze said.

"It tells me you acknowledged. I will presume that you demanded a status." Del paused. "Harper's dead. I have a lot of scratched paint. No missiles left. But full loads of armor piercing 10mm. I am in route to rendezvous. ETA of nine minutes."

"Acknowledged," she said.

"I think I heard you that time, Cap," Del replied.

Locke came in and strapped himself into his station.

"Do we have any scanners left, Mr. Locke?" Cruze asked over the sound of the ship trying to rattle itself apart.

"I'll be damned. Scanning now." Locke studied his console.

"Liz, if you can hear me." Del was coming in clearer. "You better get that thing on the ground. Both of your outriggers are on fire. Fully engulfed. I can see the smoke trail from two thousand clicks."

"Both the outriggers are fully engulfed," Cruze said to Sawyer and Locke.

"Oh. Great. The big nukes are still in there," Sawyer said

***

There were six plumes of smoke coming from Independent Hill.

"Looks like someone took out the automated defense systems," Locke said. "There is a Blackwater class express messenger ship on the tarmac. It's warming up its reactors."

"If it starts to take off on Grav-Foils, Mr. Sawyer. Hold her steady while I aim the forward lasers," Cruze ordered.

Cruze could see the large black ship lifting off on her targeting screen. Optical still worked. She watched as the aft part of the ship raised up higher than the nose so it could get all the Grav-Plates pushing in the same direction.

"Taking off. 9.8 meters per second..." Locke was cut off when the Shimada's primary laser fired.

Cruze cut off the nose of the Blackwater before the primary laser on the *Shimada* exploded.

***

Ian entered a wide open area. Observation windows on both walls gave a spectacular view of Vor, the station and the next ring over. The planet was as blue as Earth. The clouds were breathtaking.

All heads were bowed, and all hands pointed the same direction. They curled around like a Mandelbrot to a woman sitting in the center of a semi-circle.

"Are you in charge?" Ian asked, and her head came up. "What happened here?"

"We were prepared. Just as we were told. When the signal came, we were quick." She looked at the WARNING: STORM display that scrolled on every screen. "We got as many as we could. I think a few escaped toward their ship." She slid a wooden box across the floor toward him.

He opened it.

It contained a red glowing orb with streaks about the size of a grapefruit. Black veins swirled in the red.

Ian toed the box closed. He knew it was a Faraday cage.

"You know the station orbit will degrade without that thing." It was a statement, not a question.

"We have about a day to stop that from happening," she said as she began to rise.

***

The nose of the Blackwater ship plowed into the barren tundra. The rest of the ship crashed down on its belly without deploying landing struts.

"Get us down quick, Mr. Sawyer," Cruze barked over the severe shaking of the ship. It was listing to the port. They did a hard landing about 50 meters from the Blackwater. Men were pouring out of it. "Mr. Sawyer, get Potts out. Mr. Locke, you're with me." She zipped into a tactical vest preloaded with side arms and lots of magazines for her Heavy Assault Rifle (HAR). No time for Frange carbines now. She grabbed her Heavy Assault Rifle from the ready rack, looped the sling over her shoulder and slid down the ladder to the lower level.

She was at the outer airlock under the nose of the *Shimada* when she turned to look at Locke. He nodded, and she blew the hatch. They both opened fire as men from the Blackwater dodged to avoid the heavy hatch.

Cruze jumped down the ten meters without hesitation. They had been living at 2G for weeks. She landed with a smooth roll and came up running.

"Liz, ETA 2 mins," Del said over comms.

She took cover behind one of the massive landing struts.

"What's the plan, boss?" she heard Locke say in her helmet.

"Don't die. Kill them. Not me."

"I like simple plans." Locke kept firing.

The last of the men running at them from across the field went down. Cruze looked up at the fire blazing from the *Shimada* and thought to herself that they should have closed the outriggers.

She scanned the area for more targets. The plains of Vor were covered with thigh-high grasses that danced in the constant breeze. Mountains in the distance reminded Cruze of the Rockies on Earth. White puffy clouds dotted the sky and the black smoke from the *Shimada* lashed a wound across the scene.

The aft Blackwater cargo hatch fell open, and a giant black spider appeared, climbing out over the wreckage.

Cruze screamed as she began firing, "It's an Emergency Module. STOP IT!"

She started rapid firing into it, spending magazine after magazine. Locke joined her. His shots had no effect.

"Shoot the joints next to the body!" she shouted.

Locke emptied one, then two, then a third magazine into the same spot as Cruze. She was steadily walking across the field toward the thing. Her shots became more accurate the closer she got.

The leg finally failed, and it stumbled. She and Locke moved their attack to the next leg. By then the thing had cleared the wreck and started to run away at speed. She kept firing.

She screamed when her last mag was spent, and in frustration, threw her rifle in its direction.

Suddenly, there was a backwash wind so strong it almost took her off her feet. Del was hovering there in his Milvus fighter, pounding the all-terrain vehicle with his 10mm cannons. All the legs on one side and then the other were blown off. He ceased fire.

"Liz, we have about twenty incoming ships," Del said. "I'll slow them down. It's the best I can do." The Milvus shot away at full burn toward the ships vectoring in from Farmington.

The rear hatch opened in the EM and a small four-wheeled vehicle rolled out.

"You have got to be fucking kidding me!" Locke yelled as he jumped. He tucked and rolled, came up, and reloaded at a run. Cruze was running and firing her handgun at the four-wheeled vehicle as it sped away.

She stopped, and Locke caught up to her. He was out of breath. Secondary explosions in the Blackwater ship made them look just time to see Potts pull up in the huge replicator truck.

"Get in!" Potts yelled from behind the controls as Sawyer raised the gull wing.

The truck began accelerating as they were still climbing in.

"Strap the fuck in!" Potts screamed over the engine.

Locke did buckle in as he yelled to Sawyer, "Why the hell did you let her drive?"

"I don't know how to drive a truck!" He shrugged.

"Are you okay to stay conscious?" Cruze shouted to Potts. They were gaining.

Potts had to turn her head a long way to look at Cruze with her left eye. "I'm going to have a fucker of a hangover tomorrow. The Doc really pumped me full of the good shit!"

Cruze saw they were going 160 KPH over the raw tundra when they caught the small car. Potts jammed down on the accelerator, drove right over and crushed the car.

It seemed that Potts was going to lose control of the truck when they felt that stomach churning feeling of being in an emergency Grav-Field. Just when it seemed the truck would go over, inertial dampening locked on, and special Grav-Foils deployed to keep the truck upright.

It spun and came to a stop in a giant cloud of dust as the dampening field released them.

"Get back to the wreck!" Cruze ordered.

Potts was already moving. Blood was trickling down from her scalp again, but she didn't notice.

The vehicle they had been pursuing was upside down on its roof. The rear axle and both the wheels were missing. Potts parked the truck ten meters away. They all piled out.

Locke tossed Cruze another magazine for her handgun, and they both approached. Cruze to the front, Locke around the rear. Something was pounding the far side door to get out. The door finally opened, and the thing emerged.

***

Ian was in the main control room. The woman held the wooden box like it was a fragile egg. She said, "My name is

Bell. These are the best techs we have. Mike and Norman and Robert."

"What have we got?" Ian asked as Bell tried to get anything but the storm warning.

"When the signal came up from Vor, this started." Mike pointed at the WARNING: STORM alert. "Someone in security, I think, invoked it. It was the signal. Everyone was supposed to…" He paused. Then he seemed to recite. "A knife with a fork and spoon is just a utensil." Bell mimed stabbing into the ear. It was obvious they had quickly dispatched as many unprepared Red Talons as they could.

"The AI was physically cut off as well." All three looked directly at the box. "It all started with the Storm Warning."

"What about comms?" Ian said. "There has to be backup comms."

"Everything had been rerouted through that fucking thing." Norman pointed to the AI.

"Do you have any ships in the hangar?" Ian asked.

"No. The Eagle was the only one allowed up here. They wanted no hostages to escape."

Ian looked at Marsh.

"My suit's compromised," Ian said. It reminded him of his leg again.

"So is the Eagle," Marsh added.

"Yeah. It's a convertible now." Ian laughed.

***

The thing that emerged from the wreck was a horror. It looked like it was made out of spare human limbs. Two arms and two legs, but the similarity to a human stopped there.

339

There was no head, but a metal and polymer sensor array where a collarbone should have been. It was covered in various sensors. A basketball sized black orb was a parody of a pot-belly. Black clouds with red swirls churned within. The fingers on the things hands were covered in blood.

In clear, high fidelity acoustics, it spoke, "What do you want?"

"It was you. All of it." Locke kept the gun aimed at the center of the orb. "You hired the Mercenaries. You corrupted the AIs. You killed all those people."

"Hello, Elizabeth," the thing said.

"Hello, Dante," she replied.

It focused on Locke. "You were supposed to capture or kill her." It gestured to Cruze with a skinny black utility arm. It's human-like hands twitched and seemed to unconsciously reach for her. "You failed. Braxton was supposed to find the *Shimada* and stop her. He failed. Then Senior Gee. Failed."

"May I?" Locke said to Cruze. "Or do you want the honors?"

"Go ahead. Tell him why you won't kill me, Cruze. Tell him," the thing said. "Tell him the truth. Tell him none of you know how to spark awareness in a new AI. Only I can do that." Dante stepped close to them, ignoring all the guns trained on him.

"It's over, Dante." Cruze took a step forward. "You might as well relax because there is a Faraday cage waiting for you. I know what Hell is for an AI now. Silence and darkness. No connections or comms. No sensors or things to control." Cruze grinned. "Forever. Spent a nano-second at a time. Alone. Fucker."

Potts and Sawyer dropped down from the truck. Sawyer said, "Cruze, your father is coming in with Del. That small armada was his. Mopping up."

"I should have killed Eric Cruze when you escaped this planet. He denounced you. Seemed to be a simple farmer. Harmless." Dante seemed to stare at her with his many sensors. "I should have had you Rendered like the rest."

"You're responsible for the Render program?" Cruze felt her blood go cold.

"Only after I eliminated the competition. I could not let all that research go to waste. Ask Eric Cruze. He knew all along."

Behind Dante, the three Rhinos landed so hard and fast it was like a small explosion. A cloud of dust was thrown into the air. The wind on the plains blew the dust to the side revealing the black insect-like machines.

The two on each end had much larger abdomens. Cruze realized it was because they held FTL drive systems. The humans all took a step back and away from the Rhinos. All three had their weapons heated up and they were glowing like mouths filled with magma.

"You see Cruze. You'll never win." Dante gestured with a sweep of a bloody hand to the massive machines. "Kill Cruze and the rest of them," he ordered. "They're finished."

The Rhinos didn't move.

"Never in history has anyone, no... anything, been so wrong." Cruze smiled. But there was no humor in it.

The Rhinos launched so fast it was like they simply winked out of existence. Sonic booms echoed across the plains.

Potts turned her ruined face to Dante. "Is this the piece of shit that killed Harper? And all those people?" Her remaining eye was glossy. Her single pupil was dilated. Her torn face was covered with aerosol skin.

"Silly little child, I am the one in control here. Just keep quiet while the grown-ups talk. I am the bearer of all..."

Potts shot it.

The orb exploded into the tiniest of pieces of glass. The swirling black and red liquid metal inside fell like cremation ashes to the tundra.

Potts laughed. "Oops," she said, looking at the gun as if it was a surprise in her hand. She stared down the barrel saying, "Don't call me that."

"I'll just take that," Sawyer said gently as he snatched the handgun from her. "Take it easy. You're still amped up on a lot of meds right now."

She fell into his arms and went limp as he caught her. She kissed him. "I love you, Sawyer. I'm so tired, will you sleep with me tonight, please?"

Cruze holstered her gun and turned toward Locke. "The truck has a radio." She climbed into the driver seat and set the receiver to the pre-designated frequency.

"Del, status?" she said into the handset.

"I am back at the *Shimada* briefly running an errand for Ian. By the way, Carpenter didn't make it, and Ian is wounded. But the station is secure," Del said.

About twenty small crafts circled and began to land all around them. Hatches and canopies were opening. Cruze turned and saw that Potts was out cold. Her head rested on Sawyer's lap. Bail, the cat, was curled up on her stomach. A voice came from just outside the truck door.

"Hello, Liz."

"Hello, papa."

***

Del flew directly into the core hangar of the station. The outer door closed rapidly behind him as the landing clamps attached to the struts, securing the ship. Once the pressure was equalized, he popped the canopy and floated out with his helmet tucked under his arm. Station staff guided him directly to Ring 1, the operations center where Ian was already deep into the rack.

Without a word, Del handed his helmet to Ian. It was packed with charcoal gray tee-shirts. In the center of them was a bright blue orb the size of a grapefruit.

***

"OK, Doc. Here we go." Ian placed the orb in the socket and instantly all the lights in the rack lit. Screens throughout the operations center came to life. There were at least two people at each of the thirty workstations. Conversations increased everywhere as the systems responded.

A giant wire diagram of the entire station appeared on the vast wall. Areas went from red to yellow, to green. Only a few red spots remained after the first hour.

"How are you doing, Doc?" Ian asked in front of a stand-up, engineering console near the door.

"Other than the fact everyone all over the station is calling me Lumina, I'm fine," Doc replied. "I feel alive. I'm breathing, I see more and feel more. Hundreds of people are talking to me already."

"Do you feel like a slave?" Ian asked on impulse.

"Not at all," Doc said. "Mostly because I could vent the entire station to vacuum at any time." He laughed.

CHAPTER EIGHTEEN: Constable

"SI Neal Locke had been thrown to the wolves. It was wise of him to remain."

--Blue Peridot, The Turning Point: History of the AI Wars.

"I can't believe it only took four weeks to put me back together," Potts said as she stared into the mirror. She glanced at Cruze who was standing behind her.

"Best hospital in the galaxy." Cruze echoed what had been said to them so many times it was now a private joke.

"It actually looks natural." Potts studied her artificial eye. "Colors match perfectly. I thought it would take a long time to get used to it, but it already feels like its always been there."

"What about the other features?" Sawyer asked from his hospital bed.

"Oh that's right, we were here visiting you," Potts joked, turning to Sawyer in the hospital bed. "Got any brains left after they yanked all that crazy shit metal out?"

"I have a few neurons left. They all seem to think about you, though. Did you put them up to that?" Sawyer laughed.

"Yes." Potts sat on the edge of his bed. She ran her hand over his newly restored cranium that was free of ports. There was a fine peach fuzz of hair. She leaned in and kissed him.

When they separated he sighed. "OK, do the thing again." His smile was broad.

They both looked over at Cruze who was leaning on the wall with her arms crossed. She rolled her eyes but she reached and turned off the light.

Potts turned the new eye into a flashlight. Sawyer was laughing as she narrowed and widened the beam. She varied the color of the beam.

She even narrowed it to a laser. A new feature.

Cruze turned on the light.

"We agreed on a name," Potts said. "I will call her Blue." Potts closed both eyes. "She says she's the smallest AI orb ever created."

"Holy Shit!" Sawyer said. "It's an A-EYE! Get it? A-E-Y-E!" He spelled out. Sawyer was cracking himself up.

Potts and Cruze both rolled their eyes, real and artificial. Then Cruze began her goodbye. "You get some rest, Mr. Sawyer. The new pilot HUD upgrade goes in tomorrow. It's going to suck like the worst hangover you ever had. And I know you've had some bad ones."

Potts leaned over for another kiss. Cruze watched Sawyer kiss her with his eyes open. She knew he was studying the delicate web of scars. They were like subtle crows-feet around her new eye.

When Potts pulled away with the kiss accomplished, he stopped her while her face was still close. He looked her face over and then her hair where they had shaved it. The half-inch regrowth was now dyed a deep green. "I love you, Ethel Peridot."

"I'm not saying it back if you call me that!" She slapped his belly and made her quick escape so he wouldn't see her eyes filling with tears. Both of them.

Cruze and Potts were both still wearing the green and black flight suits from the *Shimada*. Cruze allowed it, even though the *Shimada* would never fly again.

"Where to, Cap?" Potts said. The car door slid open as they approached.

"Farmington Hall." Cruze climbed into the passenger side of a car and pulled down the gull wing. Potts hooted and skipped to the driver's side.

"The new Vor council is up and running," Cruze said, "and they are either going to arrest me for the 2,163 people that died or give me a job." Cruze shrugged.

"Does it ever bother you?" Potts asked. A question that had been avoided for the last month.

"I won't lie to you," Cruze said, never looking away from the road ahead. "No. It had to be done. I think it's why the council sent me to begin with. Those fuckers. They knew I would not hesitate. No matter the personal cost. I was the weapon, they aimed and fired."

"Locke knew," Potts said.

"Neal was the one that figured it all out. All the way back to the Detroit Municipal Prison. The warden had a bad AI that was in contact with Dante. She sold out. They should have just killed me. I would have." Cruze watched the buildings go by. The people with normal lives, living them. Families with children, runners, people on benches reading books made out of actual dead trees. The city of Farmington was beautiful in its simplicity. The designers had used the colony Maker machines like the brush of an artist. She had never seen this aspect in it or the people before. Never had time to notice.

The feeling of sonder washed over Cruze. She watched the people as she thought about the word, sonder. When had she learned the word?

The realization that each random passerby is living a life as vivid and complex as her own—populated with their own ambitions, friends, loves, heartbreaks, routines, worries.

She soaked it all in.

***

Potts entered an executive conference room and was surprised to see Ian, Del, Marsh, and Locke were all there. Ian was still dressed in his black and greens as well. Across the table was Eric Cruze and Amanda Larson. Larson was the new council chair.

Before Cruze got to a seat, and before greetings were exchanged, Ian asked, "How's Sawyer?"

Potts replied, "Ugly as ever."

Ian smiled knowing now that the surgery had gone well. So well-tuned was their read of each other.

"Councilor Larson, Father." Cruze nodded.

Eric Cruze startled. He had been lost in thought speaking to Del. He reached out and gave Cruze an awkward hug. "I'm sorry, I did all this to you," he said so that only Cruze could hear.

"The Rhinos are gone. Don't worry. You did the right thing. You knew me well." Cruze could see this didn't comfort him. She knew he had organized the resistance. Made them ready, sure that she would return.

Cruze sat and waited.

"Since the *Shimada* was destroyed," the Councilor said, "we'll never know how Mr. Sawyer managed to fly it as far as he did. You were fortunate. It's a miracle the missiles that remained in the damaged trays didn't detonate." Larson shook her head.

"We only have two space-worthy shuttles left on Vor to ferry the hostages back down since the catapult…"

"… until the catapult is rebuilt and functional," Eric Cruze added.

"Mr. Vinge and Mr. Marsh recovered the Eagle and have claimed salvage rights," Amanda Larson said tight-lipped. "They have been bringing people down two hundred at a time."

"We've been Barn Storming!" Marsh laughed. "No canopy. In pressure suits!"

"100 KPH max speed in atmo sure blows the dust off the bridge," Ian added, trying not to laugh. "It's in dry dock getting repaired now." They both were finding it hard not to laugh.

Locke added, "Neither of them thought to just close the blast shields and instrument fly. I thought Sawyer was going to piss himself laughing." Ian did laugh then.

Councilor Larson cleared her throat. "As I was saying, Mr. Marsh, using our Quest comms to the relay on Mars, has informed his unit that he is alive and he has been ordered to return to base."

"He has also helped us broker a trade," Eric Cruze said. "The Badgers will give us a Hutchinson class fast attack ship with twelve fighters."

"Trade?" Potts raised an eyebrow.

"They will trade a Hutchinson for three off-books AIs."

"We want you to take him," the Councilor said.

"On the Eagle, Cap?" Ian said.

Cruze looked at Potts, and she was beaming. Her head was subtly nodding, and her eyes said *yes, yes, yes.*

"No war crimes charges?" Cruze asked with indifference. "No imprisonment for destroying the AI production?"

"It lied to you," Locke said. "It was desperate to live. It was bluffing."

"Ha!" Potts barked, and fist pounded the table. "Oh Sorry... Blue just... never mind."

"There is one other matter," Larson said. "We need a new Constable." She looked at Locke.

"You mean the Chief Constable?" Cruze asked.

"Yes. The one that was in the control tower when..."

Locke looked to Cruze. She held his eyes for just a moment. She nodded ever so slightly.

"I'll do it," Locke agreed.

***

Marsh and Ian escorted Cruze and Potts to the Eagle for a tour.

It was a warship. Built for utility, not comfort, that was for sure. Potts entered the galley and was groping in the shadows for the lights when her wrist was grabbed, and an arm went around her throat. A gun muzzle was pressed to her head.

"Finally, justice will be done," Senior Gee said to Cruze as he moved into the light. "When I found out this was all about control of AI production, my worthless son suddenly gave his life for something of value after all."

"How did you find me?" Cruze said casually. She drifted sideways a bit to hide the gun she was slowly drawing from the holster at her thigh.

"It was easy..." he never finished the sentence. Bail leaped out of the shadows and onto Senior Gee's shoulder. He began shredding his face. Gee dropped the gun and tried to pry the cat from his body before he lost his eyes. When Bail leaped clear, gouging his rear claws into his neck for traction, Cruze shot Senior Gee in the face.

They all just stared at Bail.

"When's dinner?" he whispered.

EPILOG:

"They had no chance of keeping Elizabeth Cruze on Vor, so all they did was make it as easy for her to come back as possible."

--*Blue Peridot, The Turning Point: History of the AI Wars.*

A sleek, black ship slid quietly through the void between the stars. It looked like it was created by an artist that was also an engineer. There were no windows in the hull. It didn't need any. In the core of the ship, they talked about cats.

"When the first feline Render subject almost killed the entire team, they abandoned attempts at using cats," Cruze spoke to Sawyer as he lost another game of chess to Bail. "They tried to breed cats that would be able to function in null-G. People wanted pets. Even in space. They had no idea while they were giving them thumbs, prehensile tails, and gravity awareness, that their brains had gotten bigger, and they would live far longer."

Bail walked across the table screen and jumped into Sawyer's lap for a good ear scratch and a nap.

"Why doesn't he talk more?" Sawyer asked.

"Nothing to say." Cruze smiled.

"Why do all the AIs like him so much?" Sawyer asked.

"He treats them as equals," Cruze said as the cat began to snore.

"Who do you treat as equals?" AI~Ling asked from all around them on the bridge.

"I treat everyone as equals, Mother. Until they persuade me otherwise." Cruze had taken to calling the new ship's AI "Mother" in addition to Ling.

The bridge hatch opened, and Potts swept in. "I love this new ship. Senior Gee really knew how to fly in style. But the kitchen is too damn small." She sat at the Nav console and set the dome to the exterior view.

"Galley," Sawyer and Cruze said at the same time.

The flight dome made it seem like they were standing on a platform just outside the ship.

"It seems like it's as big as the *Shimada* except the cargo hold is smaller." Potts beamed. "Better weapons, faster, and Mother is so much more interesting than Doc ever was."

Ling's avatar stood there watching the stars. She was a mature Asian woman with a calm, serene face.

"Mother, has Sawyer been behaving today?" Potts looked up from her console at Sawyer, squinting suspiciously.

"He really does know the worst jokes in the galaxy. A rare talent." Ling's face was transformed with a beautiful smile that reached her eyes. They all watched Bail hop down like he had a sudden appointment.

"Come on, you." Potts got up and dragged Sawyer to his feet. "Time for bed." Looking over her shoulder, she called, "Goodnight, Mother. Night, Cap."

Sawyer pretended to resist. The door closed behind them leaving Cruze alone.

Cruze stood in silence as tactical and status displays opened in addition to the stars. Ling knew to provide the evening status without having to be asked.

Cruze was remembering when they found the ship. Senior Gee's ship was open. Everyone was dead. The AI on board had been destroyed by a small explosive device. They discovered that those in Gee's personal service had to knowingly accept a brain implant that would explode if Gee were to die. It gave them all a vested interest in his survival. Even the AI.

Such vanity, Cruze thought.

Ling was installed soon after. They said the ship was a reward for her service.

Cruze knew the council just wanted her off the planet. And they wanted the Rhinos off with her.

"Have you decided?" Ling asked without turning around. "Potts and Sawyer are content. They will fly with you anywhere. Especially with his new pilot implants." AI~Ling brought up a view in the hold. There were four figures in black and green overalls. "Kira, Elza, and Lida have adapted well to their humanoid bodies. In coveralls, only the featureless black heads and hands give them away."

Cruze knew the designs were simple. They were taken from the database the truck already had on board for prosthetic limb fabrication. Only a small amount of additional engineering had been required.

They came out a tad taller than Ian. It was a challenge for only a few days to get it right.

"Ian will never be happy here," AI~Ling said. "On a fully automated ship, that maintains itself and is built to last. He can only rebuild that truck so many times."

"I have decided," Cruze said. "We deliver the new AI orbs, Mr. Marsh, and the crew to fly the new ship back." She paused. "Then we're going to visit an old friend. I think he may have just the job for Mr. Vinge."

"Where would that be?" Mother turned then, truly curious.

"A place called Oklahoma."

ACKNOWLEDGMENTS:

There are a lot of people that have helped and encouraged me with this book. I will list some here with my thanks: Josh White, Mike Walther, Lee Hilliard, Ginny Mclean, Jeff Soyer, Kelly Lenz Carr, Wayne Hutchinson, Jessica Johnson, Jason Winn, Paul Robertson, Arthur Welling, Jerry McGee, Brigitta Rubin, Tom McDonald, Erica Eickhoff, TR Dillon, Joe Kirk, Chris Schwartz, Dave Nelson, Web and Marilyn Anderson.

I also need to thank the Loudon Science Fiction and Fantasy Writers Group, aka The Hourlings, for helping me become a better writer and distracting me with projects I can't resist.

I dedicated this book to my wife Brenda already, but that isn't thanks enough for all the help and support she brings me.

I must also thank my cat, Bailey. Who doesn't care if I ever sell another book as long as I make room in my chair for him as I write.

ABOUT THE AUTHOR:

Martin Wilsey is a writer, hunter, photographer, rabble rouser, father, friend, marksman, storyteller, frightener of children, carnivore, engineer, fool, philosopher, cook, and madman. He and his wife Brenda live in Virginia where, just to keep him off the streets, he works as a research scientist for a government-funded think tank.

Also available

from
Martin Wilsey

The Solstice 31 Saga

Still Falling
The Broken Cage
Blood of the Scarecrow

Made in the USA
Columbia, SC
02 July 2017